'TIS THE SEASON TO BE KISSED

Jenni slowly leaned in to Coop's kiss, but there wasn't anything hesitant about the way she melted. Coop kissed like he meant it.

Desire slammed into her stomach as her arms encircled Coop's neck. She could feel the heat of his mouth and the taste of his need. It matched her own. It had been so long since she had been held and desired as a woman. She just wanted to sink in to Coop and never resurface. She stretched up on her toes, bringing herself closer to his pounding heart—to his heat.

Coop groaned as his tongue swept into her mouth and seductively teased hers into submission. Her fingers sank into his thick, soft hair and pulled him closer. She wanted Cooper Armstrong and she wanted him now . . .

D0684750

Books by Marcia Evanick

CATCH OF THE DAY

CHRISTMAS ON CONRAD STREET

BLUEBERRY HILL

A BERRY MERRY CHRISTMAS

HARBOR NIGHTS

A MISTY HARBOR WEDDING

Published by Zebra Books

Mistletoe Bay

Marcia Evanick

ZEBRA BOOKS
KENSINGTON PUBLISHING CORP.
www.kensingtonbooks.com

ZEBRA BOOKS are published by

Kensington Publishing Corp.
850 Third Avenue
New York, NY 10022

All Kensington titles, imprints, and distributed lines are avail-
able at special quantity discounts for bulk purchases for sales
promotion, premiums, fund-raising, educational, or institu-
tional use.

Special book excerpts or customized printings can also be created to fit specific needs. For details, write or phone the office
of the Kensington Special Sales Manager: Attn. Special Sales
Department. Kensington Publishing Corp., 850 Third Avenue,
New York, NY 10022. Phone: 1-800-221-2647.

ISBN-13: 978-0-8217-8009-1
ISBN-10: 0-8217-8009-3

First Printing: October 2007
10 9 8 7 6 5 4 3 2 1

Printed in the United States of America

Leslie,
Friend, sister of my heart,
And fellow silver enthusiast—
this one is for you.
—Marci

Chapter One

Coop Armstrong swore as a ghost darted out of the woods directly into the path of his truck. He slammed on the brakes, kicking up pebbles and rocks behind him, as a bug-like alien creature followed the ghost into the thick woods and brush on the opposite side of the gravel driveway. Before the three-foot green-faced bug disappeared from sight, it turned and waved.

He waved back and tried not to think about how close he had come to hitting the creatures.

The Wright boys were at it again. At least there was a reason for their costumes today. It was Halloween.

For the past week he had been making deliveries and pickups at the big old house surrounded by woods on three sides and Mistletoe Bay on the fourth. The two boys had greeted him every day. To be more accurate, the boys had tried terrorizing him every day. Yesterday they had been lions or some other type of beasts waiting to attack him on the slightly slanted front porch. The day before that they had been pirates wielding curtain-rod swords and demanding all of his loot.

Whoever their babysitter was, she was doing a terrible job. The woman, who appeared hurried, hassled, and totally out of her depth when it came to the young boys, appeared to be in her late forties. The boys called her Grandmom, but she signed the name *Dorothy Wright* for the packages he delivered and picked up daily.

Learning his new route and all the side streets of the area was challenging enough. Most of the businesses along his route he already knew or were self-explanatory, but the Mistletoe Bay Company was still a mystery to him. He had no idea what the home-based company made or sold. One thing for sure, it wasn't child restraints or home repair items; 27 Bay Road had fallen into disrepair two decades ago.

The big, ramshackle old house was leaning toward the right, while the entire porch listed left. It was quite obvious, even to the untrained eye, that the house hadn't felt the blow of a hammer or a cut of a saw in twenty-five years. Since he had worked in construction for the past thirteen years he could pick out over a dozen exterior flaws within two minutes. The most pressing was the porch. He'd give the weather-beaten structure one, possibly two, more Maine winters before it crumbled into sawdust.

If the Wrights were lucky, the porch wouldn't take the front of their house with them.

He slowly drove the rest of the winding gravel driveway and parked in front of the monstrous house that looked like it could have been used as the set of a teenage horror film. And that had been before the Halloween decorations were added.

Hay bales, pumpkins, gourds, polyester spiderwebs,

and wart-nosed witches were everywhere. Plastic electric ghosts and torn white sheets adorned what three weeks ago had been brightly colored autumn trees. Peak season for the fall color was over, leaving mostly bare trees and a foot's worth of fallen leaves everywhere. A six-foot skeleton was hanging by the neck out of a second-story window and banging against the house with the cool fall breeze. The expertly tied hangman's noose deserved a merit badge. Tombstones dotted the yard, which hadn't seen a rake in the past decade.

Someone with a really sick and twisted mind had placed a five-foot stuffed panda on one of the porch rockers and had sliced open his belly, causing stuffing to spill out. If that wasn't bad enough, they had smeared ketchup—at least he hoped it was ketchup—across the wound and plucked out both of his eyes, so they dangled upon his cheeks.

The Wrights were one disturbed family, especially considering the fact that no one would be coming this far out of town to go trick-or-treating tonight. The nearest town was Misty Harbor, and that was a good two miles down the road—or by Maine's standard five miles of twisting, turning roads.

All the kids would be hitting the most populated area, which was the town. More houses meant more candy in the bags. He might be thirty-two years old, but Coop still remembered the rules of Halloween; he with the most candy wins. Nothing beat frightening a bunch of girls on the scariest night of the year, unless you could give your buddies a good scare and make them scream like little girls. Then you were cooler than cool. You were king.

As he grabbed his clipboard and the two boxes he was

delivering, Coop quietly chuckled at his memories of being king back in Sullivan for a couple of years during his misspent youth. He stepped out of the truck and silently looked at the latest addition to the tasteless Halloween decorations.

A pair of jean-clad legs and scruffy white sneakers were sticking out from under the porch. Wasn't it supposed to be striped stockings and ruby slippers instead of Keds?

Coop was halfway up the porch steps when he heard a voice and realized that the legs and sneakers sticking out from under the porch were attached to a live person—a female person, who was making reassuring promises to someone or something named Bojangles. He gave it ten-to-one odds that Bojangles was the mutt that chased his truck back down the driveway after every delivery.

Coop's eyebrows rose as he watched the legs move out from under the dilapidated porch, followed by an enticing jean-clad bottom. He had no idea whose bottom it was, but one thing was for certain: It wasn't Dorothy Wright. He sat down on the wooden step to enjoy this Halloween treat and prayed he wasn't about to be tricked.

"Come on, sweetie," purred Jenni Wright in her softest singsong voice, the same tone she used when she was passing out doggie treats. Bojangles, the family dog, had had enough trauma for one afternoon, and at fifty pounds, he was a little hard to yank out from underneath the porch. "You don't look that bad, honestly," she lied in her sweetest voice.

The dog was a disaster, and Jenni was a close second. She wiggled her way farther out from under the porch while holding onto Bojangles's collar and uttering threats against her son under her breath. She hated tight, creepy spaces, especially when they were crawling with spiders and heaven only knew what other critters. The dog was coated in pink slimy Skin So Sexy shave gel, and three-quarters of his hair had been cut off. Thankfully Bojangles had escaped the evil clutches of four-year-old Tucker before he could locate her razor to finish the job.

Tucker the terror had wanted to make Bojangles into a dragon for trick-or-treating tonight. Since dragons were hairless and Jenni had been busy out in the shop while her mother-in-law, Dorothy, had been baking pumpkin cookies in the kitchen, Tucker had decided he was old enough to give the dog a haircut and a shave.

Bojangles had other ideas.

Currently Dorothy was cleaning up big clumps of dog hair and splattered pink shaving gel from nearly every room in the house. Being the mom, Jenni got to haul Bojangles out from the nightmarish muck under the porch and into the tub upstairs. The fifty-pound mutt, who was half Old English sheepdog and half Heinz 57, was petrified of baths—almost as much as Jenni was terrified as to what could be crawling on her now.

Jenni wiggled faster and tightened her grip on the blue collar. "Come on, sweetie, we're almost there."

Bojangles dug in his front paws and howled.

She muttered a word she hoped her children didn't

hear as the dog's howl echoed throughout the small space. Knowing Tucker, he wasn't anywhere near the scene of the crime. He probably was running through the woods with his three-year-old brother, Corey, scaring whatever animal crossed his path. In the past six months, since they had moved here, Tucker had managed to frighten off nearly every critter on their two acres. The black plague had caused less destruction than her four-year-old son.

Jenni got to her knees and put every ounce of strength she had into hauling the howling mutt the rest of the way out. Bojangles gave up the fight and hurled himself straight into her arms, knocking her flat on her back and covering her with more pink shaving gel, decomposed leaves, and muck.

"Yuck! Bojangles, stop! Get off me, you big lug." She turned her face to the side to avoid a lapping tongue. The UPS delivery man was sitting on the porch steps grinning at her. Humiliation washed over her, and she tried to control the fiery blush sweeping up her cheeks. She had known this wasn't going to be her day when she had been awakened at six this morning by one of the cats hacking up a furball in the middle of her bed.

Bojangles finally noticed the man and tried to make a flying leap for him. Her fingers clutched the slippery collar as she wrapped her other arm around the mutt. "No, Bo! Bad dog!" She wrestled the dog to his back. If there had been a clean spot on her before, there wasn't now.

"Don't worry. He's all bark, no bite." The dog was acting as if he wanted to either rip the UPS man apart or go play fetch.

"We've met before."

Jenni glanced at the gorgeous man all dressed in brown as he stood up. He topped six feet and had the world's most beautiful smile. She felt that smile in the pit of her stomach. "Oh, you must be Mr. Brown." Tucker and Corey were constantly talking about their new friend, the delivery guy. Neither one of her sons or her mother-in-law had bothered to inform her how handsome brown could be.

"Brown? No, I'm afraid my name is Cooper Armstrong—Coop to my friends."

She stood up, while keeping a death grip on the collar. Cooper didn't appear to be a guy who would appreciate being covered in pink shaving gel and rotting leaves by a nearly bald dog. "My boys named you Mr. Brown after seeing a commercial about UPS."

"That explains that." Cooper looked like he was holding back laughter. "Would you like to explain how Bojangles lost his hair and what that pink stuff is all over him?"

"In a word, Tucker."

"Tucker?"

"My four-year-old son."

"He did that to the dog?" Cooper looked impressed.

"He was trying to make Bojangles into a dragon for tonight's trick-or-treating."

"A pink dragon?" Cooper chuckled. "I'll give the boy points for imagination."

A woman could wrap herself in that deep, husky chuckle and keep warm all winter long. "It's shaving gel. Tucker wanted a bald dragon."

"A ghost and a dragon?"

"How did you know Tucker is a ghost?" Up until last night, her son had wanted to be a pirate, or to be accurate, Captain Jack Sparrow from the *Pirates of the Caribbean* movie. Felicity, her seventeen-year-old sister-in-law, and her boyfriend, Sam, had come up with a string of battery-operated lights to go under an old pair of window sheers. In the darkness Tucker had glowed and shimmered, scaring his poor grandmother into dropping an entire bowl of cake batter when he had snuck up on her.

"He was either the ghost or the alien." Coop reached into his pants pocket, pulled out a dog biscuit, and tossed it to the struggling dog.

Bojangles nearly pulled Jenni's arm out of its socket jumping for the treat. "What alien? And where did you see them?" She glanced around the yard but didn't spot either boy.

She wasn't too worried. The boys knew the boundaries. It was one of the first things she did when they moved in months ago. She had purchased over the Internet two huge rolls of yellow plastic police tape, the kind that said POLICE LINE DO NOT CROSS and had strung it around trees near the house. This effectively marked the area of the woods where the boys were allowed to play. Only two areas on the property were left open—one was the driveway and the other was the treeless shoreline of the bay. The boys were under threat of eating spinach for dinner every night for a month if they went near the road or the bay.

"A ghost, and I think it was an alien, ran across the driveway on my way in." Cooper looked hesitant for a moment before adding, "You might want to have a talk with them about looking both ways before running out into the middle of the drive."

She closed her eyes and visualized the scene. "How close did you come to them?"

"Not that close, but, then, I knew there are two boys living here. I was going slow. Someone else might not be." Coop picked up the two boxes and his clipboard.

"Three, and he's a caterpillar."

"Three what?" Cooper looked confused.

"Three boys. You probably haven't met Chase yet. He's six and in first grade."

Coop whistled. "You and your husband seem to have your hands full."

"My husband passed away two years ago." She pulled the dog up the four steps, picked up his leash, and tied him to a post. She didn't want to talk about Ken and the empty hole in her heart. Two years seemed like only two months to a shattered heart. "You really think Corey looked like an alien instead of a caterpillar?" She had tried so hard on that outfit too. Sewing wasn't one of her specialties, but what did the UPS delivery guy think the two dozen feet going down the front of her son's costume were, antennaes?

"He went by pretty fast, so I really didn't have a good look at him." Cooper handed her the clipboard to sign. "Spacemen or aliens are supposed to be green, so I just assumed."

"He's supposed to be the Very Hungry Caterpillar from his favorite Eric Carle book." Next year she'd stick to making soap and buy the kids' costumes online. She signed for the boxes and handed the clipboard back to Cooper.

Bojangles tugged at his leash and howled as Tucker the ghost and Corey the caterpillar emerged from the woods. Cooper was right—her son did look like an alien. The two dozen green legs looked like wiggling tentacles as he ran toward her.

She was torn between laughter and tears. Seeing Corey's smile, she laughed.

Coop dropped the clipboard and grabbed for the porch post. It would never withstand the pressure the dog was putting on it. Any minute now the dog was going to bring the porch roof crashing down on top of their heads. "Bojangles, sit!" He held the post with one hand as he dug another treat out of his pants pocket.

The dog took one look at the approaching ghost and gave an earsplitting howl while tugging on the leash.

The post gave a small groan.

Coop dropped the biscuit onto the rotten floorboards and grabbed Bojangles's leash to take the tension off the post. The dog grabbed the treat and the post fell silent. "I hate to be the bearer of bad news, but I think your post is dry rotted." He knelt down and poked the tip of his pen into the base of the post. It went in about a half inch without a problem.

"Tell me something I don't know." Jenni frowned at the post.

"Mr. Brown, Mr. Brown!" shouted the ghost as he sprinted up the rickety steps, almost tripping on the hem of his costume. "You caught our dragon."

"Afraid not—your mother did." He turned to the woman standing beside him who was still studying the post. "I'm afraid I don't know your name." She was barely five feet four inches tall, but she was cute. No way would he have placed her as the mother of three small boys. Thick nearly black hair that hung past her shoulders was pulled back into a ponytail. At one time this morning, he would guess, she had been squeaky clean and fresh as the ocean breeze. Now she looked like she had lost a battle with a shaving cream–covered dog and had just crawled out from underneath the porch.

Her most amazing feature was her eyes. One minute they looked hazel; the next he could see amber sparkles within their depths. Tucker the Terror had his mother's hair and eye color. The younger boy had reddish hair beneath his green mask and hood.

"Oh, I'm sorry." Jenni stuck out her hand, took one look at it, and quickly hid it behind her back. "Jennifer Wright, mother to these monsters and the neurotic dragon—Jenni to my friends."

Coop smiled. The name suited her. It was plain and simple and gave you the impression of the girl next door. Of course, when he had been growing up in Sullivan, his next-door neighbor had looked nothing like Jenni. His neighbor had been a sixty-year-old lobster fisherman who was as mean as a snake and had more tattoos than a circus performer. "You don't look like your mother."

"My mother?"

"Dorothy, the woman who usually signs for all the packages."

Jenni gave a small, painful smile. "Dorothy is my mother-in-law. My parents passed away years ago."

He felt like he had just kicked a puppy. "I'm truly sorry." And he was. He could see the pain, along with the acceptance in her gaze. "I seem to be really putting my foot into my mouth this afternoon."

"It's okay. How would you have known?" Jenni

reached down and unclipped the leash from the pole. Bojangles hid behind her back and wailed when the ghost waved its arms at him.

"Tucker, stop that." Jenni reached down and patted the dog on the head. "Can't you see you have traumatized the dog enough for one day?"

Tucker pulled the sheer curtains over his head and grinned. "What's drama . . . whatever mean?"

"Traumatized. It means you scared him."

"I scared him shi—"

"That word coming out of your mouth, young man, better be 'spitless.'"

Coop looked up at the weathered underside of the porch roof and tried not to laugh.

Tucker seemed to think about it for an awfully long time before groaning, "Spitless."

"That just saved you from spending the rest of the night in your room, with no trick-or-treating." Jenni tapped her foot on the floorboards. "Since it was a close call, and you are the one who caused all this commotion, you can help me give Bojangles a bath."

"Mommmmmm!"

"Don't 'Mom' me. Go put your costume on your bed and then strip down to your Skivvies. You're the one going into the tub with him and scrubbing. I'll be doing the holding."

"But Mom, Chase says if we do it, we can say it. Besides, he knows how to spell it." Tucker crunched up the sheer curtains and crushed them to his chest.

"I'll give you points for trying to switch the blame onto Chase instead of your usual target Corey, but it's not going to work, Tucker. You know that word is bad, and if I hear it come out of your mouth, something worse than spinach will be going into it. I'm thinking oatmeal cranberry soap."

Tucker's eyes grew round with fear. "Yuck, oatmeal!" He turned and hurried into the house.

Corey, the green caterpillar, gave Coop a wave— "Bye, Mr. Brown"—and followed his brother through the front door.

The slamming of the wooden front door coincided with Jenni's sigh.

Coop laughed. "You just threatened your son with oatmeal?" Soap he understood. When he had been eight, he had had the misfortune of being in the same room where his mother's sewing circle had been meeting when he repeated a phrase his mean old neighbor had said nearly every day of his life. To this day he still couldn't use Ivory soap.

"Tucker would take soap as a challenge. I already know he despises oatmeal."

"At least you know his weaknesses." He saw a stack of boxes by the front door. "Are they to go?"

"Yes."

He picked up the first two boxes. "What are you going to do about the post?" He didn't want her to forget about it and have it come crashing down on top of someone's head.

"Put it on my list."

She tossed out the answer a little too nonchalantly. "How long is your list?" Considering the shape the house was in, he could picture an entire notebook filled with her to-do list.

"Longer than your arm."

He carried the boxes to the truck and came back for the rest. It really wasn't his business, and he had a route to finish. Maybe he could get her a list of handymen who were looking to make some extra cash. Shouldn't take more than twenty men and a year's worth of labor to spruce the place up. "Can I ask what Mistletoe Bay Company makes?" He usually picked up more boxes than he delivered. Whatever it was, he hoped it was profitable. His gut and trained eye were telling him the foundation beneath the house might be crumbling.

Jenni smiled. "Bath and body products, including the cranberry oatmeal soap I threatened Tucker with. If you would like, I can do up a sampler and you can give it to your wife or girlfriend. Call it free promotion and a thank-you for not running over my sons."

"No wife, no girlfriend, and believe me, it was my pleasure not running over your sons." Considering what his ex-girlfriend, Candace, used to spend on lotions and potions, there obviously was a market for such things. "Thanks for the offer, though. See you tomorrow."

"Bye, and thanks again."

Coop got into his truck and slowly drove down the gravel driveway while glancing into the rearview mirror. Jenni was struggling to hold on to Bojangles. The dog obviously wanted to do his daily routine of chasing him down the driveway until Coop threw a treat to him. Coop wasn't interested in the dog.

It was the enticing woman wearing a baggy sweat-shirt, jeans, and Ked sneakers whom he watched. He doubted Jenni was even thirty years old—so young to be a widow, and to be left raising three small boys. To top that, she was living with her mother-in-law. Yet when she smiled, it lit up the day and warmed the wind.

Amazing.

He shook his head as the woman, dog, and dilapidated porch disappeared from view. Wasn't his problem. So why did he keep picturing that dry-rotted post in his mind?

Jennifer Wright would have given her right arm for an hour in a hot bathtub filled with bubbles and a solid eight hours of sleep. It was a good thing no one offered the exchange. She was barely managing the business and the kids with both hands; she couldn't imagine what it would be like trying it with only one arm.

She shifted Corey in her arms and tried not to grimace when three of his caterpillar legs dug into her ribs. "That's it, boys. This is the last house."

"But Mom," moaned Tucker, "I still have room in my bag."

"Your bag is big enough to hold your bicycle." The boys had started off this evening wanting to hit every house in the town of Misty Harbor. Corey had conked out two streets ago, and she had to carry him from house to house. Chase, the wizard from the *Harry Potter* movies, had lost interest in accumulating piles of candy after the first street. He was more interested in looking at all the other kids' costumes and finding his schoolmates in the parade of kids going door-to-door.

Tucker, on the other hand, would keep ringing doorbells all night long if she let him. "You have enough candy in that bag to have you bouncing off the walls till Christmas."

She nodded to the house directly in front of them as

she put Corey back on his own two feet. "This looks like a good one. Check out all the decorations. I bet they will give out the big candy bars." The house had orange twinkling lights strung from every eave and window. The trees were bending under the weight of lights and ghosts, and there had to be at least two dozen carved and glowing pumpkins. A life-size Frankenstein was standing on the front porch holding a lantern to light the way to the door, and eerie music was coming from somewhere.

Someone obviously had a little too much time on their hands.

She smiled as the boys made their way up to the porch. Frankenstein had made a movement the boys hadn't seen. They were about to get a surprise. Chase and Tucker were going to love it. Corey was a different matter. He was almost four and idolized his older brothers, but underneath the tough act, he was still a little boy. She moved up the driveway a little bit in case Corey got scared.

Just as Tucker was about to reach for the doorbell, Frankenstein leaned down and in a creepy deep voice said, "Welcome to my castle."

Chase and Tucker jumped about a foot in the air, then laughed. Corey did what she'd thought he would do; he screamed, dropped his bag of candy, and sprinted off the porch right into her arms.

"Easy, hon. Remember, it's only a Halloween costume." She hugged Corey tight for a moment. "I told you, even adults sometimes dress up for trick-or-treat night."

Corey lifted his head from where he had buried it in her shoulder, and glanced back to the porch. Frankenstein was giving Tucker and Chase high fives. Corey relaxed slightly.

"Hey, little fellow!" bellowed the six-and-a-half-foot monster. "I didn't mean to give you that much of a fright."

Corey stopped shaking and whispered into her ear, "Is it a man inside or a kid?"

"Sounds like a man, hon. Probably some dad who wanted to have some fun on Halloween." She gave him another squeeze.

"Do you want me to give one of your brothers your candy bar, or do you want to come get it yourself?" asked the monster.

She whispered to Corey, "How about I go up with you?" Corey nodded his head. "Carry me."

"Will do." She thought her son was extremely brave to go back up there. She kept both arms around him and walked up the pathway to the porch steps.

Frankenstein bent down and picked up the bag of goodies Corey had dropped. "Here you go. Sorry for frightening you." The monster, who had a really great lifelike mask on, looked at her. "Sorry about that. My wife warned me the little ones weren't going to like it, but I couldn't resist. I dress up every year, and the older ones love a good fright."

"That's okay." Chase was down on his knees examining Frankenstein's boots. Tucker was studying the mask.

"Wow!" exclaimed Tucker. "How does it move when you talk?"

"Painfully." The man chuckled. "I forgot to shave before applying the glue."

"Glue? Wow, we have glue at home."

"Not that kind of glue, Tucker." She shuddered to think what her son would glue to his face. "It's a special kind of glue made for masks and such."

"Your mom's right, son. You have to send away for this stuff. The guys in Hollywood use it for special effects in the movies."

"Cool." Tucker looked duly impressed.

Chase tapped his knuckles on the huge black boots. "What are these made of?"

The man chuckled. "Plaster of paris. Made them myself. It's the same technique they use when you break your arm and they wrap it up in all that gauze. I just spray painted them black when I was done."

"Can I touch one of your bolts?" Tucker was looking for something to stand on so he could reach the man's neck, where two bolts were sticking out on either side.

"Boys, I'm sure Mr. . . . . ummmmm Frankenstein has better things to do with his evening than to have a bunch of boys poking at him."

"Pete Kingsman, at your service, ma'am." He bent down, and Tucker gingerly touched one of the bolts.

"It's rubber." Tucker sounded disappointed that the man didn't have a metal rod holding his head on.

"What did you think they were going to be, real?" Mr. Kingsman laughed as Chase touched the other bolt.

"How did you get your face so green?" asked Chase.

"Are you really that tall?" asked Tucker.

"That's enough, boys. Mr. Kingsman has been more than patient with you both." She knew if the questions kept coming eventually there would be one that would embarrass her to death.

Corey whispered into her ear, "Can I touch him?"

Mr. Kingsman must have had excellent hearing, because he laughed and said, "Sure, you can. Want to touch a bolt like your brothers did?"

Corey nodded his head as she slowly put him back on his own two feet. She watched as her son gathered up his courage and very slowly touched the bolt that appeared to be screwed into the man's neck. There was even a trail of blood leaking out of the bolt hole.

Mr. Kingsman smiled and slowly ran his finger down the front of his throat. He held up the green-tipped finger for all the boys to see the grease paint. "See, fake."

Corey laughed. "He's not really green." He took a step back just in case.

Mr. Kingsman handed Corey a big candy bar from the bowl near the front door. "Only leprechauns and Kermit the frog are green."

"What do you say to Mr. Kingsman, boys?" So much for her drumming it into their heads all night long to say 'thank you' to everyone.

"Thanks, Mr. Kingsman," said Chase politely.

"Thanks." Corey grinned and he dropped the goodie into his bag.

"Thanks, Frankenstein." Tucker chuckled as he sprinted down the steps.

"Thank you for taking the time to reassure Corey, Mr. Kingsman." She followed her sons down the pathway.

"My pleasure. I have grandsons about their age on the west coast. They made me feel like a real grandpop there for a little while."

"It was our pleasure." She didn't want to think about how much her own parents would have loved their grandsons. But at least she had Dorothy. She wouldn't know what to do without Dorothy, the boys' only grandmother.

"Okay, kids, to the car. It's parked around the corner. I can't walk another step." She bent down and picked up

Corey. It was getting dangerously close to Corey's bed-time, but she couldn't tell his brothers that. Chase wouldn't care much, but Tucker would hound Corey for a week for making them stop trick-or-treating earlier than he wanted.

She had wasted half this afternoon, between dragging Bojangles out from underneath the porch, bathing the hysterical mutt, and bathing Tucker after he'd made a bigger mess in her tub than the dog. Then she'd had to sop up the water all over the bathroom floor, clean the tub, and take a shower herself. By that time Dorothy had dinner ready and none of the boys wanted to eat any-thing nutritious before they went out. It had been a battle of wills, of which she probably came out on the short side.

She still had a good four hours' worth of work out in the shop tonight before she could think about heading for her own bed.

She helped Corey into his car seat and wrestled the seat belt on. All of his caterpillar legs were getting in the way. Tucker and Chase got their own belts buckled and were working out a deal on what candy could be swapped for what. She closed the door as they started to argue what was worth more, a Snickers bar or a peanut butter cup.

She smiled as she headed for the driver's side of the car. When it came to her sons, she was the world's biggest pushover. She made a mental note to work on that before they hit their teenage years.

Chapter Two

Coop was pounding in the last nail when Jenni and the kids pulled up in front of the house. He had wanted to be done and out of there before she even returned, but Dorothy Wright had had other ideas. The older woman kept plying him with fresh hot coffee, pumpkin cookies, and praises.

It really wasn't any big deal, and he had told Dorothy that the first six times she had thanked him. It was for his own peace of mind that he had returned after work with an eight-foot-long four-by-four and tools. He had kept picturing the porch roof caving in on top of a ghost, a caterpillar, and their hazel-eyed mother.

He had had less frightening nightmares after watching horror movies as a kid. A piece of lumber and some nails were a cheap price to pay for a good night's sleep.

"Wow! Hi, Mr. Brown," shouted Tucker as he rushed from the car. "What'ya doing?"

Coop tried not to chuckle as he climbed down the stepladder and took a look at the Wright family as they tumbled, rolled, and stepped out of the midsize SUV that was a couple years old. The vehicle appeared to be in a lot better shape than the house, which was good, considering he didn't know what he would have done if he'd spotted duct tape on the car, like the porch.

Instead of using nails, someone had duct taped three of the porch balusters onto the railing. The one shutter to the dining room window also was held on to the house by a dozen strips of the silver tape. Here he had thought it was part of the overzealous Halloween decorating. It wasn't.

"'Hi' back."

Tucker had a string of lights lit under his ghost costume. Coop guessed that to a kid it would appear cool. To his eye, if Tucker added some big wings and a halo he would look like an earthbound angel. He chuckled at that comparison.

A second kid followed Tucker up onto the porch. He guessed this was Chase, the boy he hadn't met yet. Chase, who was a couple inches taller than Tucker, was dressed in a purple and gold robe with shimmering stars all over it. A purple dunce cap was perched on his head and a fake gray beard was covering most of his face. Chase was also carrying a five-foot-tall wooden walking stick.

"What'ya doing?" asked Tucker again as he stuck an unwrapped candy bar up under his costume and into his mouth. Under the porch light Coop could see chocolate smears all over the sheer costume. Tucker was beginning to look like a Dalmatian ghost.

Coop glanced at the SUV as Jenni reached in the back door and unbuckled a squirming caterpillar. Corey exited the car carrying a bag almost as big as he was. It appeared to be holding an impressive amount of candy.

"What did you do—hit every house in Misty Harbor?"

Jenni was bundled up against the cold, her cheeks were pink, and she looked tired. But at least she wasn't covered in pink shaving gel and muck.

For a woman who'd just herded three kids through the streets of Misty Harbor, she shouldn't have looked that beautiful.

"Just about," answered Jenni as she climbed the steps. "What are you doing?"

He looked at the three boys and couldn't very well tell her the roof was about to cave in on them. He didn't want to frighten the boys. "Since I noticed the dry rot this afternoon, I figured I'd just give this post some additional support until you get a chance to have it replaced." He had almost purchased a new post at the hardware store after he had finished his route, but that would have been like putting a new door on one of the cabins in the *Titanic*. Without a major overhaul, Jenni's house was still going to sink.

"Thank you, but you didn't have to do that." Jenni looked embarrassed. "What do I owe you?"

"I already have a job." He didn't want Jenni, or anyone else, thinking he was trying to hit them up for money. "Consider it a good deed." He could see the uncertainty on Jenni's face. "Besides, Dorothy has already paid me with enough coffee and pumpkin cookies to fatten me up till Christmas."

"She's a great cook."

"I noticed." He also noticed that Jenni didn't have any electrical outlets on the porch. Dorothy had had to run an extension cord for him through the dining room window. As he was looking for the nonexistent outlet, he'd spotted a heavy-duty orange extension cord coming out of the living room window that the lights in one of the trees

were plugged in to. Someone had plugged the inch opening in the window with tube socks and more duct tape.

Another cord snaked its way around the side of the
house, giving electricity to the ten-foot-high blow-up
Snoopy vampire. A soft electrical hum filled the silence.

Six carved pumpkins were lined up on the porch. The
candles were nearly burnt out and the stench of scorched
pumpkin hung in the air. The candles had been so powerful that the faces had all contorted and become mushed
on the pumpkins. They now resembled aged apples.

The blind, menacing-looking panda sat in the rocking
chair in the shadows, occasionally being rocked by the
wind. It had been freaking him out all night. The wooden
skeleton was still hanging out of the upstairs window,
banging against the clapboard siding. The bones actually
rattled softly against each other with every breeze.

At thirty-two he had thought he was a little too old
to be getting the shivers on Halloween. Then again he
had never met the Wrights before.

"Tucker, put that down," Jenni said.

He glanced around at the boy and saw him holding
Coop's drill. Thankfully it wasn't plugged in. Corey was
using a pair of needle-nose pliers on one of his caterpillar legs. The older boy, who he was guessing was supposed to be a wizard or a magician, was inspecting the
four-by-four piece of lumber Coop had just put up.

He quickly took the power drill from Tucker's sticky
hands. "Whoa, you shouldn't pick up tools. They might
be plugged in and then you could hurt yourself or someone else." The drill bit had been dangerously close to
Corey's thigh.

Now, there was his nightmare for the night.

He unplugged the circular saw he had been using and put the drill back in his toolbox. The saw went to a safe spot, between his feet on the porch, away from the curious boys, because it didn't fit in his box. He shuddered to think what Tucker could do with a ten-inch circular saw.

"Boys, why don't you go ahead inside and show Grandmom how much candy you collected." Jenni took the pliers out of Corey's hands and put them in the toolbox.

The boys went running into the house. Shouts and pounding feet seemed to echo in every direction.

Coop felt sorry for Grandmom. "Are they always this vocal?"

"They're on a sugar high that will last till Thanksgiving." Jenni shook her head and unzipped her jacket. "I'm not quite sure what to say about all of this." She pointed to the post. "You didn't have to do this, Mr. Armstrong."

"It's Coop, remember?" Coop started to pack up the rest of the tools. "I need to work on some brownie points to make up for my misspent youth—karma and all that stuff."

She didn't need or like charity. Although she couldn't afford to have the entire house redone from top to bottom, she could pay a handyman to do some of the jobs to keep it from falling in on them. "I had two different men out here to help fix up the place. Neither lasted more than a week."

She sighed as she looked at the wrinkled, mushed pumpkins. Four of the candles were out, one was burning okay, and the sixth pumpkin was giving off black smoke. She walked over to the smoldering gourds and blew out the remaining candles. Burning the place to the ground might solve some of her problems with the house, but then it also would create a whole new list of them.

Jenni disliked holidays and all the hoopla that surrounded them. She felt inept, even though she knew she was quite capable of handling anything thrown her way. Two years ago she had learned the hard way just how strong she could be.

Easter wasn't too bad. It wasn't hard to hide some eggs and fill colorful baskets. Halloween was a challenge. At her age she shouldn't be climbing trees to string lights or hang ghosts. This year she had paid her sister-in-law's boyfriend, Sam, to do the climbing and the stringing. Felicity and Sam had had a ball with the boys decorating the other weekend, even though the house looked a little over-the-top.

The panda still freaked her out every time she saw it. The plastic eyes, hanging out of its face, seemed to follow her every move.

Christmas was the worst. Last year she'd had to rely on the kindness of a neighbor to help get the eight-foot tree into their house and anchored securely. Then she had nearly broken her neck trying to get the star on top. The only outside decorating she had done was nail a wreath to the front door and drape a red scarf around a half-melted snowman the boys had built the day before. Her heart just wasn't into Christmas or any other holidays.

She missed Kenneth too much.

For living in a house filled to the rafters with people and pets, she was lonely. She was a horrible person. Here she had so much to be thankful for, three beautiful and healthy boys, a mother-in-law who not only did all of the cooking, but also helped run the house and the boys. Then there was Felicity, Kenneth's younger sister, and now hers.

"What happened to them? Did Dorothy make them explode with too many cookies and cups of coffee?" Coop closed up the toolbox.

"Power tools, electricity, and my boys aren't a very good combination." Then again, Tucker could make breathing dangerous.

"Ouch." He placed the toolbox in the bed of his truck. "Want to elaborate, and was anyone hurt?"

"Mr. Carter swears Tucker took ten years off his life. Considering he was seventy-eight, he wasn't real thrilled with my son. Lesson learned; never leave exposed wiring sticking out of the wall when you leave a room."

"I didn't know Vince Carter was still doing odd jobs around town."

"He's not any longer. He officially retired."

Coop laughed. "What happened to number two?"

"An unattended caulking gun loaded with something called Liquid Nails. It took the cat months to grow back all its hair."

Coop's laughter filled the night. She chuckled for the first time about the incident. At the time it had been anything but funny, with poor Dumb stuck three feet up the dining room wall screeching its head off. The sounds that cat made were enough to raise the dead.

"Bob Sanders asked if Tucker's middle name was Damian. He packed up his tools and hasn't returned one of my phone calls since."

Coop continued to laugh as he picked up his ladder and placed it in the bed of his truck. "Don't worry about Sanders. He never did have a sense of humor."

"You know him?" Maybe if she begged nicely she could get Coop to convince Sanders to come back for a couple of days. She'd even promise to lock Tucker in the attic, if need be. "He not only unjammed three of my windows, but he got the hot water working in the sink in one of the bathrooms."

"I went to school with his two sons." He placed the saw in the truck. "Don't you have hot water in the other bathroom sinks?"

"Dorothy and Felicity's sink doesn't. But we did manage to get it to drain properly."

"Who's Felicity?"

"Dorothy's daughter, and my sister-in-law."

"She lives here too? How many people actually live here?" Coop was staring at the house like he was counting bedrooms.

"Six; me and my three boys, Dorothy, and Felicity, who is seventeen and dating Sam Fischer, Eli Fischer's son from East Sullivan. Do you know him?" Being new to an area held some disadvantages, one being not knowing family histories. Sam seemed like a very nice boy, but maybe his family tree had a few ax murderers hanging out on some branches.

"I know Eli. Good, honest man. Can't imagine the son being too much different. Hardworking family."

Dorothy would be relieved to hear that, even though she was having a hard time adjusting to her baby dating boys who drove. "There is also Bojangles, whom you met, two cats, Dumb and Dumber, an iguana, and a twenty-gallon fish tank that usually has a dead fish or two floating on the top." No matter how hard she tried, it was nearly impossible to keep any fish alive for more than a month. The boys already had next month's fish picked out.

"I'd hate to have your food bill. What do you do, own stock in Purina?"

"I'm not that lucky." She wished she owned some stock, any stock. Then again, with the way the stock market rose and fell, it would probably cause her more headaches than it was worth. How rich could she get on cat food?

"Mom!" shouted Corey from inside the house. "Tucker's taking my candy."

"I'm not!"

"Are too."

Chase, minus his beard and hat, opened the front door. "Grandmom says that Mr. Armstrong has to come in. She has something for him."

"Could you tell her that I really don't want anything, Jenni?"

"Not in this lifetime. No one says no to Dorothy. Just take whatever she's giving you. It's probably pumpkin bread or sugar cookies." She smiled at Coop as she held the door open for him. "It's how she thanks people. By giving them high cholesterol."

Coop brushed sawdust off his jeans and wiped his feet. "What, she wants to keep the doctors in practice?"

"No, but she does own a few shares of stock in some drug companies." Jenni tried to hold her smile as she entered the house. She had been hoping that some magical little elves had visited and cleaned up the place. No such luck. If possible it was worst than when she had left two hours ago.

The kids had been stripping out of their costumes,

leaving them where they landed. Candy wrappers were everywhere, and it looked like Dumber had been eating the mulberry candle she had on the coffee table again. Chunks of maroon wax were hacked up on the area rug that hadn't seen a vacuum in days. Legos and Hot Wheels were scattered everywhere, along with some of the boys' artwork.

Chase had been constructing a tower out of marshmallows and toothpicks. Tucker and Corey had been doing noodle pictures, which consisted of lots of different-shape uncooked noodles and about a gallon of Elmer's glue. Three months ago the local vet, Merle Sherman, wasn't too happy with her or the boys when Bojangles ate Tucker's noodle picture of Spider-Man. The dog wasn't too happy with the vet, or its treatment.

"Please excuse the mess." It didn't matter who it was, she always seemed to be apologizing for how the house looked. It wasn't her fault there weren't enough hours in the day or that she was born with only two hands.

Corey went running for the steps, clutching his bag of candy and screaming. Tucker was fast on his tail. "Stop!" she shouted and held up her hand. "Enough."

Both boys came to a screeching halt. "But Mom," whined Corey, who had somehow managed to get out of his caterpillar outfit, all but the green tights and a baggy T-shirt. He looked like a demented Robin Hood with his face still painted green, with purple polka dots. For some reason, Corey had insisted on the dots.

"No buts." She held out her hand. "The candy stays in the kitchen, not upstairs."

Tucker grinned and wiggled his eyebrows at his younger brother as he handed over the candy.

Corey started to cry. "He'll eat it all."

"He will not." She gave Tucker her sternest look. "You will not touch either one of your brothers' candy. Got it?"

"Yeah, but I just wanted to trade."

"No trading." She rolled her eyes. Tucker was either going to be a gangster or a politician. "Where's your bag?"

"In the kitchen with Grandmom." Tucker started to head for the kitchen.

"You and Corey head on upstairs and get ready for your baths. I'll be up in a few minutes." She gave her youngest son a hug and dried his tears. "I won't let Tucker get any. But you guys have had enough for tonight. We'll save some for the month of tomorrows to come."

Corey sniffled. "Promise?"

She gave him another hug and a kiss. "Promise." She turned him toward the stairs and lightly patted his bottom. "Now get going."

Both boys dashed upstairs with pounding feet and shouts of who would be first.

Jenni took off her coat and scarf and added them to the pile of clothes on an overstuffed chair.

Coop chuckled and then cringed as a door slammed upstairs and one of the boys started shouting. The ornate chandelier hanging in the foyer area, at the bottom of the steps, shook above his head. He stepped to his right. "Is it always like this, or is Halloween a special occasion?"

"I would love to blame all the candy, but the sad truth is I can't. They are always like this." She headed for the kitchen. "Come on back."

Coop followed while taking in everything. The living room had recently been painted a khaki color, all but the wall on which the stairs were located. That wall still had

torn and faded wallpaper from the sixties on it. It would
take scaffolding to do that wall because it went clear to
the third floor. The furniture looked comfortable and
there seemed to be plenty of it. A brick fireplace was
against the outside wall, and it looked like it hadn't been
used in years. Hopefully Jenni would know to have it
checked out before trying to light a fire in it. Ten to one
the chimney needed some work, or at least a major
cleaning.

Below his feet he could detect the rumbling of a furnace. At least the house was warm.

An orange cat came barreling down from upstairs and
into the dining room. He had no idea if it had been
Dumb or Dumber. By the noise the boys were making
upstairs he would guess that hardwood floors were
throughout the house. Jenni might consider looking into
carpeting to lessen the noise.

"Who named the cats?" He knew of the movie, but
Jenni didn't look like a *Dumb & Dumber* type person,
and the boys were too young to have seen the movie.

"They're Felicity's. She's had them for about two
years now."

"She's a movie fan?" That made sense. Their names
sounded like something a teenager would give them.

"No, let's just say they weren't the sharpest kitties in
the litter." Jenni placed Corey's candy bag on the
kitchen table.

Although the rest of the house looked questionable,
the kitchen was in top shape. White cabinets, some with
glass front doors, new countertops, and top-of-the-line
stainless-steel appliances filled the room. Baking ingredients were neatly lined up on counters, and there

seemed to be quite a collection of small appliances. Someone took her cooking seriously, and her name was Dorothy Wright.

He looked at Dorothy and knew she commanded the kitchen like a captain would his vessel. Everything had to be shipshape and in top working order. By the smell, whatever she was doing, she was doing it right. He counted five loaves of some type of bread cooling on racks, and she was busy icing leaf-shaped cookies.

"All done, Coop?" Dorothy wielded the plastic bag of yellow icing like a pro.

"Yes, ma'am." He glanced at Chase, who was sitting at the large pine kitchen table counting his candy as he dropped it into a big plastic bowl. He was up to thirty-nine and it looked like he was only halfway through his pile.

"How many people live at your house?" Dorothy was now adding red icing to the two dozen leaves spread out before her.

"Only myself, ma'am." What did it matter how many people lived at his place?

"No kids?" Dorothy glanced up from the cookies.

"No kids, no wife, not even a steady girlfriend." He chuckled at the look of disbelief on Dorothy's face. "But my parents live in Sullivan. Does that count?"

Dorothy gave Jenni a look he couldn't decipher. "You like pumpkin bread?"

"Yes, ma'am, but you already paid me in coffee and cookies." He was feeling guilty. The only reason he had supported that post was so that *he* could sleep tonight.

"Nonsense." Dorothy put down the icing and wrapped one of the loaves in foil. "Since you won't take money, you have to take food."

"I do?" He watched as Jenni dumped one of the boys' bags into a large plastic bowl. She sealed the bowl with a matching lid, slapped a piece of masking tape on it, and wrote Tucker's name.

"As my husband always said, 'Union rules.'" Dorothy wrapped another loaf.

"I never heard of that rule." He had been a union member out in California for almost twelve years.

"I've seen grown men strike over Dorothy's blueberry pie." Jenni paid her mother-in-law the compliment as she dumped Corey's candy in the other bowl. "It's the only reason we got the countertop and appliances installed. Dorothy kept feeding the crew."

"You also went on a three-hour hike with the boys," Dorothy chuckled. "Tucker was inquisitive that day."

"Is inquisitive the same as bad?" asked Chase.

Coop really did try not to laugh. Everyone seemed to have Tucker's number. Dorothy and Jenni ignored Chase's question and changed the subject.

"How many did you count, Chase?" asked Jenni.

"Seventy-two." Chase looked extremely proud of that fact, either because he could count that high, or because they had hit that many houses.

"That will last you till Christmas." Jenni picked up Tucker's bowl and compared it to Chase's. "Do I want to know how many candy wrappers are all over the backseat of my car? Your brother's stash seems to be short quite a few pieces."

"He ate some," Chase said.

Dorothy handed Coop two loaves of wrapped bread and a small container filled with cookies. "One is pumpkin, the other is cranberry nut. Since I didn't know what kind of cookies you liked, I put a couple of each kind in there."

"Thanks, but you really didn't have to." Dorothy didn't look like a grandmother to three very active boys. Her reddish hair had some gray in it and there might be a wrinkle or two by her eyes, but that was about it. No bifocals, no age-spotted hands, and no big flowery aprons like his own grandmother used to wear. Jeans, a pink long-sleeve T-shirt with a moose on it, and sneakers were this granny's baking outfit. The only flaw he could see was a smudge or two of flour on her nose.

The front door opened and the sound of a lighthearted argument could be heard.

"Come on, Felicity, you can't leave me like this," proclaimed a male's voice.

"Sure, I can. Why don't you go ask Brittany to change you into a prince." Felicity Wright entered the kitchen like a queen. To be more accurate, like a princess. She stopped and smiled. "Hi, who are you?"

Coop could see why Dorothy Wright was still a very attractive woman just by looking at her seventeen-year-old daughter. If girls had looked like that back when he had been in Hancock County High School he never would have headed for the sun and surf of California. Dressing up like a fairy tale princess instead of the wicked witch helped matters. "I'm Cooper Armstrong. I'm the UPS delivery guy and today I noticed the porch post out front was dry-rotted. I just stopped by to brace it up."

Felicity grinned at Jenni. "Did you now? How interesting."

He could see that his stopping by might not have been the smartest thing to do. His Good Samaritan number was about to get him matched up with a single mother of three. If that wasn't enough to make him run screaming from the house, nothing was. "Your mother is paying me in goodies." He held up the baked goods to prove his point.

A six-foot-one-inch frog entered the kitchen.

Green rubber flippers smacked the wooden floors. "Come on, babe, one kiss, and I betcha I turn into your Prince Charming," teased Sam Fischer as he made kissy noises toward Felicity.

Sam stopped in midpucker. "Wow, you're Cooper Armstrong." The frog held out a flipper.

"Guilty, and you're a frog." He laughed at the green-faced teenager. This must be Sam Fischer, the smitten boyfriend. Only a teenage boy on the brink of love would be caught wearing a green rubber suit. "Have we met?" He vaguely remembered Eli Fischer, the boy's father, from twelve years ago. Sam had been barely starting kindergarten.

"I'm Sam Fischer, and I just might be the one to break your record."

"What record?" asked Jenni.

"Most yards per pass in a season," replied Sam. "In 1993 he ran for an average of twenty-three yards per catch. That record still stands."

He couldn't believe that no one had shattered that record yet. Back in '93 he could move like the wind and catch just about anything thrown his way. It had been a golden year. "So I take it you're a wide receiver?"

"Number 80, same number you wore."

"Sam, is he the guy from the pictures in the showcase

you showed me?" Felicity popped a cookie into her mouth and stared at him thoughtfully.

"Yep, that's how I recognized him." Sam seemed very impressed. "Got any advice?"

"Don't drop the ball and run like hel"—he glanced at Chase, who was listening attentively to their every word—"heck."

Sam laughed and Felicity rolled her eyes.

"How's your quarterback?" A wide receiver was only as good as the quarterback would let him be. He had been lucky back in high school to have a great quarterback who could throw a long ball.

"Decent, real decent. He can hit who he's throwing for as long as he's not rushed."

"How good is your line?"

"Getting better with each game, and they are all juniors, like me. Not too many seniors on the team, so next year we are figuring to shatter a few of those records." Sam had that certain gleam in his eyes, the gleam that said he lived and breathed football.

He remembered that gleam. He had seen it in his own mirror when he had been eighteen. "Maybe I'll come by the next home game."

"Friday night at seven." Sam nearly hopped with excitement. "Can I tell Coach Fellman you'll be there?"

"I guess, but I'll only be in the stands." Why would the coach care one way or the other?

"Stop by the bench before the game starts. Coach Fellman would love to see you."

"How do you know?"

"He talks about you sometimes. He saw you play when he was a kid."

"Fellman? I don't remember a Fellman back in school."

"Bob Fellman—he was about six years behind you."

"Little Bobby?" He vaguely remembered a little kid who used to follow him around all the time. The kid was skinny as a post and barely broke the five-foot mark. "Who would have thought he'd become a coach." He shook his head in amazement. "Tell him I'll stop by."

"We'll be there too." Felicity grinned at Jenni. "The boys would love to see Sam play."

"Can we, Mom?" Chase joined the conversation.

Jenni looked at her son. "Sure."

"I got to get going," he said. He didn't like the way this was going. He'd rather be double teamed than to face a bunch of matchmakers. It didn't matter how nicely Jenni filled out a pair of jeans. "I need to unplug my extension cord from an outlet in the dining room."

"I'll show you the way." Jenni walked into the darkened dining room and flipped on the light.

"Thanks again, Dorothy." He felt like an eight hundred–pound gorilla in the room. "I'll see you Friday night, Sam." He quickly followed Jenni.

An aged, ugly, and large light hung above the fancy table. The beautiful antique mahogany dining room set was totally out of place in the room. This was definitely the room that no one had spent a dime on. The faded, peeling wallpaper had to be at least fifty years old. The hardwood floor needed to be refinished, and he wouldn't have trusted the light above the table. The thing looked ready to come crashing down.

A silver tea set sat on the buffet, and two silver candelabras were on the table with a fall-themed centerpiece. Fine antique china and crystal filled the china closet. It obviously was a room the boys were kept out of. He would hate to think what Tucker would do to his grandmother's china.

The furniture looked like something Dorothy would treasure. She probably had inherited it from her own mother or grandmother.

He walked to the front windows, where his orange extension cord was snaked under the screen and plugged into the wall socket. He pulled the plug and pushed the cord back outside onto the porch. "I would tell Dorothy not to be too concerned about Sam. He seems like a nice kid, and he's obviously head over heels for Felicity." The wooden window was a real pain to get closed. He muttered a couple of curses under his breath as he finally got it to lock tight.

"How can you tell?"

"He's dressed like a frog. That says it all." He took one last glance around the room. On the far wall there was a large, strange shape, of missing wallpaper and shattered plaster. It looked like someone had used a screwdriver or a crowbar on the paper and plaster. It was a horrible, ugly, and deep scar. It was going to take a professional to fix the mess. "What happened there?" And why was the shape hauntingly familiar?

"Remember I told you about Tucker, a caulking tube of Liquid Nails, and Felicity's cat, Dumb?"

Coop stared at the wall in dawning horror. He now knew why the shape was so familiar. It was the shape of a cat. Tucker had glued the cat right to the wall!

He muttered, "Mother of God," as he slid down the wall, laughing hysterically.

Chapter Three

For a November night in Maine, the weather wasn't too bad. Jenni had brought along plenty of blankets for herself and the boys. She hadn't been to a football game since college. Ken hadn't been a sports nut, but the boys seemed to be enjoying themselves, especially since their current idol, Sam, would be playing.

So far she had had to warn the boys only three times not to be running up and down the bleachers. They already had consumed hot dogs, chips, and sodas, and the game was just about to start. She figured by halftime she would have to remortgage the house for another trip to the snack stand. Her business had better be a huge success if she wanted to continue to feed the boys during their teenage years.

Cheerleaders, dressed in tight white, fuzzy sweaters, short blue skirts, and flesh-colored tights, were high-kicking, screaming their lungs out, and shaking their pom-poms. They also had to be freezing their butts off. The temperature hadn't been above forty degrees all day. Since the sun had set, the thermometer had been falling.

Felicity, who had come with her, was sitting with a bunch of girls on the far side of the bleachers. They all seemed to be normal teenage girls, eyeing every boy in the stadium. Except her sister-in-law, who seemed to have eyes only for Sam. Dorothy thought her daughter's infatuation with Sam was only a phase. Jenni wasn't too sure on that one.

Dorothy was the warm, lucky one tonight. She was at home by herself having a relaxing, quiet evening. Jenni's mother-in-law deserved a break from the boys and the cooking. She didn't know how she would manage without Dorothy. Raising the boys by herself would be challenging enough, but doing it while starting her own business would be nearly impossible. Dorothy was staring at the big 5-0 and should be slowing down in life.

There were reasons women that age went through menopause, and usually those reasons had names.

Jenni had seen signs that Dorothy might be starting the "change," but so far her mother-in-law denied the symptoms or the possibility. There was always some other reason as to why she was opening windows and fanning herself in October. The other day she'd caught Dorothy crying over a cell phone commercial.

Dorothy had better be starting the change, because she didn't know what she would do if her mother-in-law was going nuts. It had been hard enough to hold herself together when Ken had been killed in the fire that had destroyed half the chemical company where he had been working. Five people had died that afternoon, including a firefighter who had been trying to rescue the workers.

"Hey, Mom," said Chase, "there's Mr. Armstrong." Chase stood up and pointed down to the players' bench.

She glanced down. Coop Armstrong was shaking hands with one of the football coaches. Sam was standing right beside him, beaming. Coop really had been a football player for the local high school. She had heard all about Coop and his impressive records from Sam on Halloween night. She hadn't been too surprised. Coop certainly seemed built for the role, even if it had been over a decade ago. Coop had kept in impressive shape.

She wasn't blind. Nor was she stupid. She had seen that look of speculation in Felicity's gaze the other night and the blatant attempt to set them up as a couple. Felicity knew darn well she rarely refused Chase anything, and it had been he who had asked to be taken to tonight's game.

It had been the first time Chase had shown any interest in sports. Usually his nose was buried in a book, or he was in front of the computer in her office. Chase was just like his father, a bookworm, and one who questioned everything. Her oldest son was one of those kids who just had to take everything apart to see how it worked.

"Can we go down and see him?" asked Tucker, who was standing on the bench to see where Chase had been pointing. Corey, not wanting to miss out on anything, was standing beside him.

"No, I'm sure he's busy." She reached up and held the back of Corey's jacket so he wouldn't fall. "Let's sit down, before one of you takes a header and gets hurt."

"How come when Tucker took a header off the front porch, he hurt his arm and not his head?" asked Chase.

She was tempted to tell them that Tucker's head was as hard as a brick, but knowing her son, that would be an open invitation for him to put those words to the test. "He landed on his arm, not his head." Thankfully Doc

Sydney said it had been sprained and not broken. "Besides, the bushes broke his fall. There aren't any bushes under these bleachers, just gravel."

"So he took an armer off the porch?"

"Something like that." Jenni tugged on Corey's jacket until he sat.

"Hey, Mr. Brown!" shouted Tucker, waving his arms. "We're up here!" Tucker's voice caused half the stadium, the entire football team, and Cooper Armstrong to glance their way.

She felt like crawling into a hole, or at least sliding through the bleachers to the ground below. Tucker, when he wanted to, could shatter eardrums. Corey jumped back up on his seat and started waving and shouting too. Chase just grinned and waved.

Since they were only on the third row of seating, it didn't take Coop long to spot them. Coop and Sam both waved back. Even half the players waved back, causing quite a few people sitting around them to chuckle. She hoped the cold weather was concealing the blush sweeping up her face.

If they had been on the very top row, where the boys had wanted to sit, maybe Coop and the football team wouldn't have heard Tucker. But there was no way she was allowing the boys to sit way up there. Her heart couldn't handle the stress. They would break their necks if they fell through the bleachers. Here on the third row they just might sprain an ankle. She had learned the hard way when dealing with Tucker, always err on the side of caution.

"He's coming! He's coming!" shouted Tucker.

"Shhhhh . . . Tucker, you don't have to shout. I'm sitting right here." She also had noticed that Coop was heading their way. Now she felt like a complete idiot. She didn't want Coop to feel obliged to sit with them. She was quite capable of handling the boys at a sporting event, even though what she knew about football could be written on a three-by-five index card. The front side.

Now, baseball and bowling, she understood.

Coop chatted with a few of the locals as he made his way up to the third row of seating to Jenni Wright and the boys. He couldn't very well ignore them, especially when Tucker was shouting louder than the perky little cheerleaders with their megaphones.

"Hey, Mr. Brown, sit with us," Tucker said.

"His name is Armstrong, not Brown." Chase rolled his eyes.

"Boys, that's enough. Mr. Armstrong is free to sit wherever he wants." Jenni tugged Corey's hat over his ears. "It's a free country." She smiled at him, as if to soften her words. "Sorry about this. I'm sure you already have a place to sit."

"As it turns out, I don't." Coop winked at Chase and ruffled Tucker's hair. "Would you mind if I joined you?" He knew a lot of the locals, and the last thing he wanted to do was spend the night going over past glories and a whole list of might-have-beens.

"Not at all." The players from both teams were running onto the field. "But be warned, the boys will drive you crazy with questions about the game."

"No problem—football's my game." Coop sat down next to Chase on the end closest to the aisle. "How many games have you boys been to?"

"None," Chase said.

Tucker tried climbing over his brother to get closer to

Coop. Jenni grabbed the back of his jacket. "Whoa . . . you sit next to me." There was no way she was allowing Tucker out of arm's length. "Where's your hat?"

"In my pocket." Tucker pouted.

"Put it on. Your ears are pink." All the boys had the same style beanie, but in different colors. She never dressed the boys alike; it got too confusing to keep them straight.

"Mr. Brown doesn't have a beanie on."

"His name is Mr. Armstrong, and he's old enough to dress himself." Coop was wearing a brown leather jacket and a New England Patriots ball cap.

"I dress myself." Tucker tugged on the hat and crossed his arms in protest.

"You can't tie your own shoes." Chase had accomplished that feat when he had been only three and a half. "Mom still gives you a bath."

"Boys, stop arguing and watch the game. It just started." She couldn't believe Chase was bragging. Chase never tooted his own horn or ridiculed his brothers for not being able to do stuff he could. What was with him tonight? He wasn't acting like himself.

"How come Sam's not out on the field?" Chase pointed to Felicity's boyfriend, who was on the sidelines.

"He is sharing the ball, hon. Not everyone can play at the same time."

Coop gave her a funny look before explaining to her son, "Sam's offense, Chase. He's the one who tries to get a touchdown. Right now the other team is trying to get the touchdown, so our defensive players are out on the field trying to stop them."

"Sam can stop them." Tucker frowned at the players on the field. "Sam's strong and fast."

Coop gave Jenni a smile of understanding. "I'm sure he is, Tucker. But he's a wide receiver. That means he's really fast, and he can catch a football. We need him to make touchdowns for us."

"Oh, okay." Tucker seemed satisfied with Coop's answer. "Mr. Brown?"

"Yeah?" Coop didn't seem adverse to the name.

"What's a touchdown?" asked Tucker.

She covered up her laugh by coughing into her furry pink mittens. They were hideous mittens, but Corey had given them to her last month for her birthday. He had also made her a macaroni necklace strung on pretty yellow ribbon. Bojangles had eaten the necklace but left the ribbon unchewed, and it still was on top of her dresser.

"Mom," moaned Corey, "I have to go potty."

She tried not to groan. She had just taken them to the bathrooms behind the snack stand fifteen minutes ago. "Okay, boys, you heard him." With the Wright boys, going to the bathroom was a family affair. All of them were too young to be left on their own.

"Aw, Mom," groaned Tucker, "I don't have to go."

"We were just there," said Chase.

She stood up and held onto Corey's hand. "You both know the rules."

"How about I watch them while you handle Corey?" Coop seemed innocent to the fact he would be left alone with Chase and Tucker sitting a good six feet above ground level.

"I don't know. Tucker's awfully quick." She didn't want to embarrass her son, but Coop needed a warning.

"I was Hancock High's star wide receiver, Jenni. I think I can handle a four-year-old." Coop looked offended.

It wasn't the fact that she didn't trust Coop with her sons—it was that experience had taught her not to trust Tucker.

"Mom"—Corey held himself with his free hand and started to dance around—"I gotta go."

"All right, I'll be right back." She swung Corey up into her arms and hurried to the bathroom before her son had an accident.

Coop sat there with both boys staring at him, as if he should be saying or doing something. He had no idea what they expected him to do now that their mother was gone. Thankfully Hancock High stopped the other team from making a first down, and it was their turn to have the ball. "Sam's going out on the field."

Coop made a quick save as Tucker nearly fell off the bench trying to see. "Where?"

"There, he's number 80." He pointed to the lineup. "He's at the far end of the line."

"What's 80?" asked Tucker, still trying to see which one of the guys dressed in blue and white uniforms and matching helmets was his friend. With all the equipment football players wore, it was nearly impossible to tell one from another without the numbers.

"It's an eight and a zero," answered Chase.

"I can't see." Tucker was trying to stand on the bench. Coop couldn't have Tucker blocking people's view or falling off the bench and getting hurt. He tugged Tucker over to him and stood him in front, facing the field. "There he is," he said, pointing to a figure running down the field.

Sam Fischer had some impressive speed; the cornerback was barely keeping up. The quarterback faked a throw and then passed the ball to a running back, who was tackled within three yards. It wasn't a bad play, but if the linemen could have protected the quarterback for a few seconds longer, Sam would have beaten the corner-back and have been wide open.

"How come Sam didn't get the ball?" asked Chase.

"Where's he now?" asked Tucker, who had lost sight of Sam as the players lined back up.

"Maybe this time—watch." Coop pointed to a far end of the field. "He's over there again, Tucker."

This time the linemen gave the quarterback enough time to throw the ball long. The football went right to Sam, who caught it and ran it in for a touchdown. Their side of the stadium went nuts. Chase and Tucker cheered with the crowd.

The extra-point kick was good. The crowd and the boys cheered again.

Jenni, still carrying Corey, hurried up the steps. "What did I miss?" She looked at her two sons, expecting an answer.

Coop looked at Chase and Tucker, who both shrugged. "We don't know. Everyone started to yell, so we yelled with them," answered Chase.

"Sam caught the ball," said Tucker.

Coop started to laugh. "Sam scored a touchdown, Jenni." The boys had absolutely no idea how the game was played.

Two and a half hours later, Coop helped Jenni by carrying a sleeping Tucker to her car. Her arms were already full with a zonked-out Corey. Chase was carrying a couple of blankets. Most had hot chocolate spilled all over them.

"Tell me again how a game that has four quarters, each consisting of fifteen minutes, lasted for nearly three hours?" She had been thrilled that Sam's team had won, but it was nearly ten at night—way past the boys' bedtime.

Coop chuckled. "It has to do with Einstein's theory of relativity."

She snorted and shifted Corey higher so she could take Chase's hand. The parking lot was full, and moving cars were everywhere. A lot of them were being driven by teenagers looking to celebrate the win.

"Which way did you park?" Coop didn't even sound out of breath, while she was desperately trying not to huff and puff. Corey wasn't that heavy.

"Over there." She pointed to the right. "Did I thank you for taking the time and explaining the game to my boys?" Coop Armstrong was a very nice man. He not only had the patience of a saint, he hadn't yelled and screamed at Tucker when her son spilled half his hot chocolate all over his leg. He had calmly cleaned up as best he could in the bathroom, and then he had bought her son another cup of hot chocolate.

"Twice, but I don't know how much of it sank in." Coop glanced down at Chase, who was holding her hand. "Do you know what a touchdown is now?"

"Yep." Chase nearly tripped on the end of a blanket dragging on the ground. "And the kicker kicks, and the punter punts."

She bit her lip to keep from laughing. That was one of the lessons Coop had taught her. Here she thought anytime a guy kicked the ball, he was just kicking. As it turned out sometimes he was punting it instead. You kick field goals, but you returned punts, and no, she had absolutely no idea what any of that meant. She was more confused now than when she and the boys had arrived three hours earlier.

"What are the guys in the black and white stripes that blow the whistles called?" questioned Coop.

"Refs," answered Chase.

"Umps," she replied. She still didn't see what the difference was; both guys were out on the field calling the shots and pointing out when someone made a mistake. Referees and umpires were the same thing.

Coop and Chase both rolled their eyes.

She shifted Corey's weight again and dug into her pocketbook, searching for the keys. It was probably Einstein's theory that her keys always disappeared inside her purse, no matter how big or small it was.

"Here, Jenni," said Felicity as she stepped out from in between two pickup trucks, "I'll take him." Felicity reached for Corey.

"Thanks." Maybe now she'd be able to locate her keys. She took off the mittens and started to dig.

"Hello, Mr. Armstrong. Fancy meeting you here." Felicity's grin was wide and knowing.

"It's Coop, remember?" Coop walked the remaining steps to Jenni's dark blue SUV. "You called me Coop at the snack stand earlier."

"That's right, you were at the snack stand picking up three hot chocolates and two coffees." Felicity smirked.

"You were standing there with a bunch of girls checking out the guys." Coop smiled back.

Jenni shook her head as Coop and Felicity traded quips. She removed a bottle of water from her pocket-book and placed it on the hood of her car. Next came the travel-size box of wipes, tape measure, cell phone, and calendar. The keys still weren't there.

Jenni opened up the brown canvas bag and removed a bottle of moisturizer, a tube of hand cream, and three lip balms in assorted flavors. Next came a box of crayons, pens, and three notepads. A pair of boys' socks with dinosaurs on them, a toy catalog, three Christmas lightbulbs in various sizes, and a cooking spatula were added to the small mountain of items gathering on the hood of her SUV. Still no keys.

Felicity started to laugh, while Coop stared in awe at the pile of stuff Jenni had taken from her purse. "Jenni, check your coat pockets."

"Why, I remember putting the keys in here some-where." She dug deeper and came up with a handful of bubble gum, Legos, and a butter knife.

"What's the knife for?" asked Coop.

"The glove compartment gets stuck sometimes." Two AA batteries and a Hot Wheel were added to the pile.

"Check your pockets," groaned Felicity, "before you get to the personal hygiene products."

To save herself the embarrassment of hauling out half a dozen or so tampons, she reached into her coat pock-ets, just to prove Felicity wrong. She closed her eyes and groaned as her cold fingers wrapped around her keys.

"See . . ." Felicity's voice trailed off as Jenni quickly interrupted.

"If you say 'I told you so,' you're walking home." She

started to scoop everything back into her pocketbook. She was only half joking, but she was embarrassed because Coop was standing there watching her empty out her pocketbook while holding her son Tucker. Tucker wasn't a lightweight. The kid could pack in the food, especially if it was sweet.

"I told you so," quipped Felicity.

"Uh-oh." Chase looked at his Aunt Felicity. "You're in trouble now."

"Nah, and do you know why?" Felicity giggled. "Because I'm getting a ride home with Sam, not your mom."

Jenni replaced the last item and unlocked the doors. "Does your mom know?"

"I called her about fifteen minutes ago. She said it was okay, as long as I was home by eleven." Felicity rolled her eyes. "Can't you talk to her, Jenni? I'm the only kid in my class that has to be home that early. Some of the kids don't even have curfews."

Jenni reached for Corey and strapped him into his car seat. He never even opened his eyes. "Sorry, hon, you know your mom and I have an agreement. I don't tell her how to raise you, she doesn't tell me how to raise the boys."

Chase climbed into his spot between the two car seats and strapped himself in. Jenni closed the door and walked around to the other side of the car where Coop and Tucker stood waiting.

"But you can give her some advice—you know, about cutting the apron strings." Felicity was nothing if not tenacious.

"Nope, I'll give her my opinion if she asks for it, and

not before." She reached up and took Tucker out of Coop's arms. The man smelled of fresh air and hot chocolate—a tempting combination. "Thanks."

"You're welcome." Coop watched as she strapped Tucker into his seat. Tucker woke once, mumbled something that sounded like "holding," and went back to sleep.

Jenni laughed softly. "Is that a football term?"

"Yes."

"Great, it's bad enough I have to hear it all day and night from Sam, but now my nephews will be worshipping the pigskin." Felicity pouted. "Tell Mom I'll be home later."

"Will do." Jenni watched as Felicity went and joined a bunch of other girls who all seemed to be waiting for the players.

"Mom," called Chase.

"Yes?"

"Are we getting a pig?" Chase's voice held nothing but hope.

"No. Absolutely not." She felt like elbowing Coop in the side when he started to chuckle.

"A pig would be neat, Mom. We can name him Wilbur, like in *Charlotte's Web*." Chase was getting more excited by the minute.

"Pig?" Tucker yawned and stretched. "What pig, where?"

"Felicity said we're getting a pig, Tuck. It's going to have skin and all," explained Chase.

"She did not. There is no pig. There will be no pig." She felt like throttling Coop when his chuckles turned into a full-blown laugh. Visions of a potbellied pig snorting its way around Dorothy's immaculate kitchen and climbing the stairs on its piggy toes was enough to make her take up drinking. Did pigs even have toes?

"Why won't our pig have skin?" Tucker was fully awake now. "He has to have skin, or his guts will spill all over the floor."

"Bojangles will like pig guts. If he eats crayons and Felicity's purple eye junk, he'll like guts." Chase seemed to be calculating something in his little mind. "Mom, can pigs wear clothes? That way his guts won't drag on the ground."

"They don't make pig clothes." She tried to keep her voice at a nice, calm level. "We are not getting a pig—with or without its skin." She closed the car door on the boys' protests.

"Do you want me to explain why a football is called a pigskin?" Coop seemed amused by the whole discussion.

"Don't you dare." She already knew why. "Thanks again for everything."

"You're welcome. I'll see if I can get a couple of contractors' names for you before that porch roof comes crashing down on your heads."

"I'd appreciate it." Coop Armstrong was a real nice guy. "Just make sure they aren't too squeamish. Tucker is a child who loves a good challenge."

"Will do. Goodnight." She could still hear Coop's chuckle as he headed for the other side of the parking lot.

She climbed into the car and tuned out the boys' argument that if they couldn't have a pig, a horse would do. Tonight she actually had had a good time. Coop was both fun and knowledgeable. He also seemed to enjoy himself with the boys. That was what she missed with Ken—the togetherness.

Being a family. A complete family.

Damn it, Ken, why did you have to try to save Gloria? Weren't we important? Didn't you even think about me or the boys? One of the chemists in the lab who had made it out that fateful day had told her that Ken died a hero, trying to save Gloria Nesbitt, the sixty-year-old woman who was the head of the lab.

A dead hero didn't take his sons to football games, or put together bicycles, or get to play Santa on snowy Christmas Eves. He didn't fix the broken faucet in the bathroom, or hold her when she needed to be held, and he didn't keep her bed warm at night.

She ducked her head and quickly wiped away the tears that had filled her eyes. She didn't want the boys to see her cry. They were so happy and young. They rarely thought or asked about their father.

Jenni put the SUV in gear, focused her mind on driving, and slowly made her way out of the jammed parking lot. She had to get her family home safely.

Coop drove up the long gravel drive to the Wright house. He kept an eye out for the boys as he parked in front of the porch steps. They were known to run right out in front of him, dangle from tree branches, or plan sneak attacks up on the porch. Monday afternoon, and all was quiet. Too quiet. On a beautiful fall day, with the sun shining, Tucker and Corey should be out causing trouble.

He hoped they hadn't gotten sick from staying out in the cold Friday night. Jenni seemed to have had them bundled up pretty good the other night, but what did he know about little kids and the sniffles? If he believed all the television commercials, kids were always sick with hacking, coughing, and raging fevers that required midnight runs to the hospital in torrential downpours when the roads had been washed out.

The good news was that it hadn't rained all weekend, so there were no washed-out roads, but the bad news was that Bojangles hadn't greeted him yet. Where was the dog? There were two doggie bones in his jacket pocket with the mutt's name on them.

He grabbed his clipboard and the three boxes for the Mistletoe Bay Company. One of the boxes was heavy, a good forty pounds, while the other two were on the light side. He piled the lighter ones on top and carried them up the rickety porch steps. One of these days his foot was going through one of the wooden steps. If he was lucky, it would break only in one or two places.

His leg, not the step.

The noise coming from inside the house reached his ears before he got to the front door. Bojangles was barking his fool head off, and the boys were shouting and laughing. Dorothy was telling Tucker to do something, but Coop couldn't make out the words.

He placed the boxes on the porch. Although the rest of the Halloween decorations were still up, the deranged panda bear was AWOL. The rocking chair sat empty except for a leaf or two stuck in what he still hoped was ketchup and not dried blood. He reached up and knocked on the door. He had learned on his first delivery and pickup that the doorbell no longer worked. Usually the boys would run in and tell Dorothy he was here, or their grandmother already would be outside looking for them.

A moment later, no one had answered the door. He could still hear the shouting and laughing being punctuated by the dog's bark. He raised his hand and knocked harder.

Still no answer.

Wild thoughts went through his mind. He could picture Tucker tying up Dorothy by her apron strings and holding her hostage for cookies or the rest of his Halloween candy. Coop pressed his face against one of the sidelight windows on either side of the door. Between a lacy curtain and the wavy original glass, he couldn't see anything or anybody.

He tried the doorknob, and it twisted in his hand. He pushed the door open a couple of inches and yelled, "Dorothy? Jenni?"

"Down here" and "help" reached his ears. He was pretty sure it was Dorothy's voice. He stepped into the house and closed the door. The pounding of feet on the basement steps told him where "down here" was. He hurried into the kitchen, where the basement door stood ajar.

Corey stood on the top step grinning at him. "Hi, Mr. Brown." Corey was soaking wet. Somewhere below, Dorothy was still yelling for help.

He picked up Corey and stood him in the kitchen. "Stay right here. Don't move." Coop hurried down the steps.

As basements went, the Wrights was what he would classify as normal. Old fieldstone walls that had been patched periodically over the decades. Cracked and painted concrete covered most of the floor. An entire construction site's worth of yellow Tonka trucks and gravel took up the majority of the space.

Underneath the kitchen area was a massive cast-iron oil burner that looked like it would require its own zip code. Pipes sprang from it in every direction and tangled their way under the floor joists. The monster clanged, knocked, and seemed to make an evil hissing sound. Through a small soot-covered window, behind a black metal grate, flames danced. The grate resembled teeth.

Coop fought the urge to cross himself and turned toward Dorothy and all the commotion.

In the far corner of the basement, a small laundry center had been set up. He knew at one time it had been as neat and organized as the kitchen above. Today it was hard to tell.

Dorothy had crawled up on top of the washer and had both hands wrapped around the hose. Water was squirting through her fingers. Tucker was trying to catch the arcs of water in one of the laundry baskets. The faster the water went into the basket, the faster it drained right back out. Bojangles was barking at the spraying water, trying to drink it.

He tried not to laugh. Dorothy didn't appear to see the humor in the situation. "Can I be of assistance?"

"Mr. Armstrong, if you are done admiring the scenery"—Dorothy wiped her drenched face on the sleeve of her sweatshirt, without letting go of the broken hose—"I would deeply appreciate it if you could locate the water shutoff valve."

Chapter Four

Jenni got the job of mopping up the basement before dinner. Dorothy had taken a shower, calmed down, and was now busy in the kitchen doing what she loved to do: cook. Chase, who was now home from school, was skillfully killing aliens on her computer. Tucker and Corey were being punished for not immediately running to get her from the shop when Dorothy told them to.

Dorothy could have been lying somewhere seriously hurt. When their grandmother told them to do something, the boys had to listen. There were to be no if, ands, or buts about it. Tucker and Corey's punishment had been swift and severe, to their way of thinking.

They were both sitting on the couch with nothing to occupy their little minds but books. No television, no toys, and no talking for the rest of the night. And absolutely no dessert or leftover Halloween candy.

She wished someone would hand out that punishment to her. She couldn't remember the last time she'd read a book or had a quiet moment to herself. Mopping up two inches of water from the basement floor didn't count as peace and quiet. She was too worried that water had worked its way to the oil burner and had damaged some part or another. Underneath the hulking beast had been dried, but she still didn't trust it. Excessive moisture in the air would probably send the burner into temperamental fits—fits that contained a lot of zeros in the repair bill.

She couldn't afford to replace the ancient hunk of iron, and winter hadn't even arrived yet. The real estate agent had assured her that if she babied it, she could get a couple more years out of the burner. Vince Carter, the first handyman she'd hired, had taken one look at it, laughed, and claimed the burner was older than he was. Vince was seventy-eight, so she didn't take that as a good sign.

Thankfully, Coop Armstrong had come along and rescued her mother-in-law. Even though Dorothy claimed he took his sweet time finding the shutoff valve. Being stuck on top of the washer with both hands wrapped around the split hose had distorted Dorothy's sense of time. Five minutes to Dorothy had seemed like two hours under the water torture.

Jenni wrung out the mop for what had to be the thousandth time and was pleased to see most of the floor, although damp, contained no puddles. By the time dinner was ready she just might be done.

Dorothy had been simmering those meatballs in her homemade sauce all day long. The aroma was driving her nuts. Nothing beat her mother-in-law's spaghetti dinner, except possibly a trip to Italy. Since she'd never been to Italy, she had her doubts on that one.

Above her head she heard the boys jump off the

couch and run to the front door. Sam must be here for Felicity and a free meal. He usually stopped by at night even though Dorothy wasn't too keen on the idea of them going out on school nights. Most nights they hung around the house cranking the boys up, watching television, and emptying the refrigerator or cookie jar.

Sam seemed to take perverse pleasure in egging Tucker on—like her middle son needed more encouragement to find trouble. Tucker was like Velcro when it came to trouble.

A moment later their footsteps ran for the kitchen, and the basement door was yanked opened with enough force to put the life expectancy of the hinges into question. "Mom!" shouted Tucker. "Mr. Brown is here!"

"I hear you, Tucker. You don't have to shout that loud." The late-season tourists over in Bar Harbor probably had heard him. What in the world was Coop doing here now? He'd taken all the packages with him a couple of hours ago, along with a pair of very wet shoes and damp pants. He was probably here to sue her. She had no idea if her homeowner's insurance covered pneumonia in the UPS delivery man.

She glanced down at her stylish boots and tried not to cringe. Dorothy's spring boots were bright green with hot-pink flowers and were two sizes too big for Jenni. Since her snow boots weren't exactly made for wading, she'd had to borrow Dorothy's plastic gardening boots. Her worn, stained jeans were tucked into the boots and a baggy sweatshirt hung to midthigh. It was the perfect outfit to wear when one was mopping up a basement. She was pretty sure Cinderella had worn a similar outfit to sweep out the fireplace.

"You guys had better listen to your grandmother and get back on the couch before your mom catches you off it." Coop's deep voice held a note of amusement.

He had a right to be entertained; Coop had witnessed her very unmotherly frustration at the boys earlier. Banshees were not known to scream that loud. Maybe he wasn't here to sue her after all. Maybe he was bringing the head of social services to see the abuse for himself.

Coop started down the basement steps. "How safe is it down there?"

"You won't drown, but there's a school of trout underneath the oil burner." She watched as brown construction boots, worn jeans, and then a shiny red toolbox came into her line of sight.

The toolbox made her heart flutter.

The rest of Coop followed the toolbox. "Are they big enough to catch, or do we have to throw them back in?"

"They might feed Dumb and Dumber, but not the rest of this family." Now that the mopping was done, she could see a small sliver of humor in the situation. Now if her feet would defrost somewhat, she might even manage to crack a smile.

Coop glanced at her feet. "Nice boots."

"I have the coat and umbrella to match."

Coop looked at her as if he wasn't sure whether to believe her. "I see you have most of the water cleaned up." Coop glanced around the basement with approval. "Good thing you're not one of those people who cram everything into their basement. A lot of it would have been ruined."

"Nope, I cram it all in the attic storage room." She shuddered at the idea of the upcoming holiday season and all those boxes of decorations up there gathering dust. Not only were her decorations up there, but so were Dorothy's. "I'll be in trouble if the roof leaks."

"It doesn't?" Coop looked amazed.

"So far it's the only thing that doesn't need to be repaired or replaced." She quickly tapped the wooden table they used to fold the laundry. "Knock on wood."

Coop chuckled. "That reminds me"—he reached into his pants pocket and pulled out a slip of paper—"I have the name and number of two local guys that might be interested in doing some of that construction work for you."

"Are you serious?" She yanked the paper from his fingers. There on the crinkled white paper were two neatly printed names and phone numbers. Before she could think, she opened her mouth and teased, "I could kiss you."

A fiery blush swept up her cheeks as Coop raised a brow at that suggestion. "I didn't mean that the way it came out." The poor guy probably thought she was hitting on him. "I just wanted to say thank you. I really appreciate it."

She didn't want him running from the house in fear for his life. The way her luck with handymen was going, she'd be needing more names and numbers by Christmas.

"You're welcome." Coop put his toolbox down on the wooden table and opened it. "I picked up a new washer hose for you on the way home from work." He pulled a length of black hose from the box. "I can have it on in just a couple of minutes."

"You don't have to do that." She was thrilled to death; he was standing there with a new length of hose in one hand and a wrench in the other. A flush of genuine pleasure swept up her body. "I put a call in to a plumber in Ellsworth."

"Coastal?" Coop started to take off the old busted hose, barely paying her any attention.

"How did you know?" So much for that stupid kiss remark. He had barely given it a thought, while she was getting turned on by a shiny toolboxes and a Craftsman wrench. She was either pathetic or seriously disturbed.

"Ellsworth only has two plumbers: Coastal and Harvey Jenkins. Harvey doesn't own an answering machine. He's either there, or he's not." Coop handed her the old, brittle hose. "Coastal would take a good week to ten days to get out here for a busted washer hose."

Jenni could see why Dorothy had such a hard time holding the thing together. There was a ten-inch split down the length of the hose. She now understood why there had been so much water. "Oh." There was no way they could have waited that long to do laundry. With everything on her schedule, she couldn't imagine sitting in a laundromat for hours with three boys—especially Tucker. She'd rather have her eyelashes plucked out by chickens.

She watched as Coop expertly attached the new hose. Problem was, her gaze wasn't on the hose, or what he was doing with his hands. She was intrigued by the way his shirt stretched across his broad shoulders and the way his jeans outlined the tight curve of his rear.

The man was perfection in a pair of Wolverine boots, and she had been living out here in the woods a mite too long. One would think she didn't know what a man looked like.

"There," said Coop as he gave the hose one last tightening. "That should hold you for a while. You really should have replaced the hose when you moved in." He packed up his tools and snapped the box shut.

"No one told me that." There was a lot of stuff in life no one had bothered to inform her about, like which side of the battery jumper cables get attached to, or that dogs can heave up twice their body weight after drinking motor oil, and that little boys held peeing competitions out in the woods by seeing who could knock off the most ants from a tree's bark.

"I slipped one of the moving guys a twenty just to get the washer and dryer up and running."

"He should have told you."

"He was eighteen, at the most. He probably didn't know." She remembered coming home from the hospital with a two-day-old baby and being scared to death. Although the nurses had loaded her down with free formula, diapers, and more samples and coupons than she could use in three lifetimes, no one had handed her an instruction booklet on how to raise and take care of Chase. At least she'd had Ken to struggle along with her, and Dorothy had been a phone call away.

When Ken passed away she'd gotten plenty of condolences and cards, but still no instruction booklet on how to be the "man" of the house.

When she started her own business, tons of brochures, pamphlets, and Web sites were dedicated to helping her get her business up and running. The other night she had spent a sleepless night worrying about the stupidest thing: her sons' private parts. If she had daughters, she would know what to tell them and would know the answers to all their questions. With boys she was clueless. She was an only child, and Ken had been her first and only lover. Was there something she was supposed to explain to the boys when they reached puberty? Before puberty?

She couldn't very well search for the information on the Internet. With her luck she would be caught in some child pornography ring and arrested. She'd spent a good hour of her time ordering a couple books from Amazon.com on raising boys, praying they would have a chapter or two on that particular area. If they didn't, she would have to muster up enough courage to ask their new family doctor, Dr. Sydney.

Books were a godsend. When her old college roommate had learned she was moving to the wilds of Maine and into a rundown old house, she had sent her a box containing six rolls of duct tape and a book about a thousand uses for the sticky silver tape. Although the book was meant to be humorous, the duct tape had proved invaluable. It had been the most useful gift she had ever received. Half of her house was being held together by the wonder tape.

"Hey, you two," yelled Dorothy from the top of the steps, "dinner's ready, and, Coop, you're staying." Dorothy's tone didn't leave room for any argument.

"I am?" Coop looked amused.

Dorothy came down a couple of steps and looked at the man who probably had saved her from drowning earlier in the afternoon. "Yes, you are. We're having spaghetti and meatballs."

Jenni softly chuckled and whispered, "They actually taste even better than they smell." Since the house was filled with the heavenly aroma of simmering sauce, that was saying something.

"I'd be delighted to join you and your family, Dorothy. It smells too good to resist."

"Then get your buns up here. You too, Jenni." Dorothy turned around to march back up the steps. "Don't forget to wash up."

"Yes, ma'am." Coop and his shiny red toolbox followed Dorothy up the stairs.

So much for her scrubwoman's sex appeal. Coop was following his stomach straight to Dorothy's meatballs and hadn't so much as given her a second glance. Considering what Jenni looked like, she didn't blame him one bit.

What really fried her keister was why she even cared what Coop felt toward her. She wasn't interested in a personal relationship with the Good Samaritan or any other man. As far as she was concerned, Christmas had come early this year, and Santa had a new name: Cooper Armstrong.

Coop enthusiastically helped himself to a second serving. "Dorothy, I must admit these are the best meatballs I have ever tasted." He wasn't paying a false compliment; they were. "You have to have Italian blood in you somewhere."

"Not a drop." Dorothy flushed with pleasure.

"Where's the blood?" Tucker looked at his grandmother. "I don't see any blood."

Corey looked under the table. "What blood? Where? Who's bleeding?"

Felicity rolled her eyes. "Jenni, tell them to stop talking about blood at the dinner table. It's gross, and I'm trying to eat."

"Boys, there is no blood. It's just a saying." Jenni frowned at Chase's nearly full plate. "Aren't you hungry, hon?"

"Yeah," Chase wound some spaghetti around his fork, but anyone could see his heart wasn't in it.

Coop didn't see what Felicity was complaining about. The girl had barely touched her dinner. The teenager was too busy making eyes at her boyfriend, Sam. Ah, young love.

He turned his attention to Chase. The six-year-old wasn't quite acting like himself. Maybe the kid was coming down with something. "Hey, buddy, you feeling okay?" Chase was definitely the quiet one, but he usually managed to ask about a thousand questions.

"Yeah." Chase gave a half-hearted smile and shoved half a meatball into his mouth.

Coop refused to look at the boy's mother. Jennifer Wright was trouble with a capital *T*. So why hadn't he realized that particular fact before joining her in the basement and almost kissing her? As it was, he had nearly beaten Dorothy to the top of the steps as he raced to get out of there.

He didn't kiss single mothers, especially if they had three boys. No way. No how.

The look of pure dismay that had been on Jenni's face earlier as she had raced down the steps only to find a soaking-wet Dorothy sitting on top of the washer, and him surveying the damage, was enough to tug at his conscience for the rest of his afternoon run. Since the only thing he had waiting for him back at his apartment was a mediocre book and leftovers his mother had given him from Sunday dinner, he had decided to stop at the hardware store in Sullivan on his way home. The new hose had set him back a whole nine dollars.

It had been worth every penny just to see the look on Jenni's face when he had first shown up carrying that piece of hose. The one thing his apartment didn't have was a washer and dryer. He hated going to Sullivan's one and only laundromat. He couldn't imagine what it would be like sitting there doing laundry for six people, instead of just himself. He would rather take ballet lessons.

Usually he would show up a couple hours early for his mother's Sunday dinner, and while his clothes turned and spinned, he would do a couple chores around the place that his father no longer could do. It seemed like a reasonable trade-off, one his father didn't fight too hard against.

His father, Fred Armstrong, at one time had been the most stubborn man alive. Now it seemed his mother held that honor. Fred had suffered a heart attack eight months ago, and it had given everyone, especially his mother, a real scare. Lucille Armstrong had immediately put her husband on a low-fat, low-carb, low-calorie, low-everything diet. As his father so eloquently put it, if it smelled like a horse's behind, tasted like crabgrass, and had the consistency of a shoebox, he was now allowed to eat it.

Sunday-night dinners at his parents tasted nothing like they used to.

Dorothy's dinner invitation was a godsend. If he hadn't been fighting his sudden attraction to a certain dark-haired, mop-wielding witchy woman, he might have thought twice about accepting the invite. He didn't want to give Jenni or any other member of the Wright family the wrong impression.

He had already made the decision that he was not interested in Jenni.

The blasted woman was making his decision hard to keep. How she looked cute and adorable while cleaning up the basement in her ridiculous boots and baggy, ratty sweatshirt was beyond him. But as soon as she made that ridiculously innocent comment about kissing him, his mind had shut down and his hormones had gone into overdrive. Jenni had meant nothing by that remark, besides being extremely thankful that he had given her the names of two handymen.

So why in the hell couldn't he stop looking at her lips?

"Hey, Coop," Sam said. "Coach told the team that you would be stopping by Thursday after practice to talk to us."

"That's right." It wasn't something he was looking forward to doing, but it was a talk that needed to be had. The sad truth was, he was the perfect guy to give that particular speech. He had done it half a dozen times or so out in California. He just had never had the opportunity to give it at his old high school. He wasn't looking forward to Thursday.

"Are you going to give us some pointers?" Sam was sitting next to Felicity, but he obviously wasn't paying her enough attention. Felicity was pouting.

"What's pointers?" asked Tucker. The boy pointed at Sam, and then at his brother Chase.

Coop tried not to laugh. The boy obviously didn't get the connection.

"Not pointing, Tucker—pointers. Pointers are helpful hints." Jenni teasingly pointed back at Tucker.

"Like when we play hide-and-seek and someone says 'You're getting warmer, or colder.'"

"Something like that." Jenni smiled. "But in this case Coop will be giving the football team helpful hints about playing the game."

Tucker looked at him. "Why can't you give me pointers?"

"What would you like a pointer in?" Tucker was a little too young to be playing football. But how hard could the subject matter be? The kid was four, maybe five years old.

"Why's it easier to climb a tree than to get down from one?"

"You haven't been climbing trees again, have you?" Dorothy looked pale at the mere thought.

Jenni studied her son. "Tucker?"

"No." The boy's pout matched Felicity's.

Coop didn't want to know how high Tucker must have been in a tree before he realized he had to climb back down. It was a wonder Jenni wasn't totally gray. There wasn't a gray hair on her head, but having Tucker for a son, she probably dyed it that rich dark brown color every week. Either that or she drank heavily.

"When you're climbing a tree, Tucker, you're looking up reaching for the next branch. Your mind is concentrating on that nearby branch. When you get as high as you want, you look down, and then you realize how high you've climbed and you get scared. Those branches don't seem so close by then, and your brain is telling you that if you fall, you will get hurt." It seemed like a perfectly reasonable explanation to him.

Tucker seemed to be mulling that one over.

"How come my mom was real nice to me when I was up there, but once she got me down she whacked my bottom and made me sit in the corner for the whole day?"

"Mom said a bad word and Grandmom cried that she wanted to call the fire department again." Chase joined the conversation.

"I could imagine." He ignored the "again" and looked at Jenni. "How high was he?"

"Let's just say I passed an eagle's nest on the way up to retrieve my son. A couple feet higher and he would have needed oxygen." Jenni gave Tucker a stern look. "It won't happen again, right?"

"Right." Tucker gave his mother a pure, innocent smile. "Birds fly, boys don't."

"Right," Jenni said.

"Peter Pan flies," Corey said.

"Peter Pan isn't real, Corey." Jenni seemed to press that point hard. "Boys can't and won't fly, so don't even try it."

"Can girls fly?" asked Tucker.

"Do you think if I could fly I'd be sitting here listening to this?" Felicity obviously wasn't enjoying herself.

Coop wasn't sure what upset the girl more—the fact that Sam was paying him more attention, or the boys' ten thousand questions.

"Felicity," scolded Dorothy, "that's not nice."

"Well, they always ask stupid questions."

"They are your nephews. Very young nephews." Dorothy stared down her daughter. "Maybe you would like to enlighten us with an intelligent question."

"Sure." Felicity smiled. "Why is the earth round instead of something more aerodynamic, like a bullet shape? Wouldn't we avoid a lot of that wind resistance as we go spinning around in space?"

Jenni smiled at Felicity. "There are no aerodynamics in space. Space is a vacuum. It wouldn't matter what shape the earth was, it would still orbit the sun at the same speed."

"Geek," Felicity said. Her small smile took some of the sting out of the word.

"Thank you." Jenni looked pleased.

Coop was impressed. Not only was Jenni beautiful and smart, but she wasn't allowing the seventeen-year-old to rattle her. Felicity looked like if she set her mind to it, she could rattle a lot of people's cages. "I thought 'geek' was an insult?"

Back in college, he would have decked anyone who had called him that—not like that would ever happen. He had been a jock, a dumb-ass jock who had thought brawn beat brains every time. He had been proven wrong many times over since that ripe old age of twenty.

"Only to non-geeks," Jenni replied with a smile to Felicity. "There's nothing wrong with using your brain."

"Felicity's real smart, Coop." Sam puffed out his chest with pride. "She's only a junior but she's taking the top college-prep courses. Next year she'll be eligible to take some college courses while still in high school."

"Impressive." He gave Felicity a nod of approval and was gentlemanly enough not to stare at the fiery red blush sweeping up her cheeks.

Tucker stuck his tongue out at his aunt.

"I'm smart too," Corey said. "I can count to one hundred. Wanna hear me?"

A chorus of "no's" was heard around the table. The only "yes's" came from him and Jenni.

Corey started to count. "One, two, three, four . . ."

"Mom, make him stop," Chase pleaded.

Tucker shoved half a meatball into his mouth and then covered his ears.

"Fourteen, fifteen, sixteen . . ."

Dorothy and Felicity started to argue about Sam and her going into town after dinner. Dorothy was against it. Felicity obviously didn't like the answer—no.

Sam started making funny faces at Tucker, who nearly choked on a meatball.

"Want to hear the song we learned in school today?" asked Chase in a loud voice. All of a sudden the kid wanted some attention.

"After your brother is done counting." Jenni was leaning closer to Corey to hear him over the other conversations. "That's right, hon, keep going. You're doing great." Jenni gave her youngest son a smile of encouragement.

"Thirty-nine, forty, forty-one . . ."

"It's about a turkey named Tom." Chase wasn't giving up and he started to sing, "Gobble, gobble, gobble went Tom the Turkey."

"Sixty-seven, sixty-eight . . ." Corey was using his fingers and speaking louder to drown out his brother.

"I don't see why we can't just run into Bailey's for a few minutes," Felicity said. "They have the best sundaes. All the other kids will be there." If Felicity's pout grew any more pronounced her lower lip would land on her plate.

"Pick me a pumpkin, pick me a pumpkin, said

Priscilla Pilgrim." Chase sounded like he was singing rap, not a children's Thanksgiving song. The boy was really getting into the song.

"I said no. It's a school night. You should be doing homework." Dorothy took a drink from her wineglass.

"All the other kids . . ." Felicity's voice carried on.

"Seventy-two, seventy-three . . ."

"Tucker, I bet you can't fit an entire meatball in your mouth." Sam egged Tucker on.

Tucker took up the challenge before Jenni could stop him.

Chase's next line in the song had something to do with a chopping block, and Coop had to wonder what they were teaching kids in school nowadays.

He couldn't decide if he was developing a headache from all the noise or from holding back his laughter. The nice family dinner was now in total chaos.

Tucker looked like a demented chipmunk.

Jenni was congratulating and hugging Corey as he shouted, "One hundred!"

"Felicity, I don't mind spending the evening here." Sam patted her hand. "You can do your homework and I can catch *Monday Night Football*."

Felicity looked like she wanted to deck Sam.

Dorothy smiled pleasantly, but Coop noticed her wineglass was now empty. He should have taken up her offer to have wine with his meal instead of water.

Chase finished the last line of the song, just as everyone at the table finally fell silent. "And that's when the Indian chief said, 'Pass me a drumstick.'"

* * *

"You haven't forgiven me yet for laughing, have you?" Coop asked.

Jenni finished wiping down the counter. "You fixed the washer; I'll call it even."

"You have to admit, it was funny." Coop straightened the last chair at the table. "I haven't laughed like that in months."

"I'll admit it was, let's say, awkward." Jenni shuddered as she tossed the dishcloth into the sink. "Who teaches a first-grader about eating a poor turkey named Tom?"

"That's what you do on Thanksgiving, eat turkey and watch football."

"You don't give a name to the main dish, and not everyone watches the game." Jenni couldn't believe it. "I wasn't really paying too much attention to the song. Maybe it wasn't Tom they ate."

"Could be." Coop had an expression on his face that said he was pacifying her.

She decided to change the subject. It wasn't Coop's fault what her son was picking up in school. Here she thought he'd be bringing home four-letter words from the other kids, not songs about wielding an ax and killing a turkey from the teacher. She couldn't imagine what he'd be singing come Christmas. Reindeer burgers, mutilated elves, and Santa getting stuck in a chimney.

"Thank you again." Jenni glanced around the now-neat kitchen. "You really didn't have to help clean up, but I appreciate it." Dorothy and Jenni had an agreement— if her mother-in-law cooked, Jenni cleaned up. Jenni did a lot of cleaning up in the kitchen.

"It was the least I could do. The meal was delicious."

"Dorothy's a great cook, and she loves doing it." Her mother-in-law wasn't one for cleaning or sewing. As long as her kitchen was immaculate and the refrigerator was stocked, the rest of the house could fall down upon their ears. Dorothy also like to putter in the gardens, but so far she hadn't managed to get anything to live beyond six weeks.

Jenni had a sneaking suspicion that either the boys had something to do with that or Bojangles was watering the plants.

"It shows." Coop swiped another chocolate chip cookie from the plate sitting on the counter.

"Let me at least pay you for the washer hose." She felt funny accepting all of Coop's help. The man was a virtual stranger. She hadn't even known him a week and already he was sharing their dinner table.

"The meal was worth more than the hose. I'm the one who should be thanking you for such an entertaining evening."

"The Wright family dinners are a laugh a minute. One of these days we'll put the show on the road and make a fortune." She couldn't believe Felicity had gone into one of her snits with company at the table and that Dorothy had finished off two glasses of wine during the meal. Great, her sister-in-law's attitude was on a downward spiral and Dorothy was developing a taste for merlot.

If she could just teach one of the boys to juggle, they would have an act for every age group.

"It wasn't that bad." Coop seemed to be taking the whole thing in stride. "I've seen worse."

"When? I thought you said you were an only child." Coop had explained that he moved back to this area from California about six months ago to be closer to his parents. His father had suffered a major heart attack.

"I worked on construction crews for ten years. You should have seen our Christmas party."

She laughed as hard as he had earlier. Her beloved family was being compared to a rowdy construction crew. Somewhere her life had taken a left-hand turn instead of a right. Ever since she'd picked up not only her household but also Dorothy's and moved them all to the coast of Maine, nothing seemed to go according to her plans.

The good news was her business was taking off extremely well. Sometimes she thought too well. The orders were pouring in and she employed Felicity for about fifteen to twenty hours a week to help pick up the slack.

Her plan had been to grow the business slowly so once she would need the help, the boys would be in school full time and Dorothy would only have to work for her part time. She was grateful, because she knew most business owners would love to be in her shoes. It was just hard trying to be something to all people. There never were enough hours in a day.

Coop grinned, and he tugged on his coat and picked up his toolbox. He gave her a quick wink. "The only thing missing this evening was the stripper."

Chapter Five

Dorothy chopped carrots with a little more force than necessary. She was angry, but for the life of her, she couldn't figure out whom or what she was angry at. Tonight she was cooking a roast, throwing everything into the pan, and shoving it all into the oven. She didn't even care how it turned out.

She would like to think it was a first, but not caring about cooking was happening more and more lately. So were the tears and the anger. Helping Jenni raise three very active boys was the reason she was tired all the time, and her seventeen-year-old daughter explained the gray streaks in her hair. Felicity was turning into a stranger right before her eyes, and she didn't know how to stop it or who her own daughter was half the time.

Raising a girl was so much harder than raising a boy. Kenny had been a dream child from the day he was born. She had barely made it to the hospital and the delivery had been easy. Kenny had been an excellent student and never once gave her or his father a moment of trouble. He even married a wonderful woman, gave her three precious grandbabies, and had never once forgotten about her or his baby sister. When his father had died, Kenny had stepped right into his shoes and handled all the work and worry concerning her home.

If she had a problem, Kenny handled it, without one complaint. What mother could have asked for anything more?

While she'd grieved and missed her husband dearly, Kenny had been there to lean on. Kenny had been her strength and her rock. Only now in hindsight, she realized she shouldn't have leaned quite as much or as often.

Felicity, on the other hand, took ten hours of hard labor, and she came out mad, red, and screaming at the top of her lungs. Teacher conferences were the norm, and her daughter questioned authority at every turn. Felicity pushed buttons Dorothy never knew she had. George, her father, had spoiled her shamelessly for the first twelve years of her life, then her brother had taken over the role.

Felicity had been devastated when Kenny had died in the fire. To Dorothy's shame, she hadn't been strong enough for her young daughter. Her own world had once again crumbled around her and she had been left floating aimlessly in her grief. It had been Jenni who had stepped in and held everyone together.

Jenni was now her rock.

"Grandmom, can I have a cookie?" Tucker, who was sitting at the kitchen table practicing his ABCs added, "Please."

She was tempted to give him one for that "please" alone, but she knew she shouldn't. "I'm afraid not, hon. You're being punished. You heard your mother, no snacks."

"Can I have a drink?"

"Milk or water?" Corey was upstairs taking a nap. Tucker had outgrown that habit before his fourth birthday. They had a hard enough time just getting him to sleep at night. Kenny's middle child was always on the run, from the moment his little feet hit the floor in the morning till his mother was blue in the face from telling him to close his eyes and go to sleep every night.

"Chocolate milk." Tucker grinned.

"Sorry, kiddo, regular milk or water?" She glanced through the opening into the sun room that ran the length of the back of the house. The large room was used as the family room. Thankfully the previous owners had connected two radiators into the room, which supplied plenty of heat. Too much heat.

Then again, the entire house was too darn hot. If she hadn't opened both sets of sliding doors in the sun room to let in some cool air, Bojangles wouldn't have run through one of the screen doors to escape Tucker. Her grandson had been terrorizing the poor dog with Felicity's makeup. Jenni had heard the commotion from her shop and had come to investigate. A green plastic garbage bag and duct tape had fixed the screen door, but there was no hope for Felicity's green eye shadow, the plastic hair accessory, or the green tank top Bojangles had been wearing at the time.

Tucker was in for a world of hurt when Felicity got home from school and saw the disaster in her room.

If Dorothy found a few free minutes this afternoon, she would go upstairs and see if she could scrub off the eye liner that Tucker had used to sign the hallway walls. She should have been watching the boys more closely instead of taking inventory of what was in the pantry. Thanksgiving was coming up quickly, and she had wanted to make sure she had everything she would need.

Tucker was very proud of the fact that he could write his full name and a couple other words. Every one of them now were on display in the upstairs hallway. Corey, not to be left out of anything, had added his own artwork with Siren Green waterproof eyeliner. Of course it didn't help that Bojangles had eaten an entire tube of Felicity's cherry lip gloss before making his fashionable escape.

Bojangles, who wasn't known for his strong constitution, was sure to get the runs from that greasy treat.

One day she surely would laugh about this latest episode in what she now referred to as her Maine exile, but not today. Some days she didn't think she would live long enough to see the humor in Tucker's adventurous schemes.

Tucker frowned and gave a dramatic sigh. "Water."

She contained her smile and got her grandson a cup of water. "Want to show me what you've been working on?" Dinner was ready to go into the oven and Tucker had been working diligently on his studies.

"Stupid letters." Tucker gulped down the water like a thirsty camel.

"Letters aren't stupid. You need to learn them so you can learn to read and write." She had noticed that upstairs he had spelled "cat" with a *k*. The boy needed some more study time. She put the covered pan into the refrigerator until it was time to go into the oven.

The hulking hunk of metal in the basement called a heater was stupid. It sounded like a 747 taking off every time it kicked on, and the thermostat refused to work properly.

She walked over to the ancient thermostat and pounded on the wall. No way was it sixty-three degrees in the kitchen. Eighty-three, she would believe. One of these days the heater was going to give up the ghost and blow them all to smithereens.

She sat down next to Tucker and looked at some of his work. This wasn't how she'd envisioned her life. The first week of the new year she would be turning fifty, and she had a horrible feeling menopause was kicking in. God, she really couldn't be that old, could she?

Life was supposed to be different than this. She wanted George alive, calling all the shots and carrying their world upon his broad shoulders. He had promised to always take care of her and their children. He had promised they would travel and see the world once he retired and Felicity was through college. George had lied.

She wanted her little boy, Kenny, who had turned into a man, alive, and not only managing his own family but also helping with hers. Instead she was staring at a stranger in her daughter's body, opening doors and windows in November, and discovering new uses for duct tape nearly every day.

The big, monstrous house her daughter-in-law had bought, though situated on a beautiful piece of property overlooking the bay, was being held together with duct tape, Gorilla Glue, and prayers. The fire department's number was on speed-dial, and they had gone through two handymen since moving here a couple months ago. To top it all off, the hot water lasted for only three-quarters of a shower, no matter how fast she washed.

Dorothy was very thankful when Coop, the UPS man, stopped by the other night and fixed the hose on the washer. But little alarm bells were starting to go off in her head. She hadn't noticed any hanky-panky between Coop and Jenni, but she was watching them closely. The man had practically pushed Dorothy off the basement steps racing her to the top when she'd invited him to dinner the other night.

Either Coop had been starving, or he had been looking forward to the company.

It was bad enough trying to keep her eye on Felicity and Sam when the high school football star came visiting. Both Coop's and Sam's visits were becoming more frequent. Although she knew what Sam was after, her little girl, she wasn't too sure about the UPS guy.

The saying, "What can brown do for you?" was starting to take on a whole new meaning.

Felicity loved her nephews, she really did. She just couldn't stand them most of the time. Today she wanted to murder one, and his name was Tucker James Wright. The kid wouldn't see his fifth birthday, in two weeks, if she had any say in the matter. She'd be doing the world a favor. He was going to end up in the prison system living off the taxpayers' hard-earned money and making license plates anyway.

Tucker had all the earmarks of becoming a drain on society.

Her sister-in-law, Jenni, didn't appreciate Felicity's opinion of Tucker. Of course, the kid's mother hadn't been arguing Tucker's virtues too loudly.

The little delinquent didn't have any.

His only redeeming quality was that he was cute and

favored Jenni in appearances. Felicity was pretty sure that the prison system was filled with cute guys.

"Are you still upset?" Jenni sat a tray of bayberry oatmeal soap down on the opposite side of the workstation and then perched herself upon a stool. By the stubborn tilt of her sister-in-law's jaw, Felicity knew she would be staying awhile. Jenni looked like she wanted to talk.

"Wouldn't you be?" Felicity wasn't in a forgiving mood. It seemed all she ever did was forgive her nephews for one thing after another. After another. Today might have been the final straw. Tucker not only had ruined most of her makeup, written on walls, and totally trashed her closet. The little brat also had destroyed her favorite dark green tank top—the one that not only matched the color of her eyes but also pushed up her boobs and made her look like she had some cleavage for once.

Sam had really liked that top.

Felicity cracked a smile as she remembered the way Sam's tongue seemed to get tangled up in his words every time she had worn that particular top. She wore that stretchy green top at least once a week just to watch Sam sweat.

"See, it isn't that bad." Jenni gave her a bright, big smile back and started to wrap the bars of bayberry oatmeal soap with Mistletoe Bay labels. "We'll go shopping this weekend for a new blouse and we'll replenish your supply of makeup while we're at it."

Felicity mulled that over and continued to wrap the bars of the newest fragrance produced by the Mistletoe Bay Bath and Body Company: Snowflake. She loved the fresh, clean smell of the soap and had already confiscated a few bars for her friends at school. Jenni looked at the freebies as free advertising and test marketing. Everyone at school loved Jenni's products, and a couple of the local shops were now stocking Mistletoe Bay merchandise to cater to the new, younger customers.

"The last time I went shopping with you, I ended up wearing Corey's chocolate ice cream cone and we lost Chase in the bookstore for half an hour." She would rather do sit-ups in front of the entire boys' gym class in a two-piece bathing suit than go to the mall with her nephews.

"They'll behave this time." Jenni refused to meet her gaze. Felicity's sister-in-law kept her head bent and her fingers busy wrapping a label around each bar of soap before placing it into the appropriate box.

"Coop isn't going to find you nearly as attractive if your nose keeps growing." Felicity thought it was cute the way the UPS guy kept coming around. She just wished he wouldn't come around as much when Sam was visiting.

Over the past several months Felicity had become used to being ignored by her mother, who never seemed to have enough time for her anymore. Her nephews terrorized her and invaded her privacy every chance they got. Only Jenni paid her some attention, when her sister-in-law had a minute to breathe, like now. Sam, on the other hand, had been all hers. Or at least he had been until the former high school football star started showing up on their doorstep and talking about stupid things like shovel passes and flea-flickers.

Whatever in the hell they were.

She missed her friends at her old school and on most days hated the fact that she'd had to move to the coast and away from everyone she knew back in Augusta. If it wasn't for Sam, she would seriously consider asking her mother if she could go live with Brittany and her family back in Augusta until she went to college. Kara's family, or even Michelle's mom would take her in.

"I'll ignore that comment about Coop, and my nose isn't growing." Jenni rubbed her nose, as if she was checking to see if indeed it had grown. "What I meant to say was, I would try to make them behave."

"How? Are you packing a Taser stun gun I don't know about?"

Jenni tried to cover up her chuckle with a cough. "I don't believe in using violence to control the boys."

"That's your first mistake." She got up and reached for another tray of Snowflake soap to wrap. Jenni must have been busy today cutting all the bars. It was her job to apply labels not only to the bars of soap but also to the assorted body creams, cranberry hand wash, and brown sugar body polish. All of Jenni's products were made from 100 percent natural ingredients, and the entire state seemed to be on a going-back-to-nature kick.

By the looks of things she was going to be busy until way after Christmas.

"You would have me hit the boys?" Jenni stopped wrapping the handmade soap and stared at her in horror.

"Of course not." She felt terrible for even kidding about such a thing. Her nephews owned her heart and she would personally rip anyone apart who so much as laid a finger on them. She set the tray down and perched herself back on the stool.

She still couldn't resist teasing Jenni. "Leather restraints should do the job."

"You're horrible." Jenni laughed as she closed the first box of twelve bars of soap and started on the next.

"And you're ignoring the truth." Felicity brushed silvery glitter off her hands.

The labels for Snowflake had silver sparkles all over the printed snowflakes. Jenni had gone all out for the three holiday fragrances she was producing this year. Goodness' Sakes smelled like vanilla sugar cookies and had golden, glittery poinsettias on the label. Naughty and Nice was done in a retro pink and black argyle print with the sparkles on the pink diamond shapes, and it had a sexy flower scent.

The glitter had been a really cool marketing idea, and she had encouraged Jenni to go for it. Who knew it was going to be a freaking pain in the butt to work with. Her hands sparkled, her jeans sparkled, and her sweatshirt sparkled. Even her hair sparkled. Hell, yesterday when she was done working, she looked in the mirror and there had been golden glitter on her teeth.

Jenni had refused to work with the glittery labels. Her sister-in-law claimed that was what she was paying Felicity the big bucks for. Ha! Felicity was making the same amount as some of her new friends who scooped ice cream down at Bailey's. At least they got to see and talk to other people while they worked. She got Jenni.

Then again, the shop was totally off-limits to the boys and Jenni usually let her play whatever kind of music she wanted to. There were some perks.

"What am I ignoring?" Jenni looked around the

crowded shop as if trying to find a clue as to what Felicity was talking about.

Felicity shook her head hopelessly. "You know, he's about six-foot-two, brown hair, and deep chocolate eyes. Has a habit of dressing in brown a lot."

"Coop?"

"Is there anyone else I should know about?" She'd never thought about Jenni's love life before Coop showed up on the scene. Her sister-in-law was only thirty years old. People in their thirties dated all the time. Kenny, her brother, had been gone for two years now. In all that time she had never seen Jenni so much as look at another man. Jenni had been too busy raising the boys, taking care of every little thing for Dorothy, moving, and starting the business.

She didn't think Jenni was supposed to stop living because Kenny had.

"What about Coop?" Jenni continued wrapping soap.

"You tell me." Felicity wasn't positive, but there might have been a blush sweeping up her sister-in-law's cheeks.

"There's nothing to tell, Reds." Jenni used the nickname Kenny had bestowed upon Felicity only when she was trying to score some points or change the subject. "He's the UPS man. It's his job to come here to pick up and deliver boxes."

"What about eating dinner here the other night?"

"Your mother was the one to invite him, not me," Jenni said.

"He helped you clean up the kitchen afterward." She hadn't been born yesterday. She had noticed the way Coop seemed to purposely avoid looking at Jenni all through the meal. There was no way he, or any other man, would think Jenni was so repulsive he would turn to stone if he so much as looked at her. That avoidance, to her way of thinking, showed he was interested.

Jenni had that fresh, clean-scrubbed appearance of the girl next door that Felicity envied. Not a freckle marred her face, and her thick, long, nearly midnight-black hair had never seen a frizzy day in its life. From a distance, her sister-in-law still looked like a teenager. It was once you were close enough to see the sadness in her gaze that a person realized Jenni wasn't some college co-ed playing at being some mad scientist while stirring her pots of soap and smelling like vanilla sugar cookies all the time.

"Coop was being polite." Jenni rolled her eyes.

"Being polite is when you say, 'Thank you for dinner. It was delicious.'" She grinned at the look on Jenni's face. "Being interested is when you help the lovely widow with the dishes once the kids are out of the room." Poor Jenni—she didn't stand a chance at finding a boyfriend with Tucker around.

"Lovely widow, my butt." Jenni gave a snort. "I had just finished mopping up the basement floor, if you recall."

"What, you think I didn't notice that you changed before dinner?" She was the one who'd had to help her mother set the table while Corey climbed all over Sam. "If I'm not mistaken you also applied some lip gloss and ran a brush through your hair."

"I even took the time to wash my hands to get the stench of basement mildew and Tide detergent off me." Jenni shook her head. "I think you're reading more into this than it is, Reds. Cooper Armstrong is just a very

nice man who has taken a fancy to your mother's cooking." Jenni wiggled her eyebrows. "Maybe he's after Dorothy. Do you think he'll make a nice stepdad?"

Felicity was glad she didn't have any food in her mouth. She would have choked to death. "That would be the day. Mom's going crazy as it is, with her opening windows and constantly crying at TV commercials. Can you picture her dating, especially a younger man?"

She tried not to visualize what her fifty-year-old mother would do on a date. "Who would want to take out an old lady having hot flashes?" The mere thought of her mother out on a date was beyond her imagination. It was creepy. Disturbingly creepy.

"Shame on you. Dorothy's not even fifty yet. She's not old." Jenni gave her a stern look. "Don't you think she gets lonely?"

"Lonely?" Felicity snorted with laughter. "In that house?" The house had about eleven rooms, and there wasn't a quiet corner in any of them. Most of the time her mother was begging for peace and quiet so she could enjoy a television show or a book.

"You know what I mean." Jenni stopped what she was doing. "Don't you ever wonder why she doesn't date?"

"First off, someone would have to ask her out." Felicity couldn't imagine that possibility. "Second, she's a grandmother. Grannies don't date. They bake cookies and knit sweaters."

"Your mother doesn't knit, and of course they date." Jenni laughed and shook her head. "You can't be that naive, Reds. And just for your information, I know for a fact that Dorothy has been asked out."

"By who?"

"Joe Clayton." Jenni smiled.

"Who's Joe Clayton? And more important, what planet was he from?"

"He owns the garage on the outskirts of town. Your mom had to drop her car off there for a brake job last month. I witnessed the whole exchange. Joe asked her to dinner."

"Mom said no, right?" Surely she would have noticed her mother going out on a date.

"Right." Jenni started labeling the next box of soap. "When she picked up the car the next day, Mr. Clayton asked her to go to a movie with him."

"What is he, desperate?" The whole town was going crazy along with her mother. Maybe there was something in the town's water supply.

"No, he seemed like a very nice man. He's one of the volunteer firemen in town and he was one of the ones who came out here when Tucker got his head caught in the heating duct." Jenni shuddered at that particular memory. "He even owns his own business." Jenni grinned and wiggled her brow. "He even gave your mother a discount on the brake job."

"Isn't that illegal or something?" She remembered getting a free cotton candy from a cute boy over at Sullivan's amusement pier when she'd first moved into the area. She had been tempted to stick around until he got off work. but then she had noticed he gave away three more to other girls while she was watching him. One had to wonder how many brake jobs this Mr. Clayton discounted.

"It's his business; I'm guessing he could do what he wants."

"Not with my mother, he can't." She wasn't about to let some guy play tonsil hockey with her mother in the front seat of his pickup truck. Yuck. It was just too gross to think about.

"Felicity, she's your mother, the grandmother to my three sons, and my dearest friend. She is also a woman, a very attractive woman. Why shouldn't she date if she wants to?" Jenni looked determined to press her point. "Don't you enjoy being in the company of Sam sometimes? Doesn't your mother deserve the same opportunity to have a life outside of you, me, and the boys?"

She understood Jenni's point, but she didn't like it. "The same thing could be said about you, Jenni." As Sam always said, the best defense was a great offense. "Wouldn't you like to spend some time in the company of a cute guy? You know, go see a movie or have a dinner where you wouldn't have to cut someone's meat up for them."

"I walked into that one, didn't I?" Jenni chuckled while shaking her head.

"With both feet." It wasn't very often that she got to turn the tables on her sister-in-law. "So when are you going out with Coop?"

"I'm not."

"Why not?" She thought they made a cute couple, but more important, Coop had met Tucker, and he'd still stuck around for dinner the other night.

"Let's start with that he hasn't asked me."

"It's the twenty-first century, ask him."

"I will not." Jenni looked appalled by the very thought. "I'm not ready to date, Felicity. Let's leave it at that."

"Because of Kenny?" It still hurt to think about her

brother and all the might-have-beens. But all their pain, misery, and grief couldn't bring him back. Life went on, and although Jenni smiled more now, she wasn't totally happy.

Before Jenni could answer, the door to the shop was flung open and Corey ran into the room. "Mom, Mom, Mom!"

Jenni dropped the soap she was holding and ran for Corey. "What's wrong?"

Felicity was out of the chair and across the room in a flash. Corey knew not to enter the shop unless it was an emergency, but it was the absence of Tucker that gave her the bigger fear. Her nephew must have really done something this time.

"Tucker's on the roof, and Grandmom keeps crossing herself." Corey's words ran together while he gasped for breath.

Jenni felt her heart plummet to her knees as she sprinted for the door. Tucker was on the roof! By God, the house was three stories high. He would break his neck if he fell. She dashed down the woodland path to the front of the house. She could hear Felicity urging Corey to run faster behind her.

She sprinted around the front of the house and took in the scene. Her heart started to beat again once she saw Tucker was indeed on the roof. The porch roof. Coop Armstrong was standing below, with both feet planted in Dorothy's garden, calmly talking to her son.

"Now I want you to scoot closer to the edge, Tucker, but stay on your butt. Do not stand up." Coop's voice was steady and calm.

She watched as her son moved closer to the edge.

Tucker's gaze was on Coop, who was standing directly below him. If Tucker should fall she was positive that Coop could and would catch him.

Dorothy spotted her and Felicity and came running over. "Should I go call the fire department?" Dorothy was frantic, and though Tucker wasn't exactly smiling, he didn't look scared. Her son had the look of someone who was the center of attention—and liking it.

"No fire department, Dorothy." Coop didn't bother to turn around as he gave that order.

Jenni looked over at Coop's big brown delivery truck. It was still running, but there were no boxes around. He must have seen Tucker up on the roof as he pulled up to the house and had immediately come to her son's rescue.

Her knight in shining armor was dressed in brown and drove a box truck.

"Now I want you to lay down on your belly, Tucker. Have your head face the windows and your feet dangle about six inches over the edge of the porch toward me."

"Why? Don't I have to jump down to you?" Tucker looked over at his mother and waved. "Hi, Mom. Mr. Brown is going to catch me."

Her heart didn't like how close to the edge of the roof her son was perched. But somehow she managed to wave back calmly. "Listen to Mr. Armstrong, Tucker, and do exactly what he tells you to do." She'd kill her son once his feet were firmly on the ground.

"What's going on?" asked Chase. He had on his backpack and had just gotten off the school bus at the end of the drive. "How come Grandmom didn't meet my bus?"

Chase stared up at his brother. "What's Tucker doing on the roof? Can I go up too?"

"Being bad," Corey said as he pointed to the fire rope ladder hanging out of one of the attic windows. "He climbed out Felicity's window."

"He's taking ten years off my life, that's what he is doing," Dorothy said as she crossed herself once again. "And no, you most definitely cannot go up onto that rickety old roof with him. I'm praying that the whole thing just doesn't just collapse from his weight."

There was something Jenni hadn't thought about until that instant. The porch roof was indeed rotted and Tucker could fall through at any moment. Was it possible to feel one's hair turn gray?

"Why can't I go up?" Chase looked disappointed.

"Your brother is in a heap of trouble once Coop gets him down," Jenni whispered to her oldest son. She didn't want Tucker knowing what was waiting for him. He'd more than likely try something really stupid then, like climbing back up the ladder.

What had she been thinking when she'd purchased Felicity the rope ladder that slipped over the window sill when they first moved into the house. Why had she been worried about her sister-in-law and Chase being trapped in their third-floor bedrooms if ever there was a fire, when Tucker lived in the house? Tucker was more destructive than a fire, tornado, and hurricane combined.

She watched as Tucker, for once in his life, did as someone instructed. He got down on his belly, and his little sneakers dangled over the edge of the roof.

Coop took a step closer. "Now wiggle your way farther down, closer to the edge." Tucker wiggled a few inches. "Farther, and let your feet drop down. Coop stretched his arms high into the air. A few more inches, and Coop's big strong hands wrapped around Tucker's ankles. "That's it. I've got you. Keep coming."

She held her breath as Tucker's belly skimmed the roof and he dropped safely into Coop's arms.

Tucker looked over Coop's broad shoulder at her and grinned. "Hey, Mom, Felicity's ladder doesn't reach the ground."

"I knew that." She walked over to Coop and with shaking hands took her son and stood him on his feet. "Now, would you like to explain why you used your aunt's emergency ladder? If I recall correctly, it was under her bed, and you boys all had been told countless times not to touch it."

Felicity, who had Corey perched on one of her hips, groaned. "He was in my room again!"

Tucker looked at the ground and dug the toe of his sneaker into the dirt. Everyone was standing around outside, and no one but Chase had on a coat. In a low voice, he softly whispered, "I was looking for Fred."

"He was in my room again," wailed Chase. "Mom, you told him to stay out of it."

"Who's Fred?" asked Coop as he glanced up at the open window on the third floor.

"Did you let Fred out of his cage again?" Jenni really didn't need this today. Fred scared her.

"Who's Fred?" repeated Coop. "And why is he in a cage?" Coop frowned as Felicity paled and Dorothy crossed herself.

"He's in my room?" screeched Felicity. "Jenni, you

promised to keep Fred out of my room! He's disgusting and he gives me the creeps."

Jenni rubbed her forehead, where a headache was forming. Now that Tucker was safely on solid ground, she was coming down from the adrenaline rush. It didn't help matters. "I'm not thrilled with him either, Felicity. Calm down, we'll get him back into his cage somehow."

"Let's call Sam. He caught him the last time." Chase thumped his brother on the arm. "Stay out of my room and away from Fred. He doesn't like you."

Coop looked confused and nervous. "Okay, that's it— who is Fred?" Coop locked gazes with her. "Tell Dorothy to stop crossing herself and praying; it's getting on my nerves."

"Dorothy, please, it's okay. We'll get him." Jenni grabbed Chase by the back of his coat. "Stop hitting your brother. You know you aren't supposed to hit him. There is to be no hitting in this family."

"He knows he's not supposed to open Fred's cage." Chase stuck his tongue out at his brother. There was a look of retaliation in his green eyes.

Tucker, not to be outdone by his brother, stuck out his tongue.

"Jenni, how big is Fred?" Coop glanced up at the window.

She held up her hands until they were about ten inches apart. Fred wasn't a fast grower.

"Okay." Coop's shoulders seem to relax. "Now what *is* Fred?"

"Oh, I'm sorry. I thought you knew." Jenni couldn't

imagine what had been going through Coop's mind. "Fred is Chase's pet iguana."

"You have a loose pet iguana in the house, with two cats?" Coop held back his laughter while stating the obvious.

Jenni paled and said a very unmotherly word as she sprinted for the front door. All three boys were right on her heels.

Chapter Six

Dorothy handed her daughter a Pop-Tart.

"I thought you said you were making bacon and eggs?" Felicity frowned at the offending tart and then glanced at the stove.

"I was, until Chase couldn't find his homework." Dorothy poured herself another cup of coffee. It was her third of the morning and she still wasn't fully awake. Sleep last night had been impossible. Half the time when she closed her eyes she kept visualizing Fred crawling up on her bed, even though she knew the reptile was securely in his cage. It had taken Jenni and the boys almost two hours to find the prehistoric creature yesterday afternoon.

Fred had been basking in the warmth behind the radiator in Chase's room—apparently the last place they'd looked.

The other half of the time she was kicking off blankets and sweating like a pig in July. The darn mechanical monster in the basement must have been on the fritz again.

"What does Chase's homework have to do with me

eating junk for breakfast?" Felicity tossed the breakfast pastry onto a plate and went in search of something else to eat. "I hate Pop-Tarts."

"You love strawberries." She wasn't in the mood for her daughter's snit fit. She wanted a nap. She needed a nap.

Maybe she shouldn't have overruled Jenni when her daughter-in-law suggested they put Tucker and Corey into a preschool. Here it was only November, and she was wiped out from chasing after them all day long. Raising kids was not for the weak of heart and body. She was afraid both her heart and her body were heading for the old-age home.

"I also love chocolate chip mint ice cream. It doesn't mean I want to eat it between preservative-choked pastries every morning. Whatever happened to your favorite saying, that breakfast was the most important meal of the day?"

"Don't be dramatic. You didn't have Pop-Tarts once this week." She cradled her cup and took another jolt of caffeine. She could hear Jenni herding the boys upstairs. It sounded like a bunch of elephants doing the Watusi.

"No, I had Cocoa Puffs, and the sugar high lasted until second period at school. Then I was miserable until lunch, where I pigged out and ate Sam's dessert, along with mine." Felicity picked up a banana and peeled it. "My jeans are getting tight. I can't afford to keep eating sugar for breakfast. Whatever happened to your cinnamon French toast or that cheese omelet you used to whip up for me nearly every morning? I'd die for a piece of that toast right now."

Dorothy decided to ignore the crack about all the good stuff she used to cook in the morning. Mornings used to be her favorite part of the day. Now she dreaded them. She was now extremely partial to bedtime.

"You're not fat." Felicity was five feet nine inches tall and as skinny as a rail. Most of the time she was worried that her daughter wasn't eating enough. "You could stand to put on a few more pounds."

"Hush your mouth." Felicity twisted her neck to look over her shoulder at her butt. "God, it's sticking out!" Felicity wailed.

"It is not." Teenage girls were insane. "Maybe I should take you for an eye exam." When was the last time her daughter had been at an eye doctor? Two years? Three?

"My eyes are fine. Where's the bacon? I dreamt of bacon last night." Felicity took a big bite of the banana and glared at the empty frying pan sitting on the stove.

"It was sitting on the counter, ready for me to cook, when Chase had his emergency. I left the kitchen, and Dumb, or maybe it was Dumber, jumped up on the counter and started to eat it."

"Gross." Felicity continued eating the banana. "So, because of a cat, I get to eat like a monkey? That's not fair, Mom. Nothing is fair anymore. Corey had his turtle in the bathtub again last night. I almost stepped on it."

"You know to always check the tub first." There was no getting around it, Felicity was in a whining mood. "Buster likes to swim."

"What about Tucker?"

"What about him?" She loved her grandson dearly, but she was starting to fantasize about locking him in the basement. The other day she'd caught herself in Krup's General Store in town drooling over the deadbolts.

"He picked up the extension last night and was

making kissing sounds when I was talking to Sam on the phone."

"I thought you were doing homework." She didn't want to think about what Sam and her daughter were discussing. With Tucker on the other end, she knew it couldn't have been too bad. Jenni had talked her into allowing Felicity to date at sixteen, as long as she was in a group.

Felicity was now seventeen and allowed real dates, as long as she was home by curfew. Her daughter swore she was the only girl in the high school who had to be home by nine on a school night and eleven on the weekends. She thought she was being very lenient, while Felicity thought she was being totally unreasonable. Jenni smartly left the room whenever that particular discussion erupted.

She'd never had problems with Felicity and her occasional dates, until Sam had appeared on the scene.

Samuel Fischer was giving her an ulcer. The young couple were way too serious about each other. She had already sat her daughter down twice and had the birds-and-bees conversation. It had been one of the hardest things she had ever done. Being a widow for five years, she was a tad rusty on the subject, and for the life of her, she still couldn't figure out what birds or bees had to do with sex.

She had a feeling her daughter sat through both of those talks trying not to laugh. Hopefully it was because her daughter was trying to show her some respect and not the fact that Felicity had known all that stuff already.

"How is Sam?" Last night was one of those rare nights when Sam hadn't shown up for dinner or hours of television watching when he wasn't checking out Felicity. Maybe things were finally cooling off between them.

"He's fine. He had to help his sister, Faith, with her algebra homework while his dad took Hope shopping for a homecoming dance dress." Felicity poured herself a glass of orange juice. "Which reminds me, I need to go shopping for one myself. Sam's taking me to the dance."

So much for things cooling off. "When is it?" She would add it to the list of things to do.

"Two weeks." Felicity downed the juice. "I asked Sam to have Thanksgiving dinner here with us, but he can't. He doesn't want to leave his father and two sisters to their frozen TV dinners. Sam says his father couldn't fry an edible egg, let alone an entire Thanksgiving dinner."

Well, that explained why Sam was at their dinner table nearly every night of the week.

Since she wasn't having any luck putting some space between her daughter and Sam, maybe it was time to meet his family. She wasn't quite sure what had happened to Sam's mother, but hopefully his father felt the same way she did about the seriousness of their teenagers' relationship. She could use an ally.

"Why don't you invite Sam's father and two sisters to dinner along with Sam? It would be a shame for them to suffer through TV dinners on Thanksgiving."

"Really?" Felicity sounded excited. "You wouldn't mind?"

"I'll just buy a bigger turkey and throw a couple extra potatoes into the pot."

"You mean that?" Felicity's green eyes lit up like a Christmas tree.

"Sure, what's three more people?" When was the last time she had seen Felicity so happy with her? She couldn't remember.

Felicity flung her arms around her mother's neck and planted a loud kiss on her mother's cheek. "You're the best, Mom."

"Thank you." Her morning was suddenly looking up, way up.

"I'll tell Sam when he gets here to pick me up for school." Felicity grabbed her coat and backpack. "He's running late as usual."

"What's all this about?" Jenni stood in the opening of the kitchen smiling at them both.

"Sam's dad and sisters are coming here for Thanksgiving dinner, Jenni. Mom says I can invite them. You don't mind, do you?"

Dorothy felt a little foolish for not getting Jenni's approval first. After all, it was Jenni's house. "Sorry, Jenni. I should have asked you first."

"Nonsense. I would love to meet them, Felicity. The more the merrier."

"Great." Felicity practically danced out of the kitchen.

Jenni's smile grew. "It's been a long time since I've seen her so happy."

"I was thinking the same thing." She heard Sam pull up out front and blow his horn. The slamming of the front door punctuated Felicity's departure.

"I'll get it!" Dorothy reached for the ringing phone before the boys could abandon the television and the afternoon cartoons. For once Tucker had been behaving himself and was allowed to watch TV with his brothers.

"Hello?"

"Hello," said a pleasant-sounding man. "May I please speak to Dorothy Wright?"

"This is she." Whatever he was selling, she might listen to his sales pitch. His voice was on the husky side, and he definitely had a Maine accent.

"Hello, this is Eli Fischer, Sam's father."

"Oh, hi." Her first thought was that something was wrong, but then she realized Felicity was already home from school and working in the shop with Jenni. "Is Sam all right?"

"Sam's fine." Eli chuckled. "I'm just calling to thank you for the invitation to Thanksgiving at your place. It's very nice of you to think of me and Sam's two sisters."

"No problem. The more the merrier, as Jenni says. We usually eat around five-thirty. Will that be okay with you?"

"Five-thirty will be fine, but there's a condition on us accepting the invitation."

"What sort of condition?" Felicity had told her he couldn't cook at all, so she was hoping he wasn't going to insist on bringing dessert. She had her heart set on baking some pumpkin pies using her grandmother's recipes.

"My son swears that the old heating system in your basement is about to explode. I'm a mechanic, and there's nothing I love more than a good challenge. How about I come early so I can tinker around with it to see if I can get it to behave, or at least quiet down some?"

"I don't know." She would love for someone, anyone, to tinker around with the monster, using a battering ram and a blowtorch. "We've already had two different guys look at it, both say it's hopeless."

"Please, now I'm intrigued. Hopeless is my specialty."

She could hear the laughter in his voice. What did they have to lose but a three-ton monster in the basement? It wasn't like it wasn't on its last legs anyway. How much damage could he possibly do? "Okay, if you want to give it a shot, who am I to argue?"

"Really?" Eli sounded as happy as Felicity had this morning when she left the house.

"Really." Who was she to deprive the cute-sounding man of a challenge. "We'll see you and the girls on Thanksgiving. Come anytime you want. We'll be here."

"We'll be there." Eli paused for a moment before adding, "Thank you, Dorothy. It's very nice of you."

"Nonsense. Somehow I think we might get the better end of this deal. Bye."

"Bye."

She hung up the phone and tried to picture what Sam's father looked like. What kind of face would go with that voice? Did he look like Sam, who had dark hair and eyes and was tall and thin? Then again, what did it matter? Eli Fischer could look like a bowling ball as far as she was concerned. She was looking for an ally, not a date.

"Grandmom, can we have cookies now?" asked Corey as he came running into the kitchen with Tucker on his heels.

"I'll fix you a snack, but it won't be cookies. You boys go wash up." A grandmother's work was never done.

* * *

Jenni shivered inside her heavy coat. She wasn't cold; she was scared to death. Corey was missing.

God, what was she going to do? She'd give it another twenty minutes before calling the sheriff. Corey couldn't have gotten that far. He had been missing for only the past twenty minutes or so. Sam had already called some of his buddies from the football team to search the woods. From where she stood at the edge of the bay, she could hear them arriving.

Mistletoe Bay was gorgeous with its natural wonders. Development along the shore had been kept to a minimum, and most of what had been built was well concealed. The bay was the perfect spot to raise a family. It was also deadly.

Corey knew not to go near the water. When Dorothy had come running into the shop to give her the news that she couldn't find Corey, the first place Jenni had run was to the bay. It was the most dangerous.

Was it instinct that made her run to the edge of the water, or a premonition?

Jenni refused to think such a thing. Corey was probably still in the woods hiding from Tucker and thinking this was all a game. She studied the shoreline to her left and then to her right. Not another person was in sight, only a few hardy birds picking over what the storm might have washed up yesterday.

The storm had brought plenty of rain and howling winds, but thankfully not snow. Tucker and Corey had been closed up in the house for the past two days, and she didn't blame Dorothy for allowing them to go outside and play this afternoon. She had even given them permission during lunch to play in the woods, provided they kept dry.

They both had been playing outside since they moved here in June. All three boys knew the rules, and although Tucker occasionally bent them, they all pretty much obeyed them while unsupervised.

Dorothy had been near hysterical when she flung open the shop door. Thankfully Sam and Felicity had been right behind her and immediately got to searching the area of the woods where he was last seen. Dorothy now was sitting on the front porch with Chase, who had just gotten home from school, and a very subdued Tucker. Right now Jenni didn't have time to comfort her older sons. She needed to find Corey.

She needed to hold her baby.

She glanced at the muddy ground but couldn't detect any footprints, besides a couple of bird tracks. In the distance she could barely make out Sam and Felicity calling Corey's name. The wind was blowing off the ocean, carrying the sound away and making her eyes water. Then again, maybe she was just imagining she could hear them while praying Corey could.

"Jenni, where haven't you looked?" Coop Armstrong grabbed her elbow and dodged her blowing hair.

It took every ounce of strength she possessed not to throw herself into Coop's strong arms. She wanted so desperately to lean on someone, and Coop was the logical choice. Coop was her sons' rescuer. Today she was the one who needed to be rescued from this nightmare. She needed Coop's seeming magic that unraveled all the trouble her sons created. The only words she could get past the lump in her throat were "Please find him."

Coop pulled her into his arms and gave her a tight hug. "I promise we'll find him. Please don't cry, Jenni."

She wiped at the tears rolling down her face. She hadn't even known she was crying. She felt warm and secure in Coop's arms, but she wasn't worried about herself. She was terrified for Corey. She stepped away from Coop. "Sorry." For the first time she noticed how pale and upset Coop looked. For his being the local UPS driver, she had come to rely on him for more than just delivering her packages.

Coop gently wiped away another tear. "Don't be sorry." With shaking fingers he brushed a lock of her windswept hair away from her face and behind her ear. "Do you think he would have gone into the water?"

Her heart clutched at the fear in his voice. "Not on purpose. Corey knows not to go near the water, and it's awfully cold out today. I just came here because it posed the most danger."

"Do you see anything out of the ordinary?" Coop studied the relatively calm bay. "Do you notice anything out of place?"

"Not here, but up by the house I noticed some of the plastic yellow tape I had strung between the trees was down. The storm yesterday must have been worse than I thought. I forgot to check it before the boys went outside to play. It's all my fault."

"You mean the police tape?"

"I use it as a boundary. All three boys know not to ever cross or go beyond the tape. The woods are pretty thick, and Dorothy and I can't always see the boys from the house." She glanced back toward the house; only a small sliver of the structure could be seen through the trees. She could no longer hear Corey's name being yelled in the distance, but she knew Sam and Felicity wouldn't give up until Corey was safely home.

"Does Corey like the water?"

"To swim in, no, but he loves walking along the shore finding things the water tossed up, especially after a storm." She brushed her hair away from her eyes and studied the shoreline. It twisted and turned so often, she could see only a small patch of it, here and there. From what little she could see of it, it was empty.

"Okay, here's what we'll do." Coop nodded at the cell phone clutched in her hand. "Give me your number, I'll give you mine." He unclipped his cell phone from his belt. "You head that way, and if you find him, call." Coop nodded to the right; "I'll head this way, and I'll call you if I find him, okay?"

"What if Sam and the rest of the guys find him?"

"Dorothy knows your number, right?"

"Right." She finished entering his number. "Thanks, Coop."

"Thank me when he's home safe." Coop headed off at a brisk walk. A moment later she heard him shout Corey's name.

She quickly headed in the other direction.

Coop walked as quickly as he could. The more ground he covered, the faster he might be about to spot Corey. The bay was at high tide, leaving very little room to walk. He was left climbing over rocks, downed trees, and through brush and bushes as high as his thighs. He didn't think Corey would be able to wade through such a thick tangle of branches.

His foot sank into mud as he shouted Corey's name

again. Coop had on brown work boots. They managed to stay on his feet but now weighed a ton due to the clingy mud.

Since when had the little tyke wormed his way into his heart? For surely that was what the child had done. Coop had never experienced such panic as what he was feeling now, not even when he had flown from California to Maine after his father had the heart attack in February. Then all he kept picturing was his mother crying and sitting alone in a sterile waiting room at the hospital.

Sometimes being an only child sucked.

Corey wasn't an only child. He glanced behind him, but Jenni was now out of sight. If she was calling Corey's name, he couldn't hear her. The wind had picked up again and the sun had disappeared behind a bank of dark clouds. He shivered against the sudden chill and hoped Corey had been dressed warmly. He cupped his hands and shouted the boy's name again toward the woods.

A trio of seagulls answered his call.

How far could one little boy travel in twenty minutes, especially through this mess? If it had been Tucker, he would guess the adventurous Wright boy would be hitting the edge of town by now. Corey, on the other hand, was day to Tucker's night. Corey would do whatever his older brothers told him to do, but he wasn't the kind to go wander off and disobey his mother and grandmother. The plastic tape barrier must have been down for Corey to wander out of the area.

He refused to think about Jenni and what she must be going through at this very moment. The strong, resilient Jenni had a breaking point after all—her children. In the past weeks that he had gotten to know the Wright family, it had been Jenni who had impressed him the most.

The Wright family was a walking disaster. It didn't take a genius to realize Jenni was the overworked and underappreciated boss of the family and that she was barely holding everything together. With three small boys, a mother-in-law who kept losing sight of the boys, and a teenage girl all living in a zoo-filled house that was sagging around their ears, Jenni had her hands full. If it wasn't for duct tape, glue, and good karma, the house would have crumbled months ago.

Any sane man would be running in the opposite direction as far and as fast as his feet would go.

So why was the chaotic Wright family, especially Jenni, tugging at his heart? And when did his heart get healed enough to be tugged on?

Ever since he had returned to California, after making sure his father had recovered and was home following his heart attack, he didn't have a heart. Only a hole in his chest where it had once beat.

Candace, the woman he'd loved and was about to marry, had shattered it when he walked in unannounced to find her and his best friend in bed. His ex–best friend.

Now all of a sudden his heart had not only mended, it was beating out of his chest in fear. First Jenni had nearly broken it again with her tears, and now the missing Corey was about to cause it to explode. Did weak hearts run in his family? He was too young to go on that horrible bland diet his mother had put his poor father on.

He cupped his hands and shouted, "Corey!" The wind started to howl, and if he wasn't mistaken another storm was about to make its way onto shore. He had already walked a good distance. He'd give it a little more, and then he was calling the sheriff for reinforcements. They had to find Corey before the storm hit.

He rounded another bend and had to maneuver his way around and over a couple of boulders, but he still didn't have a clear view of the shoreline ahead. "Corey!"

Coop stood still and listened intently. In the wind he thought he heard the most wonderful two words in the English language: "Mr. Brown?"

He sprinted around some trees and over a log, shouting Corey's name as he went.

He hadn't imagined it. This time he heard "Mr. Brown?" more clearly as he hurried around the next crop of rocks and trees.

There on a huge boulder, far from the reach of the water, sat Corey. The little tyke was crying his heart out and had his arms wrapped around his knees. He hurried over to the shaking boy and swept him up into his arms. "Are you okay? Are you hurt?"

"No." Corey swiped at his running nose with his coat sleeve. "I want my mommy." Corey's words came out in big gulps as he buried his head against Coop's chest.

"I can imagine." Coop gave him another big hug and then sat the boy back down on the rock. "Hold on there, Tiger. Let's call her." He hit the send button before he finished the sentence.

"Coop, did you find him?" Jenni's voice was filled with hope and tears.

"He's right in front of me, safe and unharmed." He gave Corey a big smile. "He wants to talk to you, okay?"

"Put him on!" Jenni's shout hurt his eardrum.

He handed Corey the phone.

"Mommy?" Corey sounded so uncertain and scared.

A moment later a small smile appeared on his trembling mouth. "Okay, I'll listen to Mr. Brown. But I did what you said. I got lost, so I sat down, right where I was. Ask Mr. Brown, he saw me sitting." Corey sniffled. "Okay, love you too." Corey handed him back the phone.

"Jenni?"

"He sounds so scared." Jenni was crying again. "He never calls me Mommy anymore, only Mom."

"I told you, no more tears. He's fine." He gave Corey a thumbs-up, which caused the boy's smile to grow. "He's right, I did indeed find him sitting, right on top of a big boulder, far away from the water." He thought her advice to the kids had been great—if lost stay still, and let the adults do the finding. Corey could have been walking in circles for hours, and they might have missed him.

"He's dry, right?"

"His shoes are caked with mud, but he looks dry for now. It looks like a storm is heading in." He frowned up at the sky and could see lightning off in the distance. When it finally hit, it would hit hard. They needed to get home, where it was safe and dry.

"Jenni, call Dorothy and let her and everyone else know that he's safe. I'll meet you along the shoreline. Just keep walking until we meet." He could tell by her breathing that she was already heading back.

"Coop?"

"Yeah?"

"Thank you." Jenni's voice was barely above a whisper.

Those two small words wrapped their way around his heart and healed the latest cracks it had suffered. "You're welcome. Now call poor Dorothy. She wasn't

holding up very well when I saw her up on the porch."
Dorothy had been crying, even though she was putting
up a great front for Tucker's and Chase's benefit.

He closed the phone and clipped it back onto his belt.
"Are you ready to go see your mom, Tiger?"

Corey jumped off the rock and reached for his hand.
"Yes, Mr. Brown."

Coop stared at that small, sweetly trusting, dirty hand
and knew his world was never going to be the same
again. He reached out and wrapped his own calloused,
scarred, and big hand around Corey's soft little one. "I
think we're friends now. How about you call me Coop
from now on?"

"Okay." Corey's little hand was still trembling but
there was a look of such trust on his small face, it nearly
broke his heart.

"Want me to carry you?" Corey had managed to walk
a pretty good distance from home before realizing he
was lost. He had to be tired.

"Nope, I'm a big boy."

"That you are, Tiger, that you are." Coop matched his
steps with Corey's smaller ones as they headed for home.

Jenni had passed the midway point awhile before she
spotted Coop with Corey on his shoulders, heading her
way. She waved wildly and called, "Corey!"

"Mom!" Corey was waving back with both hands,
while Coop kept him steady on his shoulders. Her son
was so close, yet still so far away. She hurried along the
twisting shoreline trying to reach him faster. Her arms
actually ached with the need to hold him close, to see
for herself he was unharmed and safe.

Before she reached them, Coop swung her son off his

shoulders and placed him on the rocky shore. Corey sprinted right into her open arms.

She buried her face in the crook of his shoulder and cried harder. Her baby was in her arms. It was the only thing that matter at this moment in time. "You scared me, kiddo." She felt his legs wrap around her waist and knew his muddy sneakers were ruining her coat. She didn't care.

Corey hiccupped and swiped again at his running nose with the sleeve of his coat. "Sorry, I looked for the tape, but I couldn't find it."

"I know, sweetie. The storm yesterday blew it down." She hugged him tighter and planted a string of noisy kisses up his cheek while reaching into her coat pocket for the ever-present tissues. She made Corey blow his nose. "I should have made sure the tape was still up and secure before allowing you and Tucker to go outside and play today. It's my fault you got lost."

"Jenni," Coop said, "we have to be going. The storm's going to hit at any moment." Thunder sounded in the distance over the ocean.

She stood up with Corey still in her arms. She wasn't about to let go of him till tonight, or next week, or maybe when he turned ten. A raindrop plopped on her head, causing her to hurry along the shoreline for home, where Dorothy, the boys, and the entire football team were waiting for them to celebrate.

"Now you're the weather man?" Was there anything Coop couldn't do? If there was, she hadn't seen it yet.

"Doesn't take a meteorologist to read those clouds."

She shivered as rain started to fall in earnest. Corey nestled closer and ducked his head under her chin. She stopped and pulled the hood of his coat up over his head. She didn't want him getting sick.

Coop reached for Corey and plucked him out of her arms. Corey giggled at the game of being tossed around. "I'll carry him. We'll make it there faster, and drier."

She wanted to argue with him but knew he was right. They would make much better time if he carried Corey. "Okay, but I get to hold him the rest of the day."

Coop chuckled. "I think you might have to fight his grandmother, aunt, and brothers for that one." With a curt nod to her coat, he added, "Pull your own hood up before you get sick." Coop turned and hurried away.

She yanked up the hood, not because he'd told her to, but because she was getting wet.

Chapter Seven

Jenni watched as Corey took a bite of another cookie and grinned. Her youngest son was the center of attention and loving it. For once, Tucker was allowing one of his brothers to hog the limelight. That simple courtesy showed how scared Tucker had been for his little brother.

It was good to see that after all the trouble Tucker had been known to instigate or cause, he had a good heart underneath that Dennis the Menace attitude.

The storm outside finally hit full force about the time Coop, Corey, and she were a couple yards from the porch. During that last mad dash to the house, they had gone from wet to soaked. Corey had been immediately stripped and changed into dry clothes, and she had left her muddy sneakers on the front porch and was now wearing her fuzzy slippers and had damp hair.

Coop, on the other hand, had to make do with a towel and scraping the mud off his boots. The man had a route to finish and he seemed in a hurry to go. She couldn't blame him. There was an entire football team in her house, drinking hot chocolate, eating whatever Dorothy

set before them, and playing video games. The entire
defensive line was in the family room playing with Fred
the iguana and Buster the turtle. They were trying to en-
gineer a race between the two, but Buster wouldn't
come out of his shell, and Fred was ignoring them and
trying to eat the carpet.

The battle at Waterloo would have been quieter.

"Coop, don't you dare leave yet without a hug,"
Dorothy shouted from across the kitchen, where she
was pulling mini pizza bites from the oven. A couple of
tacklers rushed her and nearly emptied the baking sheet
before it made it to the counter.

Jenni watched as her laughing mother-in-law dodged
and wove her way out of the crowded kitchen. By the
looks of things, there was now an evening grocery shopping trip on her schedule and a major dent about to
happen to her bank account. She didn't mind. The football team had come running to find her son. As far as
she was concerned, they could empty every cabinet in
the kitchen. She didn't even mind that it was pouring
outside. What was a little water?

Dorothy practically threw herself into Coop's arms.
"How can I ever thank you?"

Coop was gentleman enough not to stagger, but his
brows shot up at the impact. "I believe you just did,
Dorothy." Coop's hands were gentle as he hesitantly
patted the older woman on the back. Coop shot her an
imploring glance over Dorothy's shoulder.

Jenni smiled back and glanced over at Felicity.

Her sister-in-law's jaw was sagging open and there
was a look of pure horror in her eyes as she gazed at her
mother in Coop's arms.

The small imp in Jenni wanted to make a comment, but she didn't. Felicity had been the first one out there frantically searching for Corey. Besides, Coop looked extremely uncomfortable with Dorothy plastered against his chest and her arms around his neck.

"Dorothy, ease up. I think you're choking him." Jenni came to Coop's rescue.

Her mother-in-law took a quick step back and wiped her eyes. "I'm sorry. I'm just so thankful that you found Corey, words are failing me."

"I take it you're no longer upset with me for taking so long to find the shutoff valve for the washing machine the other afternoon?" Coop reached over and plucked a paper napkin from the basket sitting on the kitchen table. He handed it to Dorothy.

"I forgave you for that as soon as the water stopped squirting me in the face." Dorothy beamed as she wiped her eyes. "If I hadn't, you are definitely forgiven now."

"I really didn't do anything, Dorothy, just walked along the shore until I spotted him sitting there." Coop looked like a man who really did not like being the center of attention or praise.

"It doesn't matter. First thing in the morning I'll be calling your company and telling them what you did. You're a hero. You need a medal or a raise or something." Jenni had never seen Dorothy look so determined.

"I'd rather you didn't." Coop looked embarrassed.

Jenni tried to hide her smile as what appeared to be a blush swept up his cheeks. "I think she's right, Coop." Even though a medal or a pay raise seemed little in the way of compensating for getting her son back. A bronze statue in the middle of the town square might be overkill, but to her, Corey was worth it.

Coop gave her a small glare before pulling on his wet jacket. "I've got to go and finish my route. Thanks for the coffee and oatmeal cookies, Dorothy. They were delicious as always."

"What are you doing for Thanksgiving?" asked Dorothy.

Jenni looked at her mother-in-law as if she had just grown another head. What was her mother-in-law thinking? Felicity dropped the wooden spoon she had been using to stir the hot chocolate.

"Thanksgiving?" Coop seemed unsure where that question was leading. "I guess eating at my parents."

"You guess?" Dorothy chuckled. "Don't you know?"

"My mom's been hunting through cookbooks trying to find some recipes."

"Why? Doesn't she know how to cook?" Dorothy seemed flabbergasted by the very thought.

"She's an excellent cook. She's just trying to find meals my father can eat now that he's on this diet because of his heart."

"What's wrong with his heart?" Dorothy seemed intrigued.

"He had a heart attack last February. The doctors want him to eat healthier, but my mother is taking it to the extreme by cooking stuff that tastes like tree bark and sand. My father hates it."

Dorothy shuddered. "Then the invitation to Thanksgiving is for not only you but your parents as well. Your poor father deserves real food once in a while. We seem to be having a full house that night—what's three more?"

"Who all's coming?" Coop looked directly at Jenni.

"Sam's father and his two sisters. It turns out Mr. Fischer isn't a very good cook." Jenni watched as Felicity refilled Corey's cocoa mug. Sam was sitting next to her youngest son and was fighting him for the last cookie.

"My dad can screw up canned spaghetti." Sam looked at Felicity and winked. "He's so stoked about coming here for dinner that he's coming early and working on the oil burner in the basement."

"What's wrong with the . . ." Coop's voice trailed off as the furnace kicked on with a horrible whining sound that vibrated the floorboards. "Forget that stupid question. My dad knows his way around heaters. I think for real turkey and pumpkin pie he'll give your father a hand in the basement, Sam."

"Cool." Sam went back to telling Corey a story about the shark that had washed up at Hancock Point last night. Per Sam, it had been twenty feet long and had jaws big enough to swallow an elephant.

Something was up between Sam and Coop. The entire football team was in her house, and besides a few "Heys" and a couple of nods, none of the players were really talking with Coop. The glint of hero worship had disappeared from Sam's gaze. She wasn't the only one who'd noticed. Felicity and Dorothy kept glancing from the players to Coop.

Coop was acting as if he hadn't noticed anything out of the ordinary.

Strange.

Coop headed for the front door. She followed on his heels, wondering how one thanks a man for finding one's son. "Coop?"

"If the words 'thank you' come out of your mouth one more time, Jenni, I'm going to be upset." Coop's strong looking hand was on the front doorknob.

Before she could think of what to say that would express her feelings without those two words, Corey came flying from the kitchen, "Mr. Brown, Mr. Brown!"

Coop bent down and smiled. "I thought you were going to call me Coop."

Corey threw himself into Coop's arms. "Thank you for res . . . cue me." Corey had obviously just been coached in the kitchen as to what to say.

She watched as Coop gave her son a big bear hug that had him squealing with delight. "I didn't rescue you, Corey. I found you. You didn't need rescuing because you listened to your mother and did exactly what she told you to do when you realized you were lost."

"Sit and be still." Corey grinned at her. "She's smart."

Coop placed the boy back on his feet and rumpled his hair. "She sure is, so always listen to her." Coop opened the front door. "See you both around, and you, Corey, stay out of trouble."

Corey laughed. "I wasn't in trouble, Coop." Her son looked very proud to be calling the UPS man by his first name. "I was lost."

"That you were." Coop gave her a wink, stepped out onto the porch, and closed the door against the howling wind and blowing rain.

She stood there and watched as Corey sprinted back into the kitchen. He almost slipped in his socks on the wooden floor. Dorothy must have done some cleaning this morning, even though now it was a little hard to tell with wall-to-wall people, especially football players.

How did these kids' parents afford to feed them? They ate like lumberjacks with bottomless pits instead of stomachs. Even Dorothy seemed overwhelmed with the job of feeding them a snack. Thankfully Dorothy hadn't invited the whole team to Thanksgiving dinner. They didn't make turkeys big enough.

So why did her mother-in-law invite not only Coop but also his parents? Sure, she was grateful for Coop going out of his way and finding Corey, but a holiday dinner invite seemed a little extreme. Holidays were for families, not a good-looking delivery man and his parents.

The whole thing smelled like "fix up Jenni with a date," but that couldn't be true. Dorothy was the last person to fix her up. Her mother-in-law still looked at her as Ken's wife, and the mother of her precious grandsons. Wives and mothers did not date.

She wasn't blind. She saw how handsome Coop was, but she wasn't into fooling herself. Coop was single, never married, and didn't have any children. There was no way he would be interested in her romantically. She just happened to be a customer on his route. That was all.

Coop was just one of those nice men who knew how to wield a monkey wrench, fix a flat tire, and untie any knot Chase had managed to tie. He also wasn't afraid of iguanas, mud, or heights. Cooper Armstrong was her boys' guardian angel, handyman, and UPS man all rolled into one stunningly gorgeous package. As far as she was concerned, Christmas had come early to Mistletoe Bay, and Coop was Santa.

What did it matter that when he had brushed away her tears with his finger earlier, her knees had gone weak and she had forgotten how to breathe? It was a normal reaction for a mother to have when her little boy was lost.

That and the fact that she had been so busy getting the boys their lunch, she had forgotten to eat hers.

It didn't matter if either of those reasons was true. That was what she was telling herself, and she was sticking to it.

"Dorothy, you're taking this harder than me." Jenni watched as Corey and Tucker played with the other kids. There were four other kids in their age group, and everyone seemed to be getting along just fine. "See, they're happy and having fun."

"I'm sure they will get along just fine." Cathy Bailey, who was in charge of the day care and preschool at the local Methodist church, handed Jenni some papers. "You can look these over when you get a chance."

Kiddie Kare came highly recommended, or her boys wouldn't have been there.

"Thanks." Jenni watched Dorothy with concern. It had taken her hours to convince Dorothy that her decision to send the boys had nothing to do with Corey getting lost. The boys needed more structure in their lives, and she was just too busy to do it. They also needed friends besides each other. Since they lived so far out of town, there was no other solution. The nearest neighbor under the age of twelve was half a mile away.

Her business was requiring more and more of her time. Since she needed the business to support herself and the boys, something had to be done. College would be starting soon enough, and it wasn't like she was spending every day with them. This way, they would have a set schedule, both in their lives and hers.

Hopefully, if she hired someone part time, she would be able to spend the evenings and most of the weekends with the boys. They could get back to being a normal family. Whatever "normal" was. In today's society, it was a little hard to tell.

Dorothy was the world's best grandmother, but she shouldn't have to spend her days, and some of her nights, running after the boys while Jenni worked. It would be too much to ask a younger woman, let alone a woman who would be turning fifty soon. Dorothy deserved to do whatever she wanted with her days—and her nights. Dorothy needed her life back.

More important was that Felicity needed her mother back. It didn't take a genius to figure out that Felicity was jealous of the boys. Jenni didn't want Dorothy to realize one day, when Felicity was away at college or out on her own, that she had missed these years with her only daughter.

The boys were her responsibility, not Dorothy's.

"I don't know, Jenni. They're so small." Dorothy watched her grandsons with concern. "You know Tucker; he tends to find trouble."

"Find trouble?" Now there was the understatement of the year. Tucker *was* trouble. "I'm sure Ms. Bailey can handle a five-year-old."

Tucker had turned five last week. In a way it had been a sad little birthday party, with only his brothers, the rest of his family, and Sam in attendance. It had been the turning point when she realized that Tucker and Corey needed some friends from the surrounding area and

town. Tucker was still sporting the black and blue eye
from where he'd run his new skateboard into the hallway closet door.

The solid wood door had won that battle.

It had been a real shame that the sink upstairs in the
bathroom hadn't won its battle. It had cost her over two
hundred dollars for a plumber to come out on a Sunday
and remove the stuck golf ball.

"We have the Higgins children here." Ms. Bailey
sounded like that explained everything. Cathy Bailey
was a very nice, motherly type in her fifties. Her husband owned the local ice cream parlor and she seemed
to know everyone in town.

"I'm sorry, who are the Higgins children?" Maybe
there was a celebrity living in town she didn't know
about. Higgins, wasn't he the man from *My Fair Lady*?

"Oh, I'm sorry, you're relatively new to the area.
Lonny and Leland Higgins are identical twins and lobster fishermen." Ms. Bailey nodded in the direction of
identical twin girls playing with Tucker. The girls
weren't dressed the same, and they even had different
haircuts, so it wasn't hard to tell them apart. "Those are
Leland's and Lisa's daughters, Lori and Lena."

"They're cute." In a tomboyish way. Both girls looked
like they could handle themselves in a preschool brawl
and would be trying out for the high school football
team in a couple years. Tucker would have his hands full
if he tried manipulating those two.

Ms. Bailey raised a brow but didn't comment.
"Lonny's son Liam is over there sitting in the 'time out'
corner, and his other son, Lawford, is over there smash-
ing Play-Doh into mush."

The Higgins kids all appeared to be self-confident and assured, and hearing all those names beginning with the letter *L* was giving her a headache. "Let me guess, Lonny's married to a Laura or a Linda?"

"No, Robin."

Jenni looked at Cathy Bailey to see if she was joking. She wasn't, but there was a gleam of laughter in her kind eyes. "That must have caused quite a commotion in the family bible."

"Lonny had been disowned by the family and written out of the will, until Robin produced the first male off-spring in thirty-eight years and named him Lawford after some great, great, something or another. All was forgiven, and even Lonny's grandmother Louise came around once little Liam was born."

"I wonder what would have happened if they'd produced girls?" She would bet the entire Higgins clan sat around the dinner table at night and did tongue twisters.

"To hear Lonny tell it, they would have kept having little Higginses until there was a boy." Cathy looked over to the corner where two-year-old Liam was still sitting quietly in the chair, but he was pulling off his clothes, one article at a time.

"I don't know, Jenni. Maybe we should take the boys home." Dorothy was biting her thumbnail, a sure sign she was upset or worried.

Jenni chuckled at Liam. Maybe Tucker wouldn't be the worst one in school after all. She watched as another teacher went over to Liam and calmly helped him get his clothes back on. "I think they have everything under control here." The kids seemed well supervised and enter-tained. At least there wasn't a blaring television acting as a babysitter. There was a small portable one toward the back of the room, but it wasn't turned on. Dorothy had gotten into the habit of having the television on day and night for the boys.

"That's Kate Audun taking care of Liam. She's well qualified to teach the afternoon preschool class and she works closely with the teachers at the local elementary school so the kids are prepared for kindergarten come next year." Cathy nodded in the direction of the very back of the expansive room. "That's our nursery back in that section. Barb Byler and Sally Newman usually handle the little ones. We also employ a couple of the local teenage girls after school and during the summer."

Jenni could see a couple of cribs set up. A very young woman was feeding a baby dressed in pink a bottle and rocking her. Another woman was feeding a little boy in a high chair. "They look like they have their hands full." She smiled at the memory of rocking her boys when they had been just tiny babies. Where did all the time go?

"We manage. Some days are easy, and some days . . ."

Jenni laughed. She knew what Cathy meant. Some days it just wasn't worth getting out of bed. "Okay, we'll get out of your hair now."

"You and Dorothy are always welcome here, any time of the day. Some of our mothers, like Doc Sydney, stop in all the time."

"Doc Sydney brings her baby here?" Now she was impressed. She'd liked Doc Sydney the few times she'd had the boys in to see her.

"That's Inga being fed her bottle." Cathy smiled. "The little boy in the process of spitting out his carrots is Doc

Sydney's nephew, Andrew Creighton. Andrew's mom, Gwen, owns and operates the Catch of the Day restaurant in town. Have you eaten there?"

"Not yet." The restaurant looked inviting, but it wasn't the kind of place she would take the boys. If their meal didn't come with a toy, the boys weren't interested.

"You must. It's simply wonderful. Try the stuffed flounder; it's out of this world."

"Really?" Dorothy looked intrigued. "That good?"

"That good." Cathy nodded toward Corey, who was running across the room, straight for them.

"Mom, Mom!"

"What is it, Corey?" She knelt down. "Try not to yell, okay?"

"Okay." Corey gave an exaggerated whisper. "I have a new friend. His name is Josh. We can stay, right?"

"Right." She brushed a lock of red hair off his forehead. Corey was looking more and more like his father every day. It was enough to break her heart all over again. "Grandmom and I will be back around five to pick up all three of you. Remember, Chase is coming here after school."

"I can show him around, right?"

"Right." She gave him a quick hug. "I'm sure he'll appreciate that. Why don't you give your grandmom a kiss goodbye and then go tell Tucker we're leaving."

Corey planted a loud kiss on Dorothy's cheek and then sprinted back across the room. He said something to Tucker, who proceeded to give her and his grandmother a quick wave and then went right back to discussing something with one of the Higgins twin girls.

"So much for him missing us." She had to chuckle. Tucker was being Tucker.

"Shouldn't we go over there and say goodbye?" Dorothy was still dragging her feet.

"No, we have plans."

"We do?" Dorothy looked confused. "What plans?"

She cupped Dorothy's arm and started to lead her from the church. "I made us an appointment."

"For what?" Dorothy kept trying to glance over her shoulder.

"At Estelle's Beauty Salon. You are getting your hair and nails done—my treat." She finally got Dorothy out of the day care center and into her car. "I'm getting my nails done and just a trim to get rid of some of these dead ends."

Dorothy perked right up. "We can do that?"

She had to laugh at the excitement in Dorothy's voice. It had been so long since they hadn't had to plan every minute of the day or shuffle the boys around that Dorothy had forgotten how to live. "Yes, we can do that, and a lot more. If you behave yourself, I think we can stop somewhere for lunch too. I'm tired of bologna or peanut butter and jelly sandwiches."

Jenni had two teenage girls coming after school today for an interview. The business was doing so well that she had to start thinking about hiring someone.

Dorothy tilted the rearview mirror her way as they drove down Main Street. "Do you think we'll have time for me to get it colored? I swear, I'm noticing more gray hair every day."

"Sure." It didn't take Dorothy long to forget the boys. Jenni pulled into a parking spot, directly in front of

Estelle's. "I heard this place is pretty good." Since moving to Mistletoe Bay, they had been hitting the hair salons at the mall in Bangor for quick trims while shopping. "One of the mothers in Chase's class recommended it to me during Back to School Night."

"It looks nice." Dorothy got out of the car and studied the front of the shop.

The white building with black trim looked to be over a hundred years old. The huge plateglass window had Estelle's name in flowing black and pink script. Pink curtains blocked people standing on the sidewalk from seeing in. She was glad they wouldn't be on display for the entire town to see as they got their eyebrows waxed or their hair highlighted. "Come on, slowpoke, it's time to be spoiled for an hour or so."

Dorothy hurried into the shop after Jenni and crashed into her back as she came to a screeching halt.

The pink was blinding. Who in the world would paint walls that color, let alone the chairs and countertops? Jenni felt like she was standing in a Pepto-Bismol bottle. Good Lord, how did anyone stand being in the place?

"Hi, you must be Jenni and Dot." A woman who could have played Mrs. Claus on a holiday float came to meet them. "I'm Estelle. Welcome."

Estelle was wearing pink spandex pants, white sneakers with pink polka dots, and a pink sweater with a white poodle, rhinestones, bows, and a bell on the front. To top off this striking outfit, she had a pink frilly gossamer apron that covered her from the bow on the poodle's head to midthigh. The woman actually tinkled when she walked. It was hard to tell, but Estelle's curly mop of white hair might have had a tint of pink to it. Then again, maybe it was the reflection of the shiny pink bow she had in it, or the walls might have been bleeding into everything around them.

"Thank you." Randy's mom had said that Estelle was a little unorthodox, but an excellent stylist who demanded nothing but perfection from her employees. There was unorthodox, and then there was preposterous. The jury was out on where Estelle fell. "I'm Jennifer Wright, and this is my mother-in-law, Dorothy." She emphasized Dorothy's name. No one called her Dot, at least no one who lived to tell about it.

"We were wondering when you two would be stopping in." Estelle's fingers played with the ends of Jenni's hair. "Please tell me you aren't cutting your hair. It's gorgeous. A little trim won't hurt, but don't take off any more than two or three inches. You have a face that can carry off the long, straight look."

"Um, thanks." Most beauty salons did whatever the customer asked, and it really didn't matter if you walked out of their door looking like Bozo on a bad hair day as long as you paid your bill.

"Lauren will do your trim and nails." Estelle nodded to a woman a couple years younger than Jenni who was finishing up with a customer. "And may I be so bold as to suggest, discreetly, of course, that you consider having Lauren give you a quick wax job." With a fingertip, Estelle traced her own brown brows. "They are a tad woolly."

"Woolly?" she gasped in horror. Her brows were woolly. She quickly walked over to the nearest mirror and looked. They weren't woolly, maybe a bit thick, but she didn't have a unibrow or anything.

"Jenni, dear," purred Estelle, who had joined her at the mirror, "they aren't that bad. Maybe we should just do a little plucking here and there."

"Estelle, you're scaring her." Lauren, the younger woman who was going to do the plucking or the waxing joined them. "Don't pay her no mind, Jenni." Lauren led her over to a chair in front of a large sink and draped a pink fabric cape around her neck. "Now, tell me what you want."

"Just a trim, a couple inches at the most." Jenni glanced at Dorothy standing in the middle of the shop looking unsure if she wanted to go or stay. "And maybe something done with my brows." Since Estelle mentioned them, there had to be something wrong with them besides a few stray hairs.

"Who's going to do my hair?" Dorothy asked Estelle nervously while glancing around at the other two hairdressers. One was giving an older woman a perm, and the other was doing the nails of a birdlike woman who couldn't have weighed more than a hundred pounds. The bright orange polish made her fingers look like claws.

"Well, I am, Dot." Estelle walked a circle around Dorothy while poking at her hair. "You have wonderfully thick hair, Dot. Why haven't you dyed it?"

Dorothy cringed. "I'm just starting to get a few grays now." Dorothy tried to smooth her hair back down. "I was thinking of maybe dying it today. You know, nothing drastic, just covering up some of the gray."

Jenni and Lauren both raised their brows at that.

Dorothy didn't have a few gray hairs, she had streaks. Jenni blessed Estelle's heart when she didn't contradict her. Her mother-in-law was in good hands.

"May I suggest going one shade lighter than your natural color, and letting me put a few strawberry blond highlights throughout?" Estelle said. "I swear it will make you look ten years younger." Estelle led Jenni's mother-in-law toward what had to be Estelle's station. The mirror was framed in a pink boa.

She couldn't hear Dorothy's reply, but she saw her smile and then frown as she looked in the mirror and traced one of her brows. It looked like Dorothy would be getting her woolly brows waxed too.

"Estelle, how come you never did anything to make me look ten years younger?" asked the woman getting a perm.

Jenni tried not to smile while Lauren rolled her eyes. The only thing that would make that woman look younger was maybe losing a hundred pounds.

With a perfectly straight face, Estelle replied, "Why, Priscilla Patterson, don't you know you can't improve on perfection?"

Jenni bit her lip and leaned back. Estelle either had the biggest heart in town, or she was on some heavy-duty medication. All she knew was she was glad it wouldn't be Estelle waxing her brows.

Twenty minutes, and three inches of hair on the floor, later, Jenni sat in front of the mirror as Lauren blow-dried her hair. She didn't have to tell anyone about herself or Dorothy; it seemed everyone in town knew everything already. It seemed they all even knew about

Corey getting lost. Norma, the woman getting her nails done, had a nephew on the football team.

Estelle and Priscilla were talking Dorothy's ears off on the other side of the room, while Jenni had the misfortune of sitting within speaking distance of Norma. Once the woman starting talking, there was no shutting her up. Not even the blow-dryer could drown out her voice.

"I heard Cooper Armstrong was the one to find him." Norma wiggled her fingers, trying to dry her nails faster under the light.

"That he did. Mr. Armstrong has performed quite a few rescues when it comes to my boys. I don't know what I would have done without him." She felt funny talking about Coop with a stranger. For some reason, it just seemed personal.

Norma gave a loud "Hhmmmpppph," then added, "He used to be such a nice boy. I'm glad he hasn't forgotten all the manners his parents and teachers taught him over the years."

"I'm sure he hasn't." What did Norma mean by "used to be"? As far as Jenni knew or had seen, Coop was still nice. She hated small-town gossip with all its hidden innuendos.

Lauren must have felt her stiffen beneath her pink fabric cape. "Hey, Norma, guess who I saw at the movies Saturday night in Franklin?"

"Who?" Norma perked up and even stopped wiggling her fingers as if the movement would affect her hearing.

"Gracie and Abraham." Lauren gave Jenni a wink. "They were in front of us when we were buying our tickets. They were holding hands and whispering like newlyweds. Of course, since they are newlyweds, I guess it's okay to act like that."

"They should act their age, that's what Gracie should be doing." Norma's thin nose actually got thinner. "Gracie is a whole year younger than I."

Lauren chuckled. "You big phony. I saw you crying into your hankie at their wedding, Norma. You don't fool me."

Norma sniffed. "I was crying over the fact that she had the audacity to wear white to her own wedding. It was scandalous."

Lauren laughed out loud. "You're just jealous because Gracie's getting some, and by the look on her face, I'd say old Abraham was doing a mighty fine job of it."

Chapter Eight

Dorothy glanced around her kitchen and wondered when she had lost control. It seemed everyone wanted to help get dinner ready—except for the men. They were all in the basement banging, muttering words she knew she was better off not hearing, and laughing. Although the heater wasn't sounding any worse, it sure wasn't sounding any better.

Coop had shown up for dinner three hours early, with his parents and two toolboxes in tow. Lucy, Coop's mother, was as nice as could be and had insisted on helping wherever she could. Dorothy had had her peel potatoes, a lot of potatoes. Now Lucy was out in the family room helping Jenni set the long makeshift table.

Who would have thought that her fine china set, with twelve settings, wouldn't have been enough? Tonight she was making a Thanksgiving feast for thirteen. One had to wonder if that was a bad omen. She hoped not.

Before Coop and his father, Fred, could get down to the basement, Sam and the rest of his family had shown up. Sam's sisters, Hope and Faith, were typical teenage girls. They had giggled a lot and were now upstairs in Felicity's room, doing makeup and such. She shuddered to think what they were going to look like when they came down. Her daughter had been known to go overboard with the glittery eye shadow on occasion. Eli Fischer didn't look like a guy who would appreciate having his very young and impressionable daughters made into streetwalkers.

It had been Sam's father who had thrown her off-kilter. Eli Fischer wasn't what, or who, she had been expecting. After talking to him on the phone the other day, she had been picturing a bigger, older Sam dressed in mechanic's bib overalls. What she got was a six-foot-two-inch, dark blond, gorgeously rough and fit male in a poorly ironed shirt. The woman in her wanted to rip that shirt off him.

To iron it, of course.

Dorothy picked up the empty platter she had set out for the turkey and fanned herself.

"Are you okay?" Lucy Armstrong asked as she came back into the kitchen. "You look flushed, Dorothy."

Nothing a little hormone replacement therapy won't cure. "I just had the oven open," she lied. She'd just committed two of the deadly sins, lust and lying. Was lying one of the seven sins? She couldn't remember. She was going to go to hell for sure. Eli Fischer was years younger than her and, by the glint of interest in his blue-gray eyes, had a lot more energy.

"Anything else I can help you with?" Lucy stood at the counter and waited for her next instruction.

"Thank you, but nothing needs to be done right now." She liked Lucy, who was in her early sixties and tended to fuss about her husband, Fred. So far Lucy had been in the basement twice on the pretense of delivering hot coffee and a few cookies. "Let's sit down and have a cup of tea."

Dorothy had put on the kettle while Jenni and Lucy had been setting the table in the back room. They wouldn't all fit in the dining room, so they had set up the table in the long family room that ran the length of the house. Felicity had been so excited to have Sam's family over, she had helped clean the room this morning. For once it looked neat and orderly.

It was a real shame it wouldn't stay that way with the boys. Her grandsons liked to spread out when they played, and currently Corey was into making tents with blankets and anything else he could find.

"It will be a mad dash the last fifteen minutes to get everything onto the table while it's hot. I could use some help then, if that's okay with you." She got out three mugs and set them on the counter. She had never cooked a Thanksgiving dinner for thirteen before. Even when her own parents and a couple of elderly aunts were still alive, they had never had more than eight at the table. Entertaining just wasn't what she had the time or opportunity to do very often.

"I'll be more than glad to help, Dorothy." Lucy glanced around the kitchen. "I must say, you have a wonderful kitchen. Who designed it?"

"I did. It's Jenni's house, but she allowed me to redo the kitchen the way I saw fit." Jenni had been so busy setting up her shop, she had been more than thankful to turn that job over to her mother-in-law. Dorothy removed the whistling kettle from the back burner. "Did Jenni say where she was going?"

Lucy sat down at the kitchen table. "She said something about the table looking bare and she went outside to see what she could find."

"She'll probably throw together some sort of center-piece." Dorothy wondered what they could use to brighten up the table. They had stopped using candles two years ago when Tucker had set his napkin on fire. "As you can tell, we don't get a chance to entertain much."

"I understand you just recently moved to this part of Maine."

"Six months ago." Dorothy cringed at the racket coming from the third floor of the house. By the sound of it, the boys had just given Sam's sisters a surprise visit from Chase's pet iguana. "As you can hear, we sometimes have our hands full."

Sam had parked his butt in front of their television and was watching the pregame show for the football game that was about to start. Bojangles was asleep next to his favorite visitor. Hearing all the football jargon on Thanksgiving Day reminded her of when George was still alive. George had loved watching football and rooting for his favorite teams.

Lucy chuckled. "I hear about the boys from Coop a lot. Did Tucker really glue the cat to the wall?"

Dorothy poured the hot water over the tea bags. "I would just like to say I was at the store when that one happened. For once it wasn't on my watch." Jenni had been home with the boys and the handyman.

"Coop misses them now that they started day care."

"Talks about them, does he?" Maybe it wasn't such a good idea inviting Coop and his parents to dinner.

Maybe the UPS man was going to read a lot more into the invitation than she had intended.

"Sometimes." Lucy chuckled. "I have to admit, meeting Tucker was kind of a letdown. I was expecting someone a little different." Lucy seemed disappointed. "He looks like Jenni and was polite as could be."

Dorothy rolled her eyes. "The day is still young. By about the time the pie is served, I'm sure his head will be rotating 360 degrees." She carried two of the mugs over to the table and sat. "As much as I love that boy, there are days . . ." She let the sentence trail off. Any mother worth her salt would know how to complete it.

Lucy laughed. "I vaguely remember days like that, and I only had the one child, Coop. He was an only child, but he filled our lives with nothing but love."

Either Lucy was making up stories, or the rumor Jenni had heard in Estelle's the other hadn't been true. By the love gleaming in Lucy's eyes, she would say the rumor mill had it wrong. It didn't appear that Coop had disappointed his parents after all. "What kind of boy was Coop? You seem to have raised a very fine young man who goes out of his way to help people."

"Thank you." Lucy sipped her tea. "He was a mama's boy until he was about eight. By the time he was in seventh or eighth grade the coaches started noticing him on the football field. From tenth grade on he was cocky and arrogant. The school let him get away with anything he wanted, because he was such a natural on the field. The town loved Coop. The girls loved Coop. Our phone used to ring all day and night with girls asking him out." Lucy shook her head.

"Call me old-fashioned, Dorothy, but I just don't agree with girls asking boys out."

"I know I never would have the nerve to ask a man out on a date." She winked at Lucy. "There are just too many ways for a girl to let a boy know she's interested."

"What ways are those?" Eli Fischer stood at the top of the basement stairs, staring right at her. "A man who's been out of practice for the past seven years might miss those signals."

Dorothy prayed for the floor to open up and to fall straight into the gaping jaws of the oil burner beneath her. Talk about embarrassing. The man must walk like a cat when he wanted to, because the basement steps groaned and moaned under the weight of Bojangles, let alone a full-grown man. She glanced at Lucy to see if there was going to be any help from that direction.

Lucy appeared fascinated as she glanced between Eli and Dorothy. "Why, Eli, have you really been on the market for the past seven years? It's truly amazing that no one has gotten her hooks into you yet."

"Lord, Lucy, you make him sound like a cod down at Cosmo's Seafood Shanty at the height of summer tourist season." She couldn't believe that Lucy had said that to Eli. The man didn't look like he needed any help in the dating department, and she was more than positive that he knew every signal in the book. Eli had probably taught his son, Sam, each and every one of them.

His son who was dating her daughter!

Maybe Eli wasn't a cod but a shark.

Eli threw back his head and laughed.

Dorothy melted at the husky sound of Eli's laugh. There was no other way to describe the warm, liquid feeling that had rushed to her stomach. Eli's laugh could put the heat into one of her hot flashes.

"What's so funny?" Jenni stood in the door of the family room and surveyed the room. She was holding a bunch of evergreens and berries. "What did I miss?"

"Nothing, Jenni," Lucy answered. "Your mother called Eli a cod."

"I certainly did not." She cringed when Eli started to laugh again.

"Hey, what's going on up here?" Coop asked. He stood behind Eli on the steps. "We send Eli up for more cookies, and you guys throw a party?"

"There's no party." Dorothy stood up and carried her cup over to the sink. She felt more in control standing in her kitchen behind the counter. "And there will be no more cookies. Dinner will be ready soon, and I don't want you men to ruin your appetite."

"Dorothy, there's a better chance of that old oil burner producing snowballs than us losing our appetite. We've been down in the basement for the past two and a half hours smelling nothing but oil and roasting turkey. We're ready to eat our boots." Coop walked into the kitchen and started to wash his hands at the sink. "Please tell us it's almost ready."

Coop was giving her that little-boy pleading look that Tucker had mastered by the age of two. She couldn't refuse Tucker any more than could she refuse three hungry men. But she could tease. "Is the monster fixed?"

Eli let out an exaggerated sigh. "The woman's heartless. Ulysses was sent out to do easier tasks."

"It's that bad?" questioned Jenni, clearly worried.

"No," Coop said.

"Yes," Eli said.

All three women looked at each other. "Which is it?" asked Lucy.

"Both," answered Fred, Coop's father, who had climbed the basement steps to join them. Fred was wiping his hands on a rag, but he smiled. "Jenni, the beast in the basement is about to give up the ghost, but I think we lovingly persuaded it to stick around, at least through this winter, possibly spring."

Eli started to wash his hands, now that Coop was done. "There's a couple parts that I would like to replace. I'll stop by next week, as soon as I can get them, and put them in. It might mean a couple more months, and better fuel efficiency this winter. But you really have to look into replacing it before next fall. Sorry, Jenni, but Maine is one place you don't want to be in January without a good heater."

"I'd really appreciate that, Mr. Fischer. Just let me know what I owe you." Jenni dumped the small pine clippings and berry branches onto the counter.

"A slice of that pumpkin pie sitting right there will do just fine." Eli glanced at the three pies sitting over by the refrigerator as if he hadn't seen a pie in years.

"After dinner you can have as many slices as you wish." Dorothy liked her guests coming to the table hungry. "What's your favorite pie, Mr. Fischer?"

"Pumpkin, and call me Eli." Eli gave her a smile that melted her knees as he dried his hands with a paper towel.

"Today it's pumpkin, but what will it be next week?" She had to give him points for being polite. Of course, with that killer smile, Eli Fischer was already off the charts in her book.

"Apple." Eli looked hesitant.

"Just let us know what day you're coming, and I'll have a freshly baked apple pie for you to take home." The poor man couldn't cook. It was the least she could do. Besides, if he thought her pumpkin pie looked and smelled good, wait until he got a gander at her home-made apple pie. In her younger days she had won quite a few ribbons with her pies, and she had only gotten better with practice.

Her grandsons gave her a lot of practice.

"You serious?" Eli looked like he wanted to get down on bended knee to thank her.

"Mr. Fischer, believe me, Dorothy is always serious when it comes to pie." Jenni chuckled as she got out a silver platter from the dining room's china cabinet and started to arrange the pine clippings and red berries.

"I can vouch for her cookies." Coop moved away from the sink area so his father would have room to wash up. "Dorothy has a habit of paying people in food—great food." Coop gave her a teasing wink. "Why do you think I'm always hanging around fixing stuff?"

"I didn't see you complaining." Dorothy checked the potatoes to see how they were doing. Another fifteen minutes and it would be feast time. "In fact, I distinctly remember you holding on to that box of chocolate chips for all you were worth."

She watched as Coop went to stand next to Jenni. "Hey, blame my dad for that one," Coop said.

"Me? What do I have to do with it?" Fred Armstrong dried his hands and tossed the paper towel in the trash.

"Mom stopped baking cookies because of the new

diet the doctors put you on." Coop's gaze was on Jenni as she left the kitchen.

Dorothy didn't like where that gaze had drifted. Jenni was her daughter, maybe not in blood, but in love. "Maybe your mother stopped baking cookies because you ate them all, Coop." The UPS man seemed to have a hollow leg where food was concerned.

"I tried a healthy oatmeal raisin recipe, and your father hated it." Lucy looked embarrassed.

"After dinner, Lucy, I have some recipes for you. They are for the healthiest cookies you can bake, but they still taste good." Dorothy winked at Fred. "But you have to promise to eat them in moderation. There is no such thing as a harmless cookie. They will clog your arteries just as fast as a greasy burger."

"Are they going to taste like hamster food or tree bark?" Fred kept looking at the pumpkin pies that Eli had been drooling over. "Am I going to be allowed a slice of pie tonight? I only ate two cookies in the basement."

Lucy looked like she wanted to say no, so Dorothy smiled at Fred. She didn't know the restrictions of his diet, but the man appeared in pretty healthy shape to her. "Yes, providing you fill your plate with lots of vegetables and no sweet potatoes. Stuffing yes, gravy no. My turkey will be moist enough that you won't need to dump gravy all over it." The man had to eat something, and it was Thanksgiving, after all.

Fred beamed and Lucy chuckled. "I think I've been outvoted," Lucy said. "No gravy or sweet potatoes, and you can have a slice of pie." Lucy got up, kissed her husband's cheek, and placed her cup into the sink. "You've been good since February, and you lost over thirty pounds."

"Thirty pounds." Dorothy nodded at Fred. "I'm impressed." Now that she was living with her grandsons, she tended to eat way too many sweets. Her caboose was now packing a few extra pounds she would love to drop off somewhere.

"Hey, Lucy lost twenty. She walks with me every day and has to eat what I eat." Fred wiggled his eyebrows at his wife. "Me getting sick was the best thing to happen to both of us."

"I don't know about that one," Lucy said.

"My parents are shrinking right before my eyes," Coop said as Jenni entered the kitchen carrying a few gourds and pinecones. "Can I ask what you're doing?"

"Sure, you can ask." Jenni turned her back and proceeded to add the finishing touches to the centerpiece.

Everyone in the room laughed but Coop.

Jenni couldn't believe how comfortable she felt with everyone crowded around the dinner table. She was used to noise, squabbles, and the occasional spilled milk. Tonight's dinner was indeed noisy. Everyone seemed to be talking, and there had to be at least five conversations going on at once. The football game had just started, and they had agreed to leave the television on in the other room so the men could listen in for the score. She just hadn't expected the TV to be blaring.

A moment of tension had occurred when Eli's daughters and Felicity had finally come downstairs to join them for dinner. Eli had taken one look at Faith, his thirteen-year-old daughter, and very politely, but firmly, told her to go wash her face. Hope, the fifteen-year-old, was allowed to keep on the lip gloss and mascara, but everything else had to go. The girls had gone and done his bidding, but Dorothy had taken Felicity aside and read her the riot act.

Felicity was still peeved at her mother, but she was behaving herself at the opposite end of the table with Sam's two sisters. Sam was entertaining Tucker, his sidekick, by trying to balance a spoon on the end of his nose. Neither Tucker nor Sam had mastered that feat.

The seating arrangements had been determined by the kids and the men, while the women rushed around in the kitchen and got everything on the table. Fred had done the honors, by carving the bird. It was the biggest turkey Jenni had ever seen, and if they were lucky there just might be enough meat left over for a sandwich or two.

Somehow, and she wasn't sure how, she ended up sitting next to Coop. Corey was on his other side, while Chase was on hers. She had tried to switch the boys, but Corey wouldn't hear it. He wanted to sit next to his rescuer. Coop had been left with the job of helping Corey fill his plate and cut his meat. Coop didn't seem to mind.

It felt strange not taking care of the boys. Chase, who was independent by nature, could manage his own plate, while Sam was helping Tucker whenever he needed it. All she had to do was enjoy the meal Dorothy had cooked. Of course, this morning she had done four loads of laundry, straightened up the basement, and scrubbed the powder room from top to bottom because one of the Higgins girls from day care had told Tucker if he shook a soda can real hard and then opened it, it would spray all over the place. Tucker had chosen the small powder room to see if it worked. It could have been worse. It could have been her bedroom or—Lord forbid—Dorothy's kitchen. At least the powder room walls were washable.

To top off that lovely relaxing morning, Bojangles had taken today, of all days, to think he was a retriever and had gone out duck hunting—or to be more accurate, seagull chasing. Not only had he gone into the frigid bay water, but he'd proceeded to dry himself off by rolling in the mud. For two cents she would have left the mutt tied to a tree outside, but her heart wouldn't let her. The whole upstairs bathroom now reeked of wet dog hair and strawberry shampoo, because she couldn't find the bottle of dog shampoo. She had just gotten out of the shower—for the second time today—when Coop and his family had shown up for dinner.

Sitting down for dinner was the most relaxing thing she had done all day. So why did she jump every time Coop's thigh accidently grazed hers? They were all crowded around the table bumping into each other. It wasn't as if he was trying to do it. So why was it bothering her so much?

The surprise of the evening was Sam's father, Eli. She hadn't really given it any thought but had assumed Eli would be a nice man, struggling to raise three teenagers on his own. She hadn't expected him to be good-looking, relatively sane, and completely smitten with Dorothy. The man hadn't stopped flirting with her mother-in-law since he'd arrived, and poor Dorothy didn't know how to handle it.

Jenni had never seen Dorothy so flustered.

"Can you pass the cranberries, Jenni?" Coop nodded toward the dish in front of Chase.

"Sure." She passed him the dish and tried not to notice how brown his eyes were. The man was too good-looking for his and her own good. Last night she had awoken from a dream all sweaty and aching. She would have liked to believe Dorothy's menopause was contagious, but she would only be fooling herself. Coop surely didn't have any romantic interest in her, and if he did, what in the world could become of it?

Absolutely nothing. She answered her own question.

"Mom, I have to go to the bathroom." Tucker got up and ran from the table after announcing to the world his intentions.

She didn't like the smile on his face, or the fact that instead of heading for the powder room, Tucker had headed upstairs. She could hear his feet pounding on the steps. "Tucker's up to something." She felt obliged to give some type of warning. There were innocent people at the table, and one had a heart condition.

Fred and Lucy seemed excited. "Really?" asked Lucy.

"By his devious smile, oh yeah." She continued to eat her dinner. She could go upstairs and see what Tucker was up to, but she didn't want to disappoint Coop's parents. They seemed to think there would be a show with their dinner. She just hoped that whatever Tucker was up to, it didn't cause any permanent damage.

A moment later Tucker's feet could be heard pounding back down the stairs, and within seconds he sprinted back into the room wearing that same guilty grin. "I'm back!"

"So I see," she said. "Did you wash your hands?"

"Yes." Tucker held up his dripping-wet hands for all to see.

"Dry them on your napkin, and finish your dinner."

She watched as Tucker quickly took his seat. He was wearing jeans, sneakers, and a sweatshirt with Spider-Man, his current hero, on the front. She hoped that whatever he had been up to didn't involve spiders. She hated spiders more than Felicity did. Sometimes she even had to get Dorothy to kill them for her. She hadn't noticed anything beneath his clothes.

No fire alarms were going off, and she couldn't hear the sound of clanging pipes in the walls, so that ruled out water. Fire and flood were off her list of possibilities. Since the table was still groaning under the weight of food, that left off famine. So what were the other plagues?

There weren't any locusts this time of year.

She continued to eat, but she was getting nervous. Tucker was into instant gratification. He wasn't one to prolong the mystery. She watched as everyone kept glancing around the room, waiting for that shoe to drop or the ceiling to cave in. The only sound she could hear was the television broadcasting the game. From where she was sitting, she had a glimpse of the kitchen. Tucker hadn't been in there. She had heard him go up and down the stairs.

What were the chances her son really did have to use the bathroom?

Fifteen-year-old Hope Fischer dropped her fork and let out a bloodcurdling scream.

Jenni's first concern was for Fred, Coop's father who was sitting right next to the girl. The man seemed to be taking in stride the fact that he probably had just had his eardrums shattered. Hope appeared frozen in her chair with her hand still halfway to her mouth.

Eli and Coop both jumped up out of their chairs,

while Sam lifted the tablecloth and looked under the table.

"Fred!" shouted Sam. "Stop that!"

Everyone at the table stared at Coop's father, who looked flabbergasted at being accused.

Lucy glared at her husband. "Fred, what did you do?" she demanded.

Fred held up his hands, "I'm not doing anything. I didn't touch her."

Bojangles, who had been asleep on the couch, came tearing into the room, barking his fool head off, and made a dash for under the table.

The tablecloth started to move.

Chase and Tucker both screamed "No!" at the same time and dived under the table. Corey laughed, shook his head, and dug into his mashed potatoes. Felicity, Hope, and Faith all put their feet up onto their chairs.

Fred and Lucy looked like they were still trying to figure it out. Jenni shrugged, said, "Iguana," and then grabbed on to the tablecloth. Felicity and Dorothy already knew the drill. Her niece instructed Sam's sister on how to hold on to the tablecloth so it wouldn't be pulled off the table, taking their dinner with it.

"Not my good china," moaned Dorothy, holding on to the table for dear life.

Lucy and Fred immediately grabbed on to their end of the table.

Coop was fast on his feet when Corey's chair was almost tipped over. Chase was yelling at the dog, Tucker was yelling at the iguana, and Bojangles was knocking into chairs and stepping on everyone's toes.

"Oh, this is ridiculous." Coop frowned at the table as

the wine in a couple glasses started to splash out. He went under the table.

Eli chuckled at the scene and winked at Dorothy. "Remember me fondly," he said before dropping to his knees and disappearing under the table.

In the distance she could hear a crowd roar.

"Who scored?" shouted Coop from somewhere under the table.

Sam got up and left the room. Lucy looked at Fred, who appeared to be contemplating joining the guys. "Don't you dare. There's enough under there."

Lucy looked at Jenni. "Does Fred bite?"

"Only when I'm hungry," growled Fred. "Who names an iguana Fred, anyway?"

"A six-year-old boy who thought he looked like a dinosaur, and named him after Fred Flintstone." Jenni felt someone grab her ankle. By the size of the hand, it wasn't one of the boys.

"Jenni, don't move that foot." Coop's hand tightened around her as he yelled beneath the table. "I want kids one day."

Lucy and Dorothy both raised their brows and stared at her. She felt a blush sweeping up her cheeks and couldn't prevent it. Her foot was seeing more action than she had in years. Life wasn't fair.

Felicity and Hope giggled. Faith looked confused, and Corey didn't seem to care one way or the other.

"Coop, you don't want to know the messy details of it all," called Sam as he entered the room and looked under the table.

Coop muttered something that caused both Chase and Tucker to giggle like girls.

"Mom, don't move!" shouted Coop.

Lucy's eyes got real big and she seemed to be holding her breath. "Fred's in my lap," whispered Lucy, hardly moving her lips.

"Smart boy," chuckled Fred.

"He has claws," Lucy said through clenched teeth as her eyes crossed.

"Eli, grab Fred," said Coop. "Chase and Tucker, keep that mutt still."

Bojangles now was doing his fun, happy bark—the one he did when he played with the boys. Something or someone knocked into Faith's chair, which caused the girl to scream. If Jenni could release the table and cloth without fear that it all would end up in her lap or on the floor, she would open the back door and the dog would come running. She couldn't chance it, but she had to give Faith credit. She had never heard anyone scream quite that high before.

"Oh my!" gasped Lucy.

"Got him!" shouted Eli. "Oowwwww! Here, take him, Chase." There was a moment or two of panic as the table once again started to shake, and then Eli and Coop came out from beneath the table. Eli had a grip on Bojangles's collar. Chase followed, holding the green, scaly Fred.

"Chase, go put him back in his cage." She frowned at the table but still didn't release it. Everyone was following her lead and kept their grip. "Tucker, please come out from under the table—now."

Tucker slowly backed out from under the table and stood. He was the picture of pure innocence.

Felicity, Hope, and Faith all glared at Tucker as they

slowly released the tablecloth and lowered their legs. Eli released the dog.

"Would you like to explain yourself, young man?" She could see Tucker's little mind trying to work up a plausible story.

"About?" Tucker was buying time. Chase was mumbling encouraging words to Fred and promising him a goodie as they left the room. Fred appeared unharmed— this time. One of these days, Bojangles was going to do more than bark at the reptile.

"Explain how Fred got under the table."

Tucker shrugged. "He must have followed me when I came down from the bathroom."

Fred and Eli chuckled.

"How did Fred get out of his cage, on the third floor? His locked cage, I might add." She watched as Tucker squirmed. Fred was out of his cage more than he was in it lately. Tucker needed a hobby.

"I don't know, Mom. Fred's pretty smart. I think he's unlocking the cage all by himself." Tucker looked pleased with himself. "Maybe we can get him on TV . . . you know, one of those amazing-animal shows."

Fred and Lucy both coughed into their napkins. Coop rolled his eyes while Eli nodded his head with approval to the small boy. Dorothy muttered something under her breath, while Sam looked like he was about to bust a seam laughing.

"Tucker James Wright, finish eating your dinner. We will be discussing Fred's latest escape and fibbing later tonight before you go to bed." She had no idea what to do with the boy. At least for now, dinner could resume at a normal pace and nothing had been broken. For Tucker, this had been one of his milder pranks.

Iguanas weren't a plague, but close.

"But Jenni, he let Fred loose in my room again today. He scared Faith and chewed on my blue eyeliner." Felicity obviously wanted to push the issue.

Sam shook his head at her, but she continued anyway. "Tucker ruins everything."

"Felicity, we can discuss this later." Dorothy looked embarrassed by her daughter.

"Can we please finish eating in peace?" Jenni now knew why they never entertained, even though the Armstrongs and the Fischers seemed to be enjoying themselves. She took another sip of her wine, something else she did very rarely—drink.

Fred and Lucy had contributed three bottles of wine to the meal, so the proper thing to do was to serve it. With Tucker at the table, they should have brought a case with a funnel.

Lucy patted her lips with her napkin. "I must say, that was exciting." Lucy smiled at Jenni.

She could see the laughter in Lucy's eyes and felt better. She just might not send Tucker off to military school after all. "Thank you."

Eli picked up his wineglass and held it out toward her mother-in-law. "Dorothy Wright?"

"Yes?" Dorothy looked like she wanted to crawl under the table.

"You're one lady who sure knows how to throw a party." Eli winked. "I like your style."

Chapter Nine

"You're going to have to forgive the mess," Jenni said as they walked the dirt path between the house and the barn.

Or what at one time had been a barn, thought Coop. Now it was Jenni's shop and he was curious to see it. "Most businesses are messy. I can't imagine making soap is a clean job." That seemed like an oxymoron to him—messy soap. "I can't even imagine how one begins to make soap."

"Sodium hydroxide, water, oils, fragrance, the usual." Jenni pointed to her left. "See, that's the dirt driveway that leads to the shop. I told you there was one."

Coop frowned at the overgrown, deeply rutted path. He would need a mountain bike to travel it, not a big brown box truck. He'd break an axle or get stuck in mud once it rained. "There's no way for me to take my deliveries back to the shop."

"I already told you that." Jenni shook her head and smiled. "You just chose not to believe me."

"It's not that I didn't believe you. I just wanted to see

for myself." He also wanted to get Jenni alone for a while, and it had seemed like the perfect excuse. His mother and Eli's daughters were doing the dishes, and Dorothy was handling the food. Everyone else had glued themselves to the television. He would rather spend time with Jenni than see the last quarter of the football game.

He wanted to talk to Jenni away from the boys, her eagle-eyed mother-in-law, and now his own parents. Jenni was living in a fishbowl and didn't even know it. She was also driving him quietly, but completely, out of his mind.

He had been dreaming of her for the past couple nights and needed to know if she tasted as sweet in person as she had in his dreams—hot, erotic dreams that had left him aching and in need of a cold shower or two. The showers hadn't been helping.

"So now you've seen my road." Jenni approached the side door to the barn. "I think I should warn you about the smell." Jenni's hand was on the doorknob, where she had just inserted a key. "It's a little overpowering at first."

"The smell? I thought you made soaps and body lotions. Doesn't it smell good?" His mother had told him that she had seen a couple of the higher-end stores up in Bangor carrying Mistletoe Bay Company products. Lucy had said she loved the Bayberry fragrance but couldn't see spending that kind of money when she could pick up hand lotion at the dollar store for a fraction of the cost. If someone looked in the dictionary under *thrifty*, his mother's picture would be there.

"The products smell wonderful. It's when you mix all those fragrances in one big building that it gets a little overwhelming." Jenni opened the door, reached in, and switched on the overhead lights. "Welcome to my laboratory."

He stepped in the barn and was truly impressed. He never would have known it was a barn from the inside. It had painted walls, wood floors, and an electric dumb-waiter that hauled stuff up and down from the top floor. It was pretty neat and organized for having boxes stacked everywhere. "You do all this yourself?"

Jenni had been right. The place was a little overpowering with all the different scents competing with each other for dominance.

"No, Felicity works for me every day after school and on weekends if we're busy. Lately we've been more busy than not. Even I underestimated the market for all-natural-ingredient products that not only smell good but work." Jenni closed the door behind them. "I interviewed two high school seniors the other day. Both of them seemed perfect, so I hired them both part time, at least through the holidays. They start Monday after school with Felicity."

He walked down an aisle and stopped at a table. Someone had been wrapping bars of soap and filling boxes. He picked up a bar and took a whiff. "Lavender."

"Not a hard one to guess." Jenni nodded at the soap he had just put back down on the table. "Especially since there's a pile of wrappers sitting right next to the tray telling anyone who could read what the fragrance is."

"Hey, I'm good. Admit it." He liked teasing her. He didn't think she got a lot of teasing around here. "I can name any soap you give me." It was a lie, and they both knew it. Any scent that was related to food, he'd probably guess; it was those darn flowers that confused him every time.

"If you can name three out of five, you're good." Jenni led the way. "I'll give you a tour of the place as we locate some unmarked soap." Jenni tossed her coat onto a stool. "This is where Felicity usually works. She wraps the soaps, labels the body creams, packs boxes, and most of the time gets the orders ready for you to pick up."

He dropped his black leather jacket on top of hers. It was a holiday and he was sick of looking at brown. Today he had worn black slacks and a green shirt. Not a thread of brown was anywhere near him.

He reached into a box and pulled out a jar. "Ocean Breeze?" He frowned at the label. "Why would anyone want to smell like salt air and dried-out seaweed?"

Jenni took the jar from his hand and opened it. "Close your eyes and smell."

He glanced at the light blue creamy mixture, then closed his eyes. Jenni must have moved the jar closer to his nose; he could smell the lotion now, and it didn't smell salty or rotting. It smelled of sea breezes and sun. "How did you do that?" All he could picture was Jenni smearing that lotion onto her legs and him going on a vacation.

Jenni grinned. "Talent," she said as she tightened the lid and replaced the jar in the box. "Come on, I'll show you where I work."

He followed her as she led the way to the back of the room, where there were huge pots, a monster of a mixer, and cases upon cases of big metal cans of oil—coconut oil, olive oil, and palm oil, to name a few. Cases of distilled water were piled high, along with more boxes of empty jars for the body cream. He picked up a empty bottle that had a pump on top from another case. "What goes in this?"

"Cranberry hand wash, the first product and best seller of the Mistletoe Bay Company. It's made with cranberry-seed oil and organic honey. It's a totally soap-free cleansing gel. A lot of people out there are extremely sensitive to soaps and chemicals."

"Sounds different." He'd never heard of anyone sensitive to soap—to chemicals, yes; soap, no. But it sounded reasonable. "So how do you come up with the scents?"

"That's the hard part. Putting different fragrances in the right combination and in the right amounts to give you the scent you're after. I developed most of my recipes when the boys were small, mostly for myself and as gifts for friends. I perfected the combinations and scents before I started the business."

Jenni glanced around the crowded room. "When the business becomes financially secure, I want to expand into the baby products end of the market. That's how the whole thing started. When Chase was born he had a reaction to just about anything I would use on him. I got tired of trying different products and watching my son go through rashes, breakouts, and pure misery."

"Why didn't you start with baby products first?" It seemed strange to him. Jenni's hazel eyes had actually lit up when she talked about starting the baby product line for the business.

"When you have a baby, you reach for a brand name you can trust. It's only after that doesn't work that you start reading labels and buying anything that is on the shelf. I need to build the name first. Besides, women buy lotions and soap on the packaging first, then the smell. Names don't really mean a thing until they discover how great it is, and then they start looking for that name brand again.

"Another reason is that all-natural products aren't cheap. In fact, they are downright expensive to make, so customers must be willing to pay a high-end price. When Chase was three months old, I would have been more than willing to pay any price for a product that worked."

"Instead you made one yourself and started a business."

"Not exactly. I'm going about it a little backward, but that's okay. My degree is in chemistry, so I'm putting it to good use."

"Chemistry? Lord, you're a geek." During his two years in college he had avoided the geek girls. Anyone who actually understood calculus and Einstein's theories scared the bejeepers out of him. Give him a hammer and a road map and he could conquer the world. Give him a computer and he would commit mayhem and bring civilization to an end.

Jenni smirked and shook her head.

He looked at Jenni, dressed in her gray slacks and shimmering gold blouse, and he had to wonder what he had been missing all these years. He might not have given the geek girls a second look twelve years ago, but he was looking now. And drooling.

"So how do you come up with a new fragrance?" he asked Jenni before he did something really stupid, like kiss that smirk off her tempting mouth.

"Mostly trial and error, and one heck of a lot of time." Jenni lifted the cover of what looked like a sheet on a tray that appeared to be about four inches deep. There were racks everywhere holding those trays. Some were covered; some weren't.

"What's that?" He walked over and took a peek. The tray was filled with a hard pink stuff. He leaned closer and sniffed. "Flowers."

"This one doesn't count because there are a few flower scents combined." Jenni covered it back up. "Tomorrow these get uncovered, and they sit until Saturday morning, when I cut them into bars." She nodded to a wicked-looking machine in the corner. "That slices a whole tray of soap in about three seconds."

"Nice." He now understood why the shop had been locked tighter than Fort Knox. Tucker and that slicer didn't belong on the same planet, let alone property. "So what's this soap called?" He nodded to the pink stuff.

"It's one of my seasonal specialties. That one is Naughty and Nice." Jenni wiggled her brows. "It's a big seller."

"I can imagine." He could imagine quite a lot with a name like that.

"Over here." Jenni went to a rack of trays with light blue soap. "Close your eyes and guess."

He closed his eyes and had to almost touch the soap with the tip of his nose. The other scents in the room were making it harder for him to get only that smell, but once he did, he knew immediately what it was. "Suicide Hill." He hadn't been there in fourteen years, but he would know that scent anywhere.

"What's Suicide Hill?" Jenni looked confused.

"A toboggan run on the outskirts of town by Sunset Cove. Haven't you been there?" He straightened back up. "I'm sorry—you and the boys haven't been in town long enough to go sledding, have you?"

"No, but I've sledded before and have even been on a toboggan a couple times in my life. But I've never been down, nor am I planning on going down, a run called Suicide Hill. I'm not that crazy."

"Now that's a challenge if I ever heard one."

"Challenge? What challenge?"

"To get you to go down it. I'm betting that before the new year I can get you to go down it, if there's enough snow by then. Some years we had to wait till January for the snow to pack down nice and deep. There's no fancy snow-making equipment out at Sunset Cove, just Mother Nature at her finest."

"I did not challenge you, Coop, and you're crazy. I won't go down it—period."

"If you say so." He grinned. "So if that's not Suicide Hill, what is it?" He pointed to the light blue soap.

"Coop, do you honestly think customers would buy a soap called Suicide Hill?" Jenni laughed and shook her head. "It's called Snowflakes."

"I like." Okay, Jenni could bathe with that soap, and he could pretend she was Suicide Hill. He'd die a very happy man.

"There's one more seasonal fragrance, but I don't have any of it in here. It's all upstairs curing."

"Curing? Soap cures?"

"Indeed it does, four to six weeks. These batches are the last of the Christmas-season specials. The body creams don't need to cure, so I can make them for a couple more weeks yet." Jenni led the way back out of her work area and toward a set of steps. The electric dumbwaiter was only big enough to carry one of those metal rolling racks holding all the trays. The racks were about five feet high.

He had to wonder how Jenni managed to get the filled trays up or down from that height.

Jenni climbed the wooden steps. He climbed behind her, enjoying the view. "Did you do all this work to the barn?" Maybe she had better experiences with a handyman out here in the shop, where the boys weren't allowed.

"I gave the walls a fresh coat of paint, that's all." Jenni stepped onto the wide-open second floor. Row after row of metal racks of curing soap and boxes filled the space. "Whoever owned it before me did all the work to the barn. They put in a bathroom, running water, a couple of windows, all the walls, and heat and central air. It's the reason I spent a lot more than I wanted to on this piece of property. The shop and of course the bay were the main selling features. The house, as you've seen, needs work. Lots of work. But it's the perfect place to raise the boys and run my business."

"Speaking of work, did you ever call either of those names I gave you the day the washer hose broke?" He hadn't noticed any improvements around the place or pickup trucks parked out front. It was Thanksgiving, and the Halloween decorations were still up out front, along with the rotting pumpkins and the electrical cords strung everywhere. Jenni should be thankful today that the house hadn't burnt down so far.

"Daniel Creighton called me back. He's got a lot of jobs lined up for his slow period, but he said he might be able to get around to doing one or two jobs early spring. He penciled me in for the last two weeks of March." Jenni started walking down the aisles of racks, inspecting the soap. "The other guy, Pete Van something or another, hasn't returned either of my two phone calls yet. I've got a feeling Bob Sanders has been down at the handyman union center spreading the word about Tucker, the glue gun, and the cat."

"There is no such thing as a handyman union center, and if there were, Pete Van de Camp wouldn't care. If he knew about Tucker he'd probably take a job just to see the boy in action." Of course Van de Camp would have to be sober enough to be out in public to hear the story. Pete wasn't known to be sober very often.

"Then there's another reason he isn't returning my calls." Jenni frowned and picked up a bar of pale bluish-green soap. "Remember, three out of five, and the first one is the easiest."

He held the soap to his nose. "Ocean Breeze. I smelled the lotion downstairs." Like he would forget that scent, or what he had been fantasizing about.

"As I said, the easiest." Jenni moved down another aisle.

He slowly followed, wondering how much he should tell Jenni about Van de Camp. "Pete has a drinking problem. A very serious drinking problem." With all the different scents in the building it was hard to think clearly. He might as well come clean with Jenni. It wasn't as if she wouldn't be hearing it around town.

Jenni glanced over her shoulder as she reached for another bar of soap. "And you felt he should be working at my house?"

"If he's working, he's not drinking. Van de Camp is a jack-of-all-trades. The man can fix, build, or repair anything. The problem is he goes off on binges for days, sometimes weeks on end. Whatever he had started will sit there until he sobers up again. Not too many people will put up with that." Van de Camp was a shadow of the man he used to be, and Coop honestly felt sorry for the guy. Van de Camp drank to forget.

"Then give me one good reason why I would want him working on my house, let alone around my children?" Jenni held the soap in her hand but didn't hand it to him.

"I was around thirteen when it happened, so that's—what—nineteen years ago? It made the news for months and affected us all." Coop remembered the extra-tight hugs from his parents and the safety drills. Lord, how he had hated all those stupid safety drills.

"Pete got up early one morning, kissed his sleeping wife and three kids, and went to work up in Bangor. He wanted his wife to be able to stay home with the kids, so he worked constantly, doing any job that came his way. He had just pulled into the job site when the state troopers arrived. The gas stove in his kitchen back home had exploded, trapping his wife and all the kids in the house. There were no survivors. Pete has been blaming himself ever since."

"Why, was it his fault?" There was horror and sorrow on Jenni's expressive face. It was enough to break his heart.

"No, it was a brand-new stove—his wife's birthday present from the week before. Turns out the stove was faulty. Lawyers won Pete a huge settlement, which to this day I don't think he has touched. He makes enough money to support his next drinking binge; that's it."

"That's horrible. Why is he blaming himself? As you said, it wasn't his fault."

"Pete felt that if he would have been home, he could have saved them, or instead of having the store, where he had purchased the stove, hook it up, he should have done it himself. He swears he would have been able to pick up on the defect if he had." Coop took the soap from Jenni's trembling fingers. "Pete's good, Jenni, but no one believes he would have found the kink in the piping that caused the explosion. It was deep inside the stove."

"The poor man." Jenni's eyes were filled with tears.

"That's what everyone said those first ten years. Now people have gotten over it, and the sympathy has worn thin around the edges. Life moves on."

"Not his." Jenni rapidly blinked away the tears. "He lost everything that day. I couldn't imagine."

"Can't you?" He watched her expression fall. "I heard that you lost your husband in a fire. I would think you would have a great understanding about Pete, and what he has gone through." He didn't want to hurt Jenni.

"I did lose my husband, but not my whole family. I still have the boys, Dorothy, and Felicity. I get out of bed every morning because they need me as much as I need them. There's a world of difference between Van de Camp and me." Jenni wiped a tear that was slowly rolling down her cheek. "As I said, I couldn't imagine what he has been going through."

"I didn't mean to make you cry." He reached out and wiped away another tear. "You have no idea what your tears do to me."

"Probably make you want to run in the opposite direction." Jenni gave him a watery smile. "You didn't make me cry, Van de Camp's story did."

"Because it's too close to home?"

"A little, but I can't imagine the pain of losing one

child, let alone three at one time"—Jenni shuddered—
"along with his wife."

"I remember the funerals, but not what his wife
looked like. I don't think I ever met his kids, but the
memory of that funeral has stuck with me for the past
nineteen years."

He could still remember the tears every man and
woman in Misty Harbor had been shedding at the time.
He could still remember the expression of shock and
grief that had been on Pete Van de Camp's face that day
in church and the remarkable fact that the man did not
shed one tear. Most of all Coop remembered his mother
holding him tight in the pew. He had been embarrassed,
until he realized there hadn't been a mother not holding
her children, no matter how old they were.

He didn't want to dwell on those memories, nor did
he want Jenni to relive hers. The past was in the past,
and he was more interested in the present. Besides, he
got his answer; Jenni didn't seem to be hanging on to
the ghost of her husband.

Coop held up the greenish soap that had little pieces
of something mixed in. "Is this number two?"

"Yep." Jenni used the sleeve of her blouse to dry her
cheeks. "My money's on you not guessing this one."

He raised a brow at the challenge and took a big sniff.
It was a wonderful fragrance, but he couldn't place it. He
closed his eyes and took a bigger whiff. It wasn't really
floral, and it didn't smell like anything he would eat. "You
didn't give it some name like 'Cloud Fluff' or anything,
did you?"

"You think it smells like a cloud? What in the world
would a cloud smell like?"

"I would think a cloud would smell like rain, and no, this doesn't smell like rain." He took another sniff. "I just don't think you should count funny names for the scent."

"That particular bar of soap is named after what's in it, and the fragrance. No funny names." Jenni grinned. "Give up?"

He held the bar out so it was in the light, and not the shadow of his body. There were green and brown flecks of something in the soap. The more he thought about it, the more he realized about 80 percent of everything out there in nature was green. It could be anything. "I give up."

"Bayberry." Jenni held up a finger on each hand. "One to one."

He took another sniff. "This is the stuff my mother likes. She saw it in Claire's Boutique in town the other day and said it smelled heavenly."

"Lucy likes Bayberry?" Jenni grinned. "Remind me to get her some free samples before we leave. I guess I should give Hope and Faith some too. After all, they did have to put up with Tucker and his tricks today."

"That would be very nice of you. My mother would love it." His mother had been driving him nuts with all her questions since he'd told her that they were all invited to the Wrights' for Thanksgiving dinner. While his father had been rubbing his hands together in glee, anticipating real fat-laden food, his mother had been putting one and one together and coming up with the prospect of having three grandsons in one fell swoop. He had burst his mother's bubble when he said Dorothy Wright had invited them all, not Jenni.

"Your parents are nice, Coop." Jenni headed farther down the aisle.

"Thank you. How many years has it been since your parents have been gone?" He realized he didn't know a whole bunch about Jenni, but he was learning.

"They passed away while I was in college."

"God, Jenni, I'm so sorry." How much pain could one person go through and still smile like Jenni smiled?

"It's okay, Coop. Life goes on." Jenni reached for another bar of soap. "I was with Ken then. Dorothy kind of adopted me, and I gained a sister in Felicity."

He now was beginning to understand the dynamics of the Wright family. He took a sniff of the soap. This one he knew. In fact he'd just had some with dinner. Anyone from New England knew that scent. "Cranberries."

"Very good, but don't get cocky." Jenni went to the next row and immediately reached for another bar. "This one you'll never guess."

He frowned at the dark, greenish soap. It didn't look very feminine or pretty. "You sell a lot of this?" He hesitantly smelled.

"A fair amount. It's mainly for rejuvenation and cleansing." Jenni leaned against a rack and grinned. "I actually have a standing order for this particular soap and body cream at two spas. One's in Bar Harbor, the other in Bangor. Both spas use it and sell it in their little boutiques."

"Spas, huh?" He took another try.

Jenni felt the chill of the metal rack against her back through her silk blouse. She didn't mind. She needed to be cooled down a couple of degrees. Cooper Armstrong had a bad habit of raising her body temperature. "Give up?" She had purposely picked a hard one for him this time, but she had given him a clue about the spas.

"You got me on this one." Coop handed her back the soap.

"Sea Kelp." It was one of Mistletoe Bay's specialty items. It wasn't pretty or floral, but it rejuvenated the skin.

"Seaweed?" Coop made a face. "Women want to bathe in seaweed?"

"Put it that way, and the answer is yes." She grinned. Coop looked so handsome today in his green shirt and black trousers. The sleeves were rolled up his forearms, exposing an intriguing amount of dark, fine hair, and there was now a black grease spot on Coop's side, by his waist. Fixing the beast in the basement wasn't the cleanest job and she was deeply grateful to him, his father, and Eli. The men deserved more than dinner and pie.

"So we're now tied."

"I'll let you pick the next bar of soap. I don't want you thinking I rigged the contest. Especially when I win." She liked Coop, and if she wasn't mistaken, he liked her back. Why else would he have used such a lame excuse as checking out her rut-filled dirt path to get her alone and out of the house?

She waved her hand down the aisle. "You pick, and I'll even be gracious enough to tell you when it has a 'cute name' or in a combination where you won't be able to tell the main scent."

"What do I get if I guess right?" Coop looked confident of his abilities.

"What do you want?" She knew she was playing a

dangerous game, but that was what made it so exciting. She tried to keep the thrill of the game from her face.

Coop studied her expression for a long moment. "I guess right, you and the boys have to go with me up to Suicide Hill the first decent snow we get."

"You expect me to allow my boys to get on a toboggan and go down a run called Suicide Hill?" If he did, Coop wasn't the man she was beginning to think he was.

"No." Coop shook his head and grinned down at her. "There are other runs there for little kids, Jenni. But I do expect you to go down Suicide Hill at least once with me."

She hadn't been sledding since before Chase was born. The last thing she wanted to do was break an arm or make a complete fool out of herself. What were the chances of Coop guessing right? There was only one soap that he had a good chance of guessing, and that was Blueberry. "Deal, but what do I get if you guess wrong?"

"Name it." Coop threw the ball back into her court.

The things that whipped through her mind could have gotten her arrested. Although her neck wasn't getting a kink in it from looking up at him, she did have to raise her chin to look him in the eyes—deep, dark brown eyes that seemed to promise her every one of those delicious thoughts.

She swallowed the lump in her throat and moistened her lips. There was no way she could voice those desires, so she asked for the first thing she could think of; a job she faced every day, and one she couldn't tackle on her own. "Your help removing the wallpaper and painting the stairway wall going up to the second floor."

Coop threw back his head and laughed. "I stepped into that one, didn't I?" Coop's eyes sparkled with laughter as he finally got himself under control and looked down at her. "Deal."

She grinned. "Go choose, but you have to do it from the center of the aisle, no getting too close." The Blueberry soap was two aisles over.

Coop slowly walked down the aisle. He stopped in front of a yellowish soap and looked back at her.

Jenni shook her head. "That's the third seasonal soap I'm doing. Go ahead and smell it. I call it Goodness' Sake."

Coop smelled the soap and grinned. "Cookies; it smells exactly like Dorothy's sugar cookies."

"It will drive men wild." She wasn't stupid. Flowers didn't turn men on, food did. If she could develop a scent that smelled like hamburgers and tasted like beer she would be able to retire filthy rich by the age of forty.

"I think I like this one the best." Coop took another whiff before replacing the soap on its tray. He continued down the row of racks, studying each one intently before selecting a white bar. "This one okay?"

"It's named after its fragrance." Lily of the Valley wasn't a well-known flowery scent, so, feeling safe, she added, "It's from my spring-summer collection." Orders were already coming in for some of her spring fragrances.

Coop closed his eyes and brought the soap up to his nose. "It's a flower." Coop sounded disappointed. "I was hoping for food."

"Men usually are." She shook her head. "But it's the woman who has to bathe with it, Coop, not a man."

"True." He sniffed again. And again. And again.

She knew he wouldn't get it. If it wasn't a rose, most men wouldn't be able to name the flower. "Give up yet? I want the wall painted a nice sage green. Something that will hide the boys handprints."

Coop frowned at her, then closed his eyes and took a big whiff.

She understood the closing of the eyes when smelling. She did it all the time. It allowed her to concentrate on the smell, and not what she was actually seeing.

Coop replaced the bar of soap and walked back to her. She couldn't tell from his face if he actually knew the scent or was willing to admit defeat. Money would be on him at least trying a guess. What did he have to lose, besides scraping forty-year-old wallpaper off a wall?

"So?" She wasn't known for her patience, unless it came to the boys. With children she'd learned that patience was more than an option, it was required.

"That anxious to go tobogganing?" He stopped directly in front of her.

"No, just wondering if I should go out and pick up the paint this weekend. Heard Sullivan's hardware store is having a great sale."

Coop moved closer. "That confident, are you?"

Her back was against the rack and he was nearly touching her. It was an interesting turn of events, one she had been hoping for since leaving the house. "Do you want to do the trim work, or use the roller?"

"Roller." Coop lowered his head and kissed her.

Chapter Ten

Jenni slowly leaned in to the kiss, but there wasn't anything hesitant about the way she melted. Coop kissed like he meant it.

Desire slammed into her stomach as her arms encircled Coop's neck. She could feel the heat of his mouth and the taste of his need. It matched her own. It had been so long since she had been held and desired as a woman. She just wanted to sink into Coop and never resurface. She stretched up on her toes, bringing herself closer to his pounding heart. To his heat.

Coop's fingers trembled as they cupped her bottom and brought her closer to his growing arousal. Her breath caught in her throat as the full extent of his desire became quite evident against the apex of her thighs.

Coop groaned as his tongue swept into her mouth and seductively teased hers into submission. Her fingers sank into his thick, soft hair and pulled him closer. She wanted Cooper Armstrong, and she wanted him now. The emptiness that had been residing inside her for so long screamed to be filled.

The slamming of the door downstairs jolted them out of their haze. They jumped apart like two young lovers whose parents had gotten home early.

"Mom!" shouted Chase.

"Mr. Brown!" shouted Corey.

"Hey, where are you?" Tucker shouted loud enough to shatter an eardrum or two.

Coop slowly lowered his empty arms and stared at her. His breathing was harsh and rapid, and his brown eyes were nearly black with desire.

She was torn between crying or giggling. She was too old to be caught in a compromising position by her sons. It was a good thing they had intruded when they did, because the way that kiss had been going, there was no telling where it would have ended.

She knew exactly where that kiss had been leading, but there was no way she was going to admit it. She knew how to say no, but with Coop she didn't want to. That admission scared her more than anything he could have done.

"We're up here, boys," she called since Coop appeared as tongue-tied as she felt. "Stay where you are . . . don't move." The boys knew they weren't allowed in the shop. There was just too much to break, ruin, or get hurt by.

"Can I shut the door?" Chase asked.

"Please do I can't afford to heat Maine." She rolled her eyes and smiled at Coop. "We'll be right down."

"What'ya doing?" called Tucker.

Coop grinned. "Your mother was giving me a tour of the place and we were playing a game."

She raised a brow.

"What kind of game?" called Tucker.

She could tell by her son's voice that he had moved a couple more feet into the shop, and that worried her, but not as much as Coop's answer. He wouldn't dare.

Coop's smile grew. "I had to guess what scent the soaps are, just by smelling."

"Yuck." Corey sounded like he was holding his nose shut. "They all smell yucky."

"Don't worry, Corey, he lost the game." She headed for the stairs. "Coop now has to help me remove that wallpaper in the stairwell and paint the walls." She grinned over her shoulder before hurrying down the wooden stairs. "What brings you boys out here?"

"Mr. Brown's dad sent us," Corey said. Her youngest son was peering into a case of hand wash. Corey didn't look impressed.

"He said to tell Coop that his team lost and that you owe him ten bucks." Chase was over by the work table with both hands behind his back, examining the area.

Tucker ran halfway up the stairs to meet Coop, who was coming down. "I'm supposed to tell you that everyone is waiting on you and my mom." Tucker looked like he wanted to get into something. Anything.

"I guess we have to be going, Jenni." Coop walked over to his coat and put it on. "You have a very nice shop." Coop's eyes were dancing with secrets.

"Mr. Brown?"

"Yes, Corey?"

"I'm supposed to tell you that your dad wants pie. Pumpkin pie."

Coop laughed with her son. "Did he now." Coop ruffled Corey's red hair. "Then I guess we'd better get moving. He can get cranky if not fed."

"You guys go ahead. I have to get some samples." She found an unsealed box of Bayberry soap and picked up a couple bars. She started looking for the body cream to go along with it for Lucy. "Tell your grandmother to start serving her pie. I'll be right there." Somewhere in the mountain of boxes were opened cases of Snowflake for Faith and Naughty and Nice for Hope. The girls deserved a little something for having ten years scared off their lives by Fred the iguana licking their legs.

"We'll wait, won't we guys?" Coop looked at her sons. "A gentleman always waits for a lady."

Tucker looked ready to argue.

"Of course, if you want to, you can head back to the house without us." Coop stared at Tucker.

"Naw, I'll wait." Tucker stepped farther into the shop. "Can I go see the back room?"

"No, you know that room is strictly off-limits, especially after the last time you visited." She glared at her son. "Right?"

Tucker scuffed the toe of his untied boot against the wooden floor. "Right." He sighed.

"Do I want to know what happened last time?" Coop looked intrigued.

"No, Doc Sydney says thinking about it just causes undue stress." She found the Bayberry body cream and added two jars to her growing pile.

Tucker plopped his butt onto the last step. "I said I was sorry."

"Mom, can I go back? Sam's waiting for me." Chase had his hand on the doorknob and was ready to bolt.

"Sure, just be careful not to trip in the dark." There was a low-wattage light outside the shop door, and one could see the lights from the back family room, but the path through the overgrown brush wasn't lit. "Take Corey with you."

"I want to wait for Mr. Brown." Corey was glued to Coop's side.

"Okay, Chase you can go, but be careful."

Chase shot through the door like an arrow. She gathered up a couple of the cranberry hand wash and three jars of the brown sugar body polish before finding the Snowflake case of soap. She added it all to the pile.

"Can I help you with something?" Coop was eyeing the growing mountain of jars and soap.

"Grab me three of those smaller boxes over there." She pointed to the right. "Thanks."

She finished grabbing what she needed and carried it all over to the table. "This should do them nicely." She started to divide up the goodies. "Tucker, why don't you carry this box back and give it to Faith with an apology for scaring her like that." She handed her son a box.

Tucker took the box. "It wasn't my fault she didn't like Fred."

"I told you that Fred is one of those pets that are an acquired taste. He's like brussels sprouts; not everyone is going to like him." She pulled on her jacket but didn't bother to zip it. The last thing she needed was her winter coat. Coop had started her furnace just fine. She went to pick up the other two boxes, but Coop beat her to it.

Tucker dashed out the door with Corey right on his heels. "Slow down, Tucker. That box has glass jars in it." She could hear them banging against each other as her son ran. If he made it to the house with one thing in that box intact, it would be a miracle. She had only herself to blame if she had to make another trip out to the shop tonight. She knew better than to give Tucker glass.

"Did you just compare Fred to a vegetable?"

"I had to think of something Tucker could relate to, and he relates to brussels sprouts. The boy hates them." She glanced around the shop one last time before turning off the lights and locking the door behind them.

They were halfway down the path when she heard the sliding door to the family room slam shut behind the boys. "One of these days they are going to pull that door right off its tracks." She said the first thing to pop into her mind to cover up the awkwardness she was feeling at being alone with Coop. What was she supposed to say to a man who had just kissed her senseless?

"You won't get an argument out of me on that one." Coop was quiet for a moment before asking, "What are you doing Saturday night?"

Her feet halted on the dirt path. "Saturday night?" Her mind drew a blank. Saturday night was just like any other night, except the boys got to stay up half an hour longer because it wasn't a school night. After the boys were tucked into their beds she usually went into the office and did paperwork. "Why?" Why would Coop care if she was printing out shipping labels or ordering in more supplies?

If she wasn't mistaken, Coop rolled his eyes. In the shadowy darkness it was hard to tell. "I thought if you weren't busy we could go out to dinner or something. Maybe see a movie in Franklin."

"As in a date?" She couldn't believe it—Coop was asking her out. She hadn't been asked out on a date since college, and her last date had been with Ken.

That invitation from the comb-overed character named Wendell, or something like that, the first week she moved to town didn't count. The man was a complete idiot. Five minutes after she had turned him down, he had been hitting on Dorothy. Whatever Dorothy had said to him had made him go pale, and neither one of them had been bugged by the president of the chamber of commerce since.

Would she even remember what to do on a date?

"Yes, Jenni, as in a date." Coop sounded unsure of himself. "I never asked a woman out that has kids. Do you need more time to find a babysitter or something?"

"Coop, that's not what threw me. I can find a babysitter." She had no idea what Dorothy would say to her dating again. It had been two years since Ken had passed away; surely Dorothy knew that one day she would start dating again. "It's just that I haven't been on a date since college."

"You haven't dated since you lost your husband?" Coop sounded amazed, if not in downright shock. "It's been—what—two years?"

"Over two, but yes." What did it really matter how long it had been? The question was, how was she going to tell the boys she was going out without them?

"Yes, what? Yes, you'll go to dinner with me, or yes, you haven't dated in over two years."

"Yes to both."

Coop smiled. "Really?"

"Really." Her smile matched his. She wasn't naive enough to think anything would come of a simple dinner date and heated kisses. She wasn't looking for a future with Coop, or any other man. She had three boys to raise and a business that was just starting to take off. But she was human, and, as Coop's nuclear kisses had just demonstrated, a woman. She wanted as many of those kisses he was willing to share before he came to his senses.

Dorothy knew Cooper Armstrong would be trouble from the first day he and Jenni had met. The man couldn't keep his eyes off her daughter-in-law and he always was around when the boys were causing trouble. Boys would be boys, and men would be men.

Jenni was going out with Coop tonight on a date. A real date, and she had only herself to blame for this turn of events. After all, she had been the one to invite Coop and his parents for Thanksgiving dinner. She had been so thankful when Coop had found Corey safe and sound that she would have knitted him a stocking and invited him to spend Christmas with them—if she knew how to knit.

Now Coop had taken the holiday meal as an open invitation to date Jenni. She didn't know what exactly had happened out in the shop the other night, but she could guess. She wasn't born yesterday.

She could hear Jenni arguing with the boys in her bedroom while she got ready. The boys didn't understand why they couldn't go along for dinner. Tucker had even promised to behave himself. Dorothy had heard the uncertainty in Jenni's voice, but her daughter-in-law had held firm. That alone told her how much Jenni wanted to go on this date. Jenni wasn't known to be a tower of strength when the boys ganged up on her like that. They usually got what they wanted.

To top that one off, Jenni hadn't even bothered to ask her to babysit. Jenni was not only going to pay Felicity and Sam to watch the boys, but she also was giving Sam money to run into Sullivan to pick up pizza for everyone. In other words, Jenni didn't need her.

"Mom?" Felicity walked into her bedroom unannounced.

"Yes?" She continued to put away the laundry in her dresser. She had spent the morning in town food shopping, and the afternoon in the basement catching up on her and Felicity's laundry.

"Have you seen my new jeans?" Felicity pulled open the closet door and started to search through the slacks hanging there.

"In the last four months I've bought you at least five new pairs of jeans. Which pair?" Like she would be able to tell the difference. Denim was denim and her daughter probably had over a dozen pairs of jeans thrown around her room upstairs in the attic. "They aren't in there. That much I do know."

"How do you know?" Felicity pushed aside a bunch of blouses and continued to search.

"Because I only own three pairs of jeans, unlike some people in this room. I'm wearing one pair, and the other two pairs are hanging right there in front of your nose." She cringed as her daughter shoved aside three silk blouses she had picked up from the cleaners just yesterday. "Be careful, Felicity. I prefer my blouses without wrinkles." Her daughter was constantly losing and misplacing things.

"Are you sure you did all the laundry today?" Felicity closed the closet door and frowned at the neatly folded basket of towels.

"Would you care to rephrase that question?" She closed the last drawer with a little bit more force than necessary. "You're seventeen, Felicity. You're old enough to start doing your own laundry if you don't like the way I do it."

Maybe she had been babying her daughter a little too much. Here she had thought she was helping Felicity out with her laundry. Between school and working part time for Jenni, Felicity had very little time to relax. She had done Kenny's laundry until he went away to college, and then when he did manage to come home to visit, he always brought what seemed like a semester's worth of dirty laundry home with him. "Mom, you know I didn't mean it that way." Felicity rolled her eyes. "It's just that Sam is going to be here any minute and I need to change."

"What's wrong with the jeans you have on?" The pair looked perfectly fine to her. They were better than fine; they didn't have any holes in them. It had taken Felicity four months to talk her into buying a brand-new pair of jeans with holes already in them. Today's fashions were ridiculous and depressingly dark.

"I wore these Tuesday to school." Felicity looked appalled.

"And they were washed on Thursday." She shook her head as she carried the basket of towels into the bathroom. "They're clean."

"I worked five hours today in them. They smell like soap and have glitter all over them." Felicity followed her into the bathroom and brushed her thigh. "See?"

When they had first moved into the house, Jenni and

she had gotten into their first fight. Jenni had insisted that Dorothy take the master bedroom with its adjoining bath. The house was Jenni's, so she believed Jenni deserved it. While she had been busy with the movers in the kitchen, Jenni had directed the placement of the bedroom furniture. Jenni had won that argument by default. Dorothy wasn't strong enough to move the furniture and switch Jenni's and her bedroom sets.

Felicity and she now shared this one bathroom, while Jenni and the boys had the main, out-of-date bath, off the hallway. Most of the time the turtle spent his day in the bottom of her tub because Corey swore that Buster hated pink. The color made the turtle sick, and the main bath of the house was a putrid shade of 1960s pink, down to the commode, sink, and floor and ceiling tiles. At least her and Felicity's bath was white, ancient, chipped white. The walls were papered in a current 1970s style of crushed-velvet paisley. Retro was alive and well in the Wright house, and she hated it.

Pink sparkles now glittered on the white throw rugs she was using in the hopeless cause of toning down the room. "Don't do that, Felicity. They get everywhere."

"Yeah, like on my jeans." Felicity studied her face in the mirror and moaned in dismay. "I'm getting another zit."

She stood beside her daughter, who was at least three inches taller, and marveled at the woman she was becoming. It was scaring her to death. In two years Felicity would be away at college. Felicity wasn't anything like her brother, Ken. With her daughter she wasn't sure if she would come home for visits, dirty laundry or not. "You are not. Stop poking at it."

"See? You said it; you see it too." Felicity moved closer to the mirror above the sink.

"I see a freckle. In fact I see a whole face of freckles. You got them from your father's side of the family." The red hair ran on both sides, but George had been blessed with the Irish freckles. "Your father used to rock you in the chair and claim all those freckles were from where the angels kissed you."

"Dad was Irish; he was full of baloney." Felicity grinned at herself.

"Hey"—she lightly smacked her daughter on the arm—"watch it, sister. I'm Irish too."

"Mom, so am I." Felicity glanced over at the tub, where Buster was playing in the half-inch of water at the one end. "I forgot to tell you about tonight and Sam."

"Speaking of Sam"—maybe now was the time to have the heart-to-heart with her daughter—"you're a beautiful girl, Felicity. Do you really want to be spending all your time with one guy? Sam's a really nice boy, don't get me wrong." She could see the anger building in her daughter's face. "What I'm saying is that you barely know anyone else at school. Maybe you should be, I don't know—what do you young kids call it nowadays?—playing the field."

"It's called being a 'sleaze-ut,' Mom. Is that what you want me to be?"

"Of course not." She didn't need to be seventeen again to figure out that a "sleaze-ut" was a sleazy slut. "What I'm trying to say is that maybe you and Sam shouldn't be so serious. You barely know each other." All she had been hearing from Felicity for the past three months was Sam, Sam, and more Sam. Her daughter's world was starting to revolve around one guy, and she was way too young to be acting so serious. "You have your whole world ahead of you."

"What's that got to do with Sam?" Felicity crossed her arms. "What's wrong with him?"

"Nothing is wrong with him, hon. He seems like a very nice and polite boy." It was time for her to do some backpedaling. "Your nephews love him, and his family seems really nice."

"Great, glad you like his family." Felicity was being sarcastic. "Because what I forgot to tell you is that not only is Sam coming tonight, so are his father and sisters. Sam said something about his father having one or two parts he wanted to put on the furnace in the basement, so they decided to make a night of it."

"Here?" Eli Fischer was coming here tonight. The house was a disaster, and so was the kitchen. She had baked a chocolate cake this afternoon while doing the laundry, but she hadn't had a chance to frost it yet. Tonight she had been planning on giving the kitchen a good scrubbing while Sam and Felicity occupied the boys.

She didn't even want to think about what she was wearing. She wasn't fit for company.

Before she could think of what to do first, there was a pounding on the front door that vibrated the whole house. One of these days they had to get the doorbell fixed before the walls came tumbling down. The boys heard the pounding, sprinted from Jenni's room, and started running down the stairs, shouting, screaming, and, knowing her grandsons, probably pushing each other. It was a miracle no one had broken their neck yet, the way the boys raced up and down those steps.

"I'll get it!" shouted Tucker.

"No, me!" answered Corey.

"Boys, no pushing!" Jenni came out into the hallway to yell down the stairs.

She and Felicity joined Jenni at the top of the stairs as Chase made it to the front door first and flung it open.

The Fischer family tumbled into the house with pizza boxes, bags of chips, bottles of soda, and what looked like a month's worth of DVDs. Eli stood at the bottom of the stairs, glanced up at them, and grinned. "I declare it movie night!" He held up an economy-size box of microwavable popcorn, boxes of Milk Duds, and a bottle of wine.

Chase, Tucker, and Corey all stood there with their mouths hanging open, probably thinking that Christmas had come early to Mistletoe Bay.

Jenni snapped her seat belt and watched as Coop walked around the front of her SUV and then got into the driver's seat. The man was not only gorgeous, but attentive and a perfect date as well. She couldn't remember the last time she had been this relaxed over a meal.

What Cooper Armstrong did to a suit should be illegal. The man oozed sex appeal. All through dinner she kept getting whiffs of his aftershave and it was driving her nuts.

Coop started the car and turned on the heat. "Give it a minute to warm up." Coop's gaze was on her legs.

She nervously shifted her legs as the scent of his aftershave filled her car. Coop had taken one look at her shoes and declared his pickup truck unacceptable. She had handed him the keys to her SUV without an argument. "It's okay, Coop. I knew it was cold out when I got dressed." She had debated long and hard what to wear tonight. Since she didn't have time to go shopping, she was left with only a couple suitable choices. The knee-length red silky dress worn because she had shoes to match. Bojangles had chewed the heel off her good navy dress shoes and the ears off her bunny slippers.

The next free moment she had, she was doing some major shopping and buying a lock for her bedroom door. She didn't know who was worse, the boys spilling her one and only bottle of perfume tonight before she'd had a chance to put any on, or the animals. At least the boys didn't chew her shoes, but her bedroom now reeked like a whorehouse.

She had been left in the awkward situation of asking her mother-in-law if she could use some of her perfume. Although Dorothy had excellent taste in perfume, it wasn't hers, but it beat Felicity's odd assortment.

"You don't have to go straight home, do you?" Coop started to drive. "I wanted to show you something."

"Now that's a loaded question if I ever heard one." She chuckled at some of her thoughts.

"Don't tease, Jenni," Coop groaned. "I'm trying to be on my best behavior tonight."

It was on the tip of her tongue to ask why, but she already knew the answer. Cooper Armstrong was trying to impress her, and she thought that was sweet. Of course, he didn't need to make a good impression on her; she was already impressed. She had been in awe of him since he'd rescued Tucker off the porch roof and captured the iguana underneath the dinner table. "So what did you want to show me?"

"Sunset Cove." Coop drove out of the restaurant's

parking lot and headed out of town. "It's the best place to go sledding for the boys, once we get a good pack of snow."

"That's where Suicide Hill is, isn't it?" She'd take the boys sledding, but there was no way she was tobogganing down that hill. "How come I've never heard of it before?"

"It's a town secret." Coop clicked the heater on, now that the car was warmed up. "We don't advertise it because of the tourists. It's nice for the locals to have a place of their own. During the summer months it's great for swimming and just bobbing around in a rowboat pretending to fish."

"Sounds nice." Mistletoe Bay was far enough out of town that most of the tourists didn't bother with it. "Doesn't anyone live there?"

"Sure, there's a few houses, but there's also a lot of open spaces. Teenagers use it as a hangout area, and the sheriff knows to patrol it regularly."

"So what you are telling me is that my sister-in-law and Sam have probably been there. Now there's a thought that would give Dorothy more gray hair."

"Felicity seems to have her head on straight." Coop chuckled as he made a left turn. "I think you should worry more about Eli taking Dorothy there."

"Eli does seem to enjoy flirting with her, doesn't he?" She remembered the banter going on in the kitchen between the two when she and Coop had left for dinner. "He's quite a few years younger, though."

"In case you didn't notice, Jenni, Eli didn't seem to care. I would say the man is smitten."

"Smitten." She couldn't help but laugh at the image.

"Now the question is, what's he smitten about—
Dorothy or her cooking? The man does like to eat."

"All men like to eat, Jenni." Coop turned off the street
and onto a gravel road. "I still can't believe you hadn't
eaten at the Catch of the Day before tonight."

"I never had the opportunity before tonight. It's not
the kind of place one would take Tucker for a meal." She
glanced around as the cove came into view. The crisp,
cold night air was clear and bright, allowing the nearly
full moon to reflect off the still water of the cove. "This
is beautiful."

At her house you couldn't see the water of the bay
from any first-floor window. A couple of the windows
on the second floor allowed a few glimpses between the
trees. It was Chase's third-floor window that had a clear
view. One of these days, when she had some extra
money, she was going to hire a landscaper to thin out a
lot of the branches to open up the view from the second
floor, and possibly remove a few trees and bushes so
they could all enjoy the view from the back family room.

Coop stopped the SUV and turned off the headlights.
"This is where everyone has picnics and swims in the
summer. There's a small sandy beach right at the water's
edge, and little kids can wade out pretty far before it
drops off."

She could picture what it must look like during the
summer months when the trees had leaves and the occasional flower dotted the underbrush. "I bet the water
is still cold."

"Nicely chilled, but on hot summer days, it hits the
spot." Coop pointed off to the right. "Over there is a
rope tied to that big tree leaning over the water. It's the

perfect Tarzan rope, and the water beneath it is deep enough that you don't have to worry about banging your head on anything. Every spring the volunteer fire company holds a clean-up day out here. It's more like a party, but they always put up a new rope for the kids and wade into the cove to remove anything hazardous they can find." Coop turned back on the headlights and drove back out the gravel road back to the paved street. "It's sorta like Misty Harbor's unofficial park."

"Where's the sledding?" She hadn't see any hilly area that looked cleared enough to sled down.

"I'll show you. It's at the farthest end of the cove." Coop passed a couple of homes that backed right up to the water. "Everyone in town knows to drop off extra firewood, branches, and logs out at the hill. During the winter months they feed the fifty-five-gallon drums that keep everyone warm. A few of the local residents along here even keep the gas-powered generator filled. There's a donation box up there to help cover the cost."

"Why do you need a generator?" She leaned forward and stared out into the darkness. The only thing she could see was the occasional house, and trees. The actual water of the cove was nowhere to be seen.

"Someone strung a line of lightbulbs up there so you can see the course at night."

"Sounds nice." She could tell they were heading up a hill. "Does the cove freeze during the winter? I haven't been ice skating in years."

"No, but there's Sarah's Pond for that." Coop glanced over at her. "Don't tell me, you don't know where that is either?"

She shook her head. She would laugh, if it wasn't so

pathetic. Here she could have been taking the boys to Sunset Cove last summer, but she hadn't even known it existed. Instead they had waded in the bay on those hot summer days. "I'm a lousy mother."

"You are not." Coop pulled the SUV onto another gravel road that wound its way into the woods. "Why do you think that?"

"I should have gone out exploring the town more. This is our home now."

"You never would have found the swimming beach or Suicide Hill by exploring, Jenni. They are pretty well hidden, as you can see." Coop pulled to a stop in what seemed to be a big, clear parking lot filled with gravel and ruts. "We can't get out and see everything with those"—he nodded to her high heels—"shoes on. You'll break an ankle."

"Sorry, I didn't realize hiking would be required." She unbuckled her seat belt and leaned forward so she could see out the windshield better. "So this is Suicide Hill?" In the beam of the headlights she could see a clear area that went all the way down to the edge of the cove. The run didn't look dangerous or steep, but having water at the end of the run didn't seem like a smart idea to her. Tucker would take the frigid water as a challenge. "It doesn't look bad, except for the stopping."

Coop chuckled as he unbuckled his seat belt. "There will be piles of hay bales and a snowbank so thick and high around the shoreline that no one would go into the water. It's perfectly safe."

"Well, if that's the case, I will go down Suicide Hill with you." She'd sledded steeper runs by the time she was Chase's age. At the edge of the light she could make out a couple of those fifty-five gallon drums Coop had told her about. They were well away from trees, and there were quite a few piles of wood laying around waiting for the first snowstorm.

"You will?" Coop's voice held laughter.

"Sure." She'd never figured Coop to be such a wuss when it came to tobogganing.

"I'll hold you to that." Coop leaned forward and gave her a quick, teasing kiss. He pointed over her shoulder and out the passenger side window. "Suicide Hill starts up there"—his finger indicated the top of the small mountain next to them—"and ends down there." His finger moved until it was pointing at an area of the cove that was far to the right of them.

She frowned out the window. In the shadowy moonlight, all she could see were trees. "Where's the run?"

"On the other side of the trees. The run starts at the very top, and there's at least two hairpin turns in it. Most beginners never make it past the first one."

"What stops them, the trees?" No wonder they called it Suicide Hill.

"Sometimes, but usually fortified snow banks prevent any major injury." Coop leaned in closer. "You don't have to worry, though. I'd mastered the run by the time I was fifteen. I won't let anything happen to you." Coop's voice held nothing but teasing and laughter.

"You tricked me." She nodded to the safe little hill in front of them. "So what's that?"

"The kiddie run." Coop was still laughing when he kissed her.

Chapter Eleven

Coop started to unload the cart stacked with boxes. He might not be able to drive his truck to the door of Jenni's shop, but he could push a dolly over the rough dirt path. He didn't mind the extra work, and besides, he got to see Jenni. By next week, if they got the snow that was being forecast, he wouldn't be able to use the dolly.

Jennifer Wright was turning his world upside down. Three months ago he would have told anyone who would listen that that particular feat was impossible. One little five-foot-four-inch woman with the most delectable mouth had not only proven him wrong, but she had dropped him to his knees and he was about to cry "Uncle."

"Thanks, Coop. I appreciate the extra effort." Jenni took the last box and sat it by the door. "One day when I become rich, I'll have that driveway paved."

"How thankful?" Coop backed her up against the closed door and stared at her mouth. He couldn't care less about the condition of her driveway. He had to rush through his morning deliveries and had cut his lunch short to make sure he made Mistletoe Bay Company's stop before Felicity got home from school. As it was, he had about ten minutes alone with Jenni before they would be interrupted.

Jenni's smile was pure wickedness. "Gee, you want a tip or something?"

He stepped closer without taking his gaze from her lips. "Or something." He didn't even want to think about how many company rules he was breaking right about now. He didn't care about anything but kissing Jenni. His dreams last night had been hot, erotic, and entirely unsatisfactory. He wanted the real thing. He wanted Jenni.

The tip of Jenni's tongue slipped out from between her lips. With a slow and deliberate movement, she slowly ran it across her upper lip.

A groan rumbled up his throat. "You're doing that on purpose."

Jenni's smile grew. "Of course." Her thin arms wrapped around his neck as she stood on her tippy toes. "You're too tall."

"You're too short." He brushed the side of her mouth as his hands spanned her waist. A woman with three children shouldn't be this hot, be this desirable, or smell this tempting. Jenni smelled like sugar cookies warm from the oven. The fragrance alone was making his mouth water.

"Five-four isn't short." Jenni's moist lower lip pouted playfully as her fingertips teased the back of his neck and wove their way into his hair.

He lightly nipped that lip. "Six-two isn't tall." Jenni's fingers felt hot against his chilled neck.

"Coop?" Jenni pressed herself against his chest, trying to get closer.

"Hmmm . . . ?" He skimmed her jaw with tiny nibbles. Jenni Wright was like a fine wine; she needed to be savored, not gulped.

Jenni turned her head and tried to capture his mouth. "Kiss me."

"I thought you'd never ask." He finally did what he had been dying to do since saying goodnight to her last night. He kissed her.

There was nothing sweet or slow about their kiss. They were beyond that point, but nowhere near where his body was craving to be. He wanted Jennifer Wright in his bed, naked and smiling. They were both too old to be playing this frustrating game of sneaking kisses when no one was looking. The Wright household had more eyes than a optometrists convention.

Jenni lightly bit his lip and moaned.

The woman was playing with fire, and she knew it. Before he slipped over the edge, and his smoldering campfire turned into an inferno, he slowly broke the kiss and reached for the last tattered threads of his self-control. "Jenni"—he brushed one last kiss over her moist lips while trying to catch his breath—"Felicity will be here any moment." The last thing he wanted to do was give an impressionable teenage girl a sex education 101 class.

Jenni looked like she wanted to argue, but she didn't. Jenni slowly lowered her arms, and he stepped back.

He smiled gently. At least he knew whatever he was feeling, Jenni was too. This fierce heat was between them, but there was something else, something powerful and so new to him that he couldn't put a name to it. Desire, lust, and just plain old horniness, he understood. Whatever was happening between him and Jenni was different and it was starting to scare him.

Jenni worming her way into his heart, he could handle. Chase and Corey made his blood drop a few degrees. Tucker, on the other hand, made it freeze. The five-year-old had used his grandmother's toothbrush on Bojangles's teeth and hadn't bothered to tell her about it until two days ago. Dorothy was currently working her way through her third bottle of mouthwash.

"How's the remodeling coming along?" All week long Pete Van de Camp's beat-up old pickup had been parked in front of the house. It was a record for Pete.

Coop had made a habit of stopping by just about every night on the pretense of checking Pete's work. In truth his visits were for Dorothy's cooking and Jenni's kisses.

"Pete seems to be holding it together, and for some strange reason, I think he's bonding with Tucker."

"Tucker? Your Tucker?" If Tucker had been left out in the woods, wolves wouldn't even raise him.

"Yes, my Tucker." Jenni grinned. "It's kinda cute. Pete let him chip away at the tile in Dorothy's old bathroom the other day when he got home from school."

"He gave Tucker tools?" Coop glanced out the window next to the door. He could make out the section of the second story that was Dorothy's bathroom. "It's still standing." He would have placed money on at least one gaping hole, if not scorch marks damaging the wooden siding.

Jenni whacked him on the arm. "Tucker's not that bad." Jenni chuckled at herself. "Most of the time."

"If you say so." He would be the last to admit that he kind of liked Tucker. The boy had what John Wayne referred to as "grit." "Hasn't Tucker tried to electrocute, glue, or decapitate Pete yet?" Maybe the boy was going soft in his old age. Or maybe Pete was working drunk out of his skull.

What did he know about kids? Absolutely nothing. He was an only child. Jenni was the first woman he'd ever dated who had a child, let alone three.

"There was the one incident with the pliers, but that didn't count. Tucker was only trying to imitate Felicity and pluck the cat's eyebrows." Jenni opened up the first box and pulled out a packing slip.

"Felicity plucks the cat's eyebrows?" He had lived with his ex-girlfriend for seven years. When Candace wasn't plucking her brows, she was getting them waxed, shaped, and sometimes dyed. Then she would spend two days pouting because he never seemed to notice. A woman's eyebrows weren't high up on his pay-attention-to list. As long as Candace hadn't been sporting a unibrow, he couldn't understand what all the fuss was about.

Jenni glanced up, glared at him, and then rolled her eyes. "Just be thankful you didn't hear Dumber's scream." Coop was pulling her leg again, so she pulled his back. Thankfully Pete had caught Tucker before he could get the cat's head steady.

Coop shuddered. "I thought you said Pete and Tucker were bonding?"

"They are. Pete promised not to pluck Tucker's

eyebrows with a monkey wrench if Tucker promised not to try that number again." She sliced through the tape on the next box—more empty jars. "Tucker will hold to his promise not to, because he never does the same thing twice." Her son had more creativity than that.

"So Pete's working out okay? No problems?" Coop lifted up the next boxes onto the work table for her.

"He's doing a great job in Dorothy's bathroom. The only problem is, she and Felicity now have to share my and the boys' bathroom, and it's getting crowded real fast." She didn't want to think about the athletic abilities she now needed just to take a shower. Between boats, toys, six bottles of shampoo and just as many of conditioner, not to mention bars of soap, bottles of body wash, buffs, puffs, and Lord knew what all else, there was barely any room to stand, let alone move.

Last night she had showered with Buster the turtle floating on an orange plastic Frisbee with a few chew marks around the edges. Buster was fascinated by bubbles.

Coop was polite enough to try to hide his laughter. "How much longer will it take before Dorothy's bathroom is operational?"

"Pete got the tub into place this morning. He's putting up the wallboards or whatever it is that he needs before tiling." Dorothy was having a ball picking out the tile and fixtures, even though she would never admit it. Dorothy had fought her on which room of the house should be done first. For the first time in their relationship, Jenni had pulled rank on her mother-in-law. After all, it was Jenni's house.

"Is she still feeding Pete?" There might have been a hint of envy in Coop's voice; she couldn't tell.

"Every chance she gets. You jealous?" Coop was at their dinner table more nights than not. He loved Dorothy's cooking, just like every other male in the world. "If you are, you'll have to stand in line behind Eli."

"Eli's not handling Pete's presence very well, is he?" Coop glanced at his watch and frowned.

"Pete doesn't look at Dorothy the way Eli does. Eli has nothing to be jealous about. Pete eyes her rump roast, while Eli eyes her . . ." She stopped in midsentence as the door to the shop opened and Felicity walked in.

"Hi, Coop," Felicity said as she hung up her winter coat. A few snowflakes fell to the ground. "Fancy seeing you here." Felicity's grin was infectious and all-knowing.

"Had a delivery." Coop nodded to the stack of boxes on the work table.

"I just bet you did." Felicity wiggled her brows. "It's starting to snow again."

Last night they had gotten about two inches of the white stuff. "They aren't predicting any real accumulation till late Saturday night or Sunday morning." Jenni glanced at Coop. "We might have to cancel our date if it starts early."

"Nonsense. That's why they invented four-wheel drive." Coop didn't look too pleased with the prospect of calling off their date.

Jenni tried not to smile. It was good to know he was looking forward to some alone time as much as she was. She watched as Felicity headed for the back room, and she gathered up her courage. "I was thinking, instead of us eating out, I could cook you a meal."

"Don't you mean cook everyone a meal?" Coop zipped his jacket, not seeming to like that idea.

"No, I was thinking about cooking it at your place." She knew he had an apartment over in Sullivan somewhere.

Coop's eyes lit up. "It's a pretty small kitchen."

"I'll manage." When she and Ken had first gotten married their entire apartment hadn't been any bigger than her current family room. Every time she had washed dishes in the kitchen sink, she had unintentionally splashed Ken on the sofa with sudsy water.

"I don't have a lot of gadgets and cooking equipment. Just the basics, the very basics."

"Are you trying to talk me out of it?" For some perverse reason she wanted to show Coop she could cook a meal and that she wasn't totally helpless in the kitchen. It might not be as fancy as Dorothy's but it would be delicious. Ken never once complained about her cooking.

"No." Coop glanced at Felicity as she came out of the back room carrying a tray of light purple soap. "I just don't want you to go to too much trouble."

"I'll bring everything I need." She wasn't stupid. She knew what was going to happen if she spent hours alone with Coop in his apartment. By the look in Coop's eyes, he knew it too. She might as well have put a sign around her neck that read, I WANT TO SLEEP WITH YOU!

Felicity sat on the chair and tried not to glare at Sam. It wasn't his fault that Tucker and Corey were all over him and wouldn't leave him alone. Well, not 100 percent his fault. Her nephews never left Sam alone when he came over. Chase was sitting on the end of the couch laughing at his brothers and Sam's antics.

This was not how she was supposed to be spending her Saturday night. It was pretty bad when her widowed sister-in-law was out having more fun. At least Jenni was allowed out of the house, while she was confined for the night because of a few snowflakes.

It was more than a few, but before the first thousand flakes had hit the ground, her mother had pulled the plug on Sam and her plans to go see a movie in Franklin. Sam's father hadn't helped matters when he had agreed with her mother.

"Sam, are you hungry yet?" She knew it was a stupid question. Sam was always hungry. Her mother had roasted a chicken tonight, with all the trimmings. It had been the size of a small turkey, and there had been barely anything left on the platter. Jenni and Coop hadn't even eaten with them. They had disappeared fast, after promising the boys that they would take them sledding tomorrow. A curious person would have to wonder what kind of plans they had beyond a meal and a DVD Coop claimed he'd rented.

She wasn't a curious person—much.

"In a minute, Felicity." Sam rolled Tucker off the couch and onto the floor. Corey had his arms around Sam's neck and was riding his back as an animated movie played on the television. Chase turned up the volume as the boys yelled and squealed and basically rolled around like idiots.

She was dating an idiot.

She wondered if anyone would hear her scream out her frustration?

There was no way she could watch one more kids' movie without throwing something through the screen.

Tonight her mother, Hope, and Faith were supposed to be watching the boys. Sam and she weren't even supposed to be there. She had fulfilled her family obligation last night by sticking around after dinner and helping everyone carry down box after box after box of Christmas decorations from the attic. The entire family room was floor-to-ceiling boxes.

This was going to be their first Christmas in this house, and all together. She liked the idea of waking Christmas morning with all the boys there ripping into their presents. Christmas with just her and her mom wasn't what one would call exciting. Waiting for Jenni to show up with the boys had been the highlight of her mother's and her morning.

She didn't even mind moving out of the only house she had ever known and into this one. The third-floor bedroom was kind of neat and a lot bigger than her old room. Since the room had been nothing but ancient plaster and wide pine flooring, her mother and Jenni had given her permission to do what she wanted on a three hundred-dollar budget.

Three hundred bucks went a long way if you managed it right and did the work yourself. She had painted all the walls and trim using three shades of green and had purchased a real funky shag rug. Retro curtains with a matching comforter completed the look. In the end, she'd had enough cash left over for a really cool lamp and some posters. The white princess furniture of her youth had been sold back in Augusta, and she now had a room she felt comfortable in.

Plus she loved living right on the bay.

But she missed her friends back in Augusta, and her

school. She was making new ones here, and then there was Sam, who made up for a lot of things. She knew adjustments had to be made. She was just tired of being the one who always had to make them. Why couldn't *she* watch a movie she wanted to watch once in a while?

She got up and headed for the kitchen to see what was up in there. Maybe she could do something with Hope and Faith besides teach them makeup tricks and talk about hot boys and hotter music. She heard the laughter before she entered the room.

Party time was in the kitchen, and she hadn't even been invited.

She stood in the entryway and watched as her mother instructed Sam's sisters on how to make brownies from scratch. Both girls were hanging on her mother's every word, and her mother had never looked happier. There was a flush to Dorothy's cheeks that had nothing to do with the heat of the oven and everything to do with the man sitting at the counter, shelling walnuts. Eli Fischer was having the time of his life and sitting there as if he belonged.

"No, no, no." Dorothy laughed. "Keep the beaters in the bowl." Her mother's arms encircled Faith as she showed the younger girl how to use the mixer.

"How come she gets to use the mixer?" groused Hope.

"Because you got to melt the chocolate, and she didn't." Dorothy helped Faith with the spatula. "Keep pushing everything into the beaters so it blends nicely. You don't want lumpy brownies, do you?"

"Hey, what's this about lumpy brownies?" Eli popped a nut into his mouth.

"Stop eating them all, Eli, or there won't be enough."
Dorothy grinned at Eli and went back to helping Faith.

Her own mother didn't even see her standing there.
She had become invisible, and that wasn't even the
worst thing. When her mother smiled at Sam's father,
the man had winked back, causing her mother's flush to
become more pronounced.

Her mother and Sam's father were flirting with each
other. The whole world had gone insane since Thanksgiving.

She turned around, grabbed her coat off the hook by
the front door, slipped her feet into her boots, and
stepped out onto the front porch. The biting cold and
wind made her eyes water as she slowly walked around
the side of the house and down the path to the edge of
the bay. She loved the bay at night. It was so peaceful
and quiet that she headed for her favorite spot: a huge
boulder not far from the water's edge.

Using the sleeve of her coat, she brushed off some
of the snow and sat with her knees pulled up to her
chest, blocking some of the wind. Her finger trembled
as she yanked up the collar of her coat and brushed
away a tear that was rolling down her check. Damn
wind.

A few minutes later she heard Sam coming before she
saw him. The snow crunched beneath his boots. He quietly brushed off a spot next to her and sat. "You okay?"

"Fine." What was she supposed to say—that she was
a super-bitch and had a raging case of PMS?

"What's got you upset?" Sam pulled out his gloves
from his jacket pocket and handed them to her.

"Nothing, just needed some fresh air." She slipped on his gloves and felt like a bigger ass.

"Nice night for it." Sam's voice held sarcasm as he moved forward a couple inches to block the wind from directly hitting her. "You're not going to go all girly on me, Felicity, are you?"

"What's that supposed to mean?" Didn't Sam think she was girly enough?

"It means you're not going to make me sit out here freezing my ass off trying to guess what's upsetting you." Sam's voice softened as he cupped her cheek. "One of the things that I like best about you, Ms. Augusta, is the way you say what you mean, and mean what you say. No mind games."

Sam used the nickname he'd given her the week they'd met. He had claimed that Felicity couldn't really be shortened, so he had mistakenly called her "Reds." She hated that nickname and wasn't afraid to let Sam know it. From then on out, he'd called her Ms. Augusta. "I'm just being foolish, Sam."

"About me?" Sam's warm fingers stroked her chilled face. "You're upset that I put Corey's DVD in? I know we must have watched it a hundred times already, but it was either *Cars* or *Winnie-the-Pooh*. No offense against the big old yellow bear, but I would go insane if I had to sit through another one of his movies. The voice alone makes me want to pick up an ice pick and stab something."

"I like Pooh." She rested her cheek in the palm of his hand and smiled.

"I know you do. We'll put in the Pooh movie once this one is over."

"Not tonight." She really didn't want to see it again. She wanted to go in to Franklin and cuddle up with Sam over a large tub of popcorn and a gory horror flick.

"You're mad that I was wrestling with Tucker?" Sam dropped his voice into an awful Arnold Schwarzenegger imitation. "I vas showing 'im some moves."

She pushed his arm. "That's awful." She tried not to laugh. Only Sam could pull her out of such a deep funk. "Can I ask you a question, without you getting all upset?"

"Sure, wait a minute." Sam's voice sounded hesitant. "You're not going to ask if you can see other guys, are you?"

"What ever gave you that idea?" She pushed Sam away and tried to read his face in the darkness. She couldn't. There wasn't enough light. "Why in the world would I want to see other guys?"

"Then what's the question?" She could hear the smile in Sam's voice.

"I was just wondering why your father and sisters are always around now. Don't get me wrong, I like your dad and sisters. But they just seem to be at our house all the time now."

"Your mom was the one to invite them to dinner tonight and to help out babysitting the boys while Jenni and Coop go out." Sam shrugged. "Besides, my dad loves your mom's cooking."

"Do you think your dad likes my mom?" She didn't doubt that Eli Fischer loved her mother's cooking. That wasn't the issue here.

"Sure. Your mom's cool."

"I mean, *like* like. As in like her as a girlfriend? I

think they were flirting with each other tonight, and your dad winked at her." There, she'd said it. The biggest ick factor in her life was now out in the open.

"So what if they were? They're both adults, Felicity." Sam shook his head. "It's a little strange, I guess, but I have never seen my dad happier."

Felicity felt her heart sink. Sam didn't get it after all. He had been her last hope of an ally in a world gone crazy.

Jenni rinsed the bubbles off the plate and handed it to Coop. "This is a beautiful set of dishes." She loved the dainty violets and greenery on the ivory-colored china, but she didn't think Coop would pick out such a set for himself. Besides, they were antiques and probably could fetch a pretty penny.

"They were my late Aunt Bernice's, my father's sister." Coop dried the plate and then put it back into its proper place, on the top shelf of the kitchen cabinet. "My mom gave the set to me when I moved here from California. She didn't need two sets. She already had her original set of china from when she and dad got married." Coop glanced around the kitchen and the connecting living room. "She cleaned house, and most of the stuff in here came from her, or some dead relative. Mom's sort of a pack rat, and she packed it all off on me." Coop shook his head and chuckled. "It saved me a small fortune, but most of it isn't my style."

"That explains the violets." It also explained the retro enamel kitchen table with chrome and vinyl chairs. Coop didn't strike her as a retro type of guy. The couch was beige and overstuffed, but the leather recliner looked new and barely broken in. The large-screen television had Coop's name all over it. She could see Coop's everyday brown and dark green dishes on the bottom shelf. She thought it was cute that he wanted to impress her with the "fine china." "What made you move back from California, your father's health?"

She knew about Fred Armstrong's heart attack and thought it was sweet of Coop, an only child, to move back close to his parents when they needed him. It said a lot about a guy. Ken, though not a mama's boy, cared deeply for his mother, and made sure she had whatever she needed, especially after his father passed away.

"Partly." Coop frowned as she handed him the next dish to dry.

"What was the other part?" Coop knew all about Ken and how she'd come to inherit his mother and sister. "Did you miss Maine? I'm sure living in southern California was a major adjustment for you." She loved Maine and had lived here all her life, but there were times when she wondered what it would be like to live somewhere else. One glance out the kitchen window told her tonight just might be one of those times. It had started to snow in earnest about half an hour ago. Big, fat flakes drifted from the skies, covering everything in sight. The Weather Channel was predicting at least a foot by morning.

"That's why I headed for California when I left college. It was the farthest distance I could get by car."

Coop put away the bowl she had served the potatoes in. Tonight she had baked honey-glazed salmon, garlic mashed potatoes, and a medley of fresh vegetables. Coop had complimented her throughout the meal.

"So why come back?"

"Dad and Mom needed me, and there was nothing left for me in California."

Getting answers from Coop was like asking Tucker what had happened. "What had been in California for you?" Something must have kept him there for over ten years, besides the constant sunshine and bikini-clad girls on the beach.

"Candace, the woman I lived with for seven years." Coop reached for the silverware sitting in the drainer. "She worked in advertising, and I did construction work. Met her at a party one night on the beach. We dated for about four months, and then she moved in." Coop polished the flatware until it gleamed, then dropped it into the drawer next to the sink, one piece at a time.

It sounded like a thousand other love stories to her. So what had gone wrong?

"Mom called one night. Dad had had a heart attack, and they weren't sure he was going to make it. I booked the first flight out of there, kissed Candace goodbye and told her to handle the homefront, and went to be with my mom. Dad pulled through and was back home within two weeks."

"I like your father and mother. They seem like real nice people." Fred had really seemed to enjoy himself on Thanksgiving, and Lucy had even sent her a thank-you card for all the Mistletoe Bay products she'd gone home with that night.

"They're the best."

Which left open the question, why had he dropped out of college and headed for California instead of coming back home? Coop obviously cared for his parents, and they him.

"The whole time I was here pacing hospital hallways, hunting down doctors, and making sure my mother was taking care of herself, I thought. I realized how short and precious life was, and that for the past seven years I had been wasting it. I realized when it was time to ante up your chips in life, the only thing that mattered was family. I wanted a family. I wanted the wife, the kids, the mortgage. I wanted that special someone to be by my side throughout all of life's ups and downs.

"When my father was well enough for me to go home, I bought an engagement ring and flew back to Candace."

She had a horrible sinking feeling she wasn't going to like the rest of Coop's story.

The sound of a spoon landing in the drawer broke the silence. "It was the classic Hollywood betrayal. I walked into our apartment unannounced with a bouquet of roses, a bottle of champagne, and a diamond ring that the jeweler swore would make any woman say yes." A second spoon landed in the drawer.

She could barely choke out the next question even though she was pretty sure she already knew the answer. "What happened?"

"Candace was entertaining"—a fork landed in the drawer—"my soon-to-be-ex–best friend, Gary, in our bed."

"Sorry" seemed so inadequate, but what else was left to say? "I'm sorry Candace broke your heart, Coop."

She handed him the saucepan she had been scrubbing. With a soft smile she said, "She was a fool."

Coop surprised her by grinning. "She didn't break my heart, Jenni. Banged it around a bit, yes; shattered it, no." He started to dry the pot. "Candace did more damage to my dreams than my heart."

"Dreams have a habit of changing, growing in a different direction, or just fading away." She liked the fact that Coop could smile about Candace's betrayal now and that he hadn't turned into some woman-hating grump. "Dreams are fed by life, and life is constantly changing." She'd learned that one firsthand.

"That it is." Coop placed the pot inside the still-warm oven. It was where he stored all his pots and pans because the tiny kitchen was, well, tiny. "What's one of your dreams?"

"Opening the Mistletoe Bay Company." She grinned as she finished with the last pan and pulled the plug in the drain. "With the help of Dorothy and Felicity, I accomplished the first stage of the dream. I never would have been able to do that and take care of the boys."

"What's stage two?" He dried the pan and added to his collection already in the oven.

"A baby-product line, I think." She reached for the towel he was using and dried her hands. Coop's dream of a family was wonderful, and something she had achieved. Now, though she had the boys, it wasn't a complete family, but she had learned to play with the hand she'd been dealt.

"You think?"

"Well I'm working on that, and a line of more natural-ingredient products." She walked over to his couch and

sat. A pile of DVDs was sitting on the coffee table. Coop
had explained earlier that he had gone out to rent a
movie but couldn't decide what she would want to
watch, so he had gotten an assortment. She picked up the
small pile and started to glance through them.

"You can get more natural than oatmeal cranberry
soap?" Coop sat next to her.

"Sure. I'm working with pine and some sea scents
right now. Men are looking for excellent products that
wouldn't leave them smelling like a funeral parlor." She
couldn't help laughing at the assortment of DVDs in her
hand. Coop had rented *Casablanca,* one of the *Lord of
the Ring* movies, *Blazing Saddles, Braveheart,* and the
current Oscar contender for best picture. "This is quite
an assortment."

"I told you I couldn't make up my mind, and I don't
know yours all that well—yet."

She smiled. "I like that 'yet.'" It made it sound like
Coop wanted to continue this relationship. She knew
whatever developed between her and Coop would never
work out in the end. Coop had dreams of starting a
family, while she, on the other hand, was raising hers.

She didn't come with a cute matching set of baggage,
she came with a warehouse stacked to the rafters with
worn, torn, and banged-up crates. Coop would come to
his senses soon enough, but in the meantime she was
going to hoard every memory they had together.

Coop moved closer. "So which movie did you want
me to put on?"

She could feel his gaze on her mouth. "It doesn't
matter." She leaned toward him and wrapped her arms
around his neck. "I don't think I'll be paying much

attention to it, or to anything else." Who cared about a movie when she had Coop all to herself for a couple hours?

Coop's mouth skimmed her jaw. "Why not?"

Strong arms gently wrapped around her. "Because, Cooper Armstrong, I can't think when you kiss me."

Coop grinned and lowered his head. "So stop thinking," he whispered against her lips.

Chapter Twelve

By the time she came up for air from their first kiss, she was in Coop's bed with over half of her clothes gone. She had no idea how she'd gotten there or where her blouse, bra, and slacks had disappeared to, but it really didn't matter. She was right where she wanted to be, and Coop's mouth was hot against her breast.

Coop Armstrong had the hands of a magician.

Her eyes crossed as he gave her nipple a gentle bite. "Coop, we have to slow down." She wanted to savor this moment so she could pull out the memory of it on long, cold winter's nights.

Coop's mouth nuzzled the valley between her breasts as his large, warm hands caressed her thighs. "Name three good reasons why we have to."

What did he, with his fingers tugging on the elastic of the sexiest pair of panties that she owned, want her to think? She rubbed her toe up the back of his jean-clad leg. Somewhere between the living room and the bed she had lost her socks. She knew for a fact she had been wearing them while she had washed the dishes. "You have too many clothes on." Her fingers were itching to caress his skin.

Coop raised his head and grinned. "I love how your mind works." Coop's hands left her body and immediately started yanking his shirt over his head.

Her hands skimmed up his chest and marveled at the strength and warmth of his chest. Years of construction work had toned Coop to near perfection. "Protection?" She felt Coop tremble beneath her fingertips and prayed it was because he was excited, and not unprepared.

Coop leaned away from her and the bed. His one hand fumbled with his belt buckle; the other was rummaging through the drawer in the nightstand. "Check."

She softly smiled as Coop stepped out of his pants and yanked off his socks. So much for slowing things down. Coop stood in the pool of light by the side of the bed, totally aroused and unashamed. The man was magnificent, while she had given birth three times. Thankfully, no one had bothered to turn on the bedroom lights, and the only light was coming in from the living room, highlighting Coop and the bottom of the bed.

"Are you done looking yet?" Coop inquired. "What's the third reason?"

Coop chuckled while she blushed. She knew exactly where her gaze had been. She tried to scoot back farther onto the bed, away from the light, but Coop clamped his hand around her calf. "I told you I can't think when you kiss me." What was she supposed to say? *I have faint stretch marks.* That would only call attention to them.

"I'm not kissing you." Coop's fingers trailed up both thighs to hook into the waistband of her silk panties. He slowly started to peel them down.

The slowness was killing her. She wanted Coop, and she wanted him now. "So hurry up and kiss me."

Coop practically tore off the triangle of silk. "I thought you'd never ask." He grabbed a foil packet and joined her on the bed.

Before she could tunnel her fingers through the whirling hairs on his chest, his mouth was on hers, hard and demanding. She arched into his kiss and slid her thigh over his hip. It had been over two years since she had been touched. Loved. Wanted.

Coop's scorching mouth was everywhere at once. There didn't seem to be an inch of her he didn't want to taste or kiss. "Lord, Jenni, you're beautiful" was breathed against the curve of her hip.

She felt his finger penetrate her opening and she nearly climaxed. She cried his name as she pushed against his hand, demanding more. Her hands tried to pull him closer as her thighs opened wider.

Coop positioned himself between her thighs as he cupped her cheeks. His breath was coming fast and furious. "Jenni, I'll go slower the next time," his mouth teased hers open as he started to enter her with one long thrust, "promise."

The thickness of his arousal slid into her as she locked her ankles behind him, arched her hips, and climaxed.

Coop joined her in release before she felt the last tremors of her own body fade.

Somewhere in the distance she thought she had heard a loud cry and hoped like hell it hadn't been her. She had never cried out in bed before, and she didn't want to start now. It was pitiful enough that Coop was going to think she was easy, considering this was only their third date.

It had taken Ken six months to get her into his bed.

Jenni closed her eyes as Coop eased to his side and tucked her head upon his shoulder. She felt a tear slide down her cheek. What kind of mother was she? How was she ever going to face Dorothy?

She was going to go to hell.

Coop was trying to catch his breath when he felt a tear splash onto his chest. His heart nearly leaped out of his rib cage. "Jenni?" He reached over and turned on the light on the nightstand and watched as she frantically fumbled with the sheets until they were up to her chin.

His passionate siren from three minutes ago was gone. In her place was a pale, beautiful woman with tears clinging to her impossibly long lashes. With a hand that refused to be steady, he wiped at the tears. "Did I hurt you?" It was his worst fear. Jenni was so tiny and petite, while he wasn't what anyone would call dainty.

"Of course not." Jenni rapidly blinked but didn't look away.

He let out a breath he hadn't even known he was holding. "Why the tears? And don't tell me they're tears of joy. I can see they aren't." He felt like a heel. He had never made a woman cry in bed before. What in the world was wrong?

"I . . . ummm . . ." Jenni looked confused, embarrassed, and appalled all at the same time.

He felt his gut clench. Maybe she hadn't been feeling what he had, but there was no way in hell he was asking her if it had been as good for her as it had been for him. He had felt her climax pulsating around him as he had thrust into her. She couldn't have faked that. "Jenni, come on, please talk to me." He slowly reached out and brushed a long strand of her hair behind her ear. He took it as a good sign that she didn't flinch from his touch. "I didn't go too fast, did I?" He vaguely remembered her asking him to slow down, but with Jenni lying naked across his bed, that had been an impossibility.

"No." Jenni bit her lip. "I'm not the kind of woman who usually does this, Coop."

He nodded. "I figured that one out weeks ago, Jen." He used the pad of his thumb to lightly tug her lower lip out from beneath her teeth. If anything was going to mark that luscious mouth, it was going to be him. "Whatever this is growing between us, Jen, it's going both ways."

"What I'm trying to say is that I haven't done this sort of thing since Ken died." Her misty-green eyes locked with his. "Ken was my first and only lover."

He refused to acknowledge the spark of jealousy that singed his gut when he thought of Jenni making love to another man. Ken had been her husband and was the father of her three boys. "Two years is a long time for a very beautiful woman to be alone." His fingers caressed the delicate curve of her jaw and then lightly skimmed her knuckles—her white knuckles, which were still clutching the sheet.

"I'm a mother, Coop." Jenni kept trying to read his expression. "Mothers don't do this." Jen waved toward the bed and the tangled sheets.

He laughed. He couldn't help it. "Go tell that to about a hundred million mothers, Jenni. I'm sure they will disagree with you." He could tell she was upset, but surely not because they'd made love and she was a mother. "I've met the boys, your mother-in-law, Felicity, and half the San Diego zoo in your house." He reached for the sheet and started to tug. "You're a woman first, a mother second. A very desirable woman." He could see that her nipples were hard beneath the sheet. His penis stirred. "I want you again already."

Jenni held the sheet firm and glared at the light. "I gave birth to three boys, Coop."

"I know." He wasn't about to force Jenni to do anything she wasn't comfortable doing. "Are you worried about the boys?" Maybe she wanted to go home. "Do you want to call and check on them?"

Jenni shook her head. "Could you turn out the light?"

"Why?" He wanted to see every incredible inch of her this time when they made love.

Jenni rolled her eyes. "Coop, childbirth has a way of changing a woman's body, and it's not for the better."

"Jen, your body is perfect, trust me. If it got any better I'd be embarrassing myself." He couldn't imagine what she was talking about. Granted he'd never had a lover who had given birth before, but unless they tattooed an EXIT sign inside of her thighs, there hadn't been any difference that he'd felt or tasted.

"Perfect? You're nuts."

"Nuts about you." He gave the sheet a harder tug, and this time Jen released her grip. Pale, round breasts that had filled his palms perfectly came into view. The only thing wrong with them was they were too far away. He bent forward to place a kiss on one of the pouting nipples. "As I said, perfect."

Jenni sighed as her arms reached for him.

Coop spent the next two hours showing Jenni just how beautiful her body was, and how nuts he was about her.

* * *

Jenni nervously paced at the bottom of the hill as she waited for Corey to make his first solo run on a sled. She could see him standing at the top of the hill in his little red snowsuit with his brothers beside him. All three of her boys held the ropes of their sleds as they not-so-patiently waited their turn.

"Relax, Jen. He'll be fine," Coop said as he came up beside her and rested his gloved hand on the small of her back.

"I know, but it's always so scary letting them go. My baby isn't a baby any longer." She was half sad about that fact, half elated. She glanced at the small mountain of hay bales covered in snow, effectively blocking the kids from sledding right into the frigid waters of Sunset Cove. The worst that could happen was Corey might crash into that mountain, but he wouldn't get wet.

"No, he's now officially a kid." Coop chuckled as one kid tried to ride his sled down the hill on his knees. The kid didn't make it very far before sliding down the rest of the way on his back. "Before you know it, Corey will be dating."

She scrunched up her nose at the thought. "Hush your mouth." She didn't want to think about her boys getting any older. She wanted them young, sweet, and full of mischief. Okay, the mischief part she could do without, but she loved being the one to tuck them in at night, the one they ran to when they got a scrape and needed a bandage and a kiss to make it all better, and the one they made mushy Valentine's Day cards for.

Right now she loved being the most important woman in their lives.

Corey's turn was next. She watched as Chase got on his sled to one side of Corey; Tucker had the other side. His big brothers were going to protect Corey. It did her heart proud to know that she had raised them right, at least in one regard.

Tucker's nursery school teacher, Mrs. Audun, had called her Friday afternoon with a concern. Tucker and the Higgins twin girls had been whispering and planning something all week long. Kate Audun wanted Jenni to find out what it was and when it would be happening so she could have the fire department and an ambulance crew on standby. Jenni thought the teacher was overreacting, but just in case, she was planning on having a talk with Tucker tonight before he went to bed.

With the boys in school and day care for the past couple of weeks, they were finally getting a routine down. Dorothy finally had some time to herself, which she spent handling the renovations of her bathroom, cooking up a storm, and smiling. She had never seen Dorothy so happy, and it wasn't all due to the boys' being in day care. Eli Fischer and his daughters were becoming regular fixtures around the house.

The best thing about day care was the fact that the boys were making friends, and Jenni wasn't being distracted a couple dozen times a day with catastrophes, chaos, and confusion. For seven blissful hours a day she could concentrate on the business, and it showed. For the past two weeks, she had accomplished more work than during the entire month of October. And she was spending more time with the boys without having her mind preoccupied on all the work she still needed to do out in the shop.

It was a win-win situation that Tucker would ruin if he got expelled.

She watched as Corey took his position on the sled, then raised his head and waved down to her and Coop. She grinned, even knowing he would never see it, and waved back. Coop was waving beside her.

All three boys started down the hill at the same time. It wasn't a sharply steep hill, but it was long. On the far right-hand side of the hill was a natural bump that gave the more experienced sledders some air time. She had warned the boys not to go near the jump.

It appeared that every kid in Misty Harbor had the same idea as Coop had last night when he told the boys they would be going sledding come the afternoon. A foot of freshly fallen snow made for a great start to the sledding season, and because they had waited till lunch time, the roads had all been cleared and the sun was now shining.

They couldn't have asked for a better day. Or better company. She glanced at Coop standing beside her and saw the anxiety on his face as he watched the boys. She immediately returned her attention to the hill. Corey was doing wonderfully, heading straight down the hill, like she had shown him half a dozen times. Chase was right beside him. It was Tucker, as usual, heading straight for trouble. She knew allowing the boys to rub the runners of their sleds with an old candle had been a bad idea. Tucker was going way too fast and he was heading straight for the jump.

In horrible slow motion she watched as her son's sled

hit the bump and both went airborne. She could see Tucker's body leave the wooden sled, but his hands still gripped the steering bar. Someone screamed, and it might have been her. She took a step forward, only to be brought up short by Coop, who had encircled her waist with his strong arms.

Tucker's sled landed back down on the snowy hill. She blinked, and Tucker was still on his sled, skidding into the mountain of hay. Cheers erupted from every teenager standing around the jump. Her knees went weak, and she would have fallen if Coop hadn't had such a tight grip on her.

"He's okay, Jen." Coop's voice was low and hoarse against her ear. "Tucker's fine."

She blinked and then swung her head a couple of yards to the left, where Chase and Corey were tumbling out of the hay, laughing their butts off. Her heart started to beat again. She let out a sigh of relief.

"Did you see me, Mom?" yelled Corey as he wiped snow off of his face and out of his tousled red hair.

Somewhere in the mound of hay was his new hat, the one with Thomas the Tank Engine on it. "You were fantastic, hon." She couldn't very well tell him that she'd missed most of his run because of his suicidal brother. "Don't forget your hat. You don't want to catch a cold." She wasn't really worried about colds or his hat. She just needed time to catch her breath and to kill her middle child.

"Coop, could you please keep an eye on Chase and Corey while I go have a few words with Tucker?" She thought her voice was calm, cool, and collected.

By the look on Coop's face, she wasn't fooling him. Coop glanced over at Tucker.

The boy was surrounded by half a dozen bigger kids, all congratulating him as if he'd just won the qualifying run for the Olympic bobsled event. Short of tying Tucker's sled to the bumper of her SUV, there wasn't going to be a way to keep him away from the jump now.

"You're not going to kill him, are you?"

"If I answer that question, they could get me on pre-meditated murder." She started across the snow-packed ground to where Tucker stood. She had to dodge a couple of out-of-control sleds and nearly ended up on her butt twice, but she made it to within five feet of him. "Tucker James Wright, I would like a word with you."

Tucker glanced over at her and grinned. "Did you see me, Mom? I went flying."

"So I saw." She was going to keep replaying that horrifying scene of him flying through the air every night in her dreams until he was married and settled down.

Every one of the kids congratulating him had to be in elementary school already. One little girl, who looked about six or seven and was dressed in all white and pink, batted her eyelashes at him. Her son had turned five just last month and he already had a snow-bunny groupie.

She shook her head, reached into the gang, and grabbed ahold of the back collar of Tucker's jacket.

Tucker must have realized he was in trouble, because his smile fell. "Oh, Mom," he groused.

"Excuse us." With her free hand she grabbed ahold of the rope from his sled and pulled them both a good distance away.

Tucker kicked at the snow with the tip of his brand-new

boots, boots that now looked like they had walked across Antarctica on some polar expedition. What in the world had he done to them? Tucker had worn them a grand total of only three times so far. She didn't know what was going to go first, all her money or her mind.

"I told you not"—she hissed the word between clenched teeth—"to go over that bump. It was too dangerous." She distinctly remembered telling him at least three times.

"I didn't get hurt, Mom." Tucker wiggled all his legs and arms and put that "but you love me" smile on his face. "See? All in one piece."

She had Felicity to thank for that particular saying. Whenever there was a loud commotion and her niece beat her to the scene, Felicity always yelled that he was in one piece. Who "he" was never had to be clarified.

"You might not be once I get through with you." She was so upset not only with his blatant disobeying of her but also with the chance he had taken. Hundreds of kids every year got injured or died from sledding. "Do you want to ruin the day for your brothers and go home now?"

"No." Tucker's lower lip started to tremble. "I didn't mean to make you mad, Mom."

"What did you mean to do?"

"Show Mr. Brown what a good sledder I am." Tucker looked over to where Coop and the other two boys stood. They were laughing about something, which made Tucker frown.

The boys had been competing for Coop's attention all afternoon long. "Well, I'm not going to ruin the rest of your brothers' day, but as for punishment for you, young man, no toboggan run."

"Mom?" Tears welled up in his hazel eyes. "You said we could go down with Mr. Brown."

Felicity, Sam, and his sisters were on Suicide Hill with a large toboggan. Jenni had been so busy with the boys that she hadn't been paying attention to the death-defying run. She had told the boys they would do one run down the hill, as long as Coop was with them. There would have been room on the toboggan for her, Coop, and all three boys smashed in the middle, but now it didn't matter.

"I said we will go down, as long as everyone behaves themselves. You didn't behave, so no toboggan." She felt like such a meanie, but she was at her wit's end with Tucker. One of these days her son was going to get seriously hurt.

"Mom," sniffed Tucker.

"No, you may continue to sled on this hill, but if you so much as look at that jump, your butt will be in that SUV heading for home so fast, it will take a week for your head to catch up to it."

Tucker's eyes widened.

Great, she had now resorted to threats. She was a horrible mother. "Now scoot."

Tucker grabbed hold of the rope and scooted right over to his brothers.

Fifteen minutes later, Coop passed each of the boys and Jenni a hot chocolate. "Careful, the lady said it was real hot." Jenni and the boys were standing around one of the fifty-five-gallon drums that had a fire going and were taking a break. Jenni had gotten the tin of cookies that Dorothy had sent along out of the SUV.

"There's Sam!" shouted Tucker as he waved wildly.

Coop looked over to see Felicity, Sam, and his two

sisters making their way to them, pulling their toboggan. By the bright red cheeks and smiles, he would say they were having a good time. "Hi, guys. how was the run?" He hadn't been on a toboggan in a dozen years and he was itching to show Jenni his ability to master the five-foot-long sled and the ice. He just hoped he hadn't forgotten anything.

"Great," answered Hope. "Last night the fire department came out and squirted it down. It's solid ice beneath the snow." Hope was watching a group of teenage boys head over to the makeshift hot chocolate and coffee stand. "Come on, Faith. Let's get something to drink."

Coop tried not to chuckle at Sam's expression. The big-brother look was hardening the boy's face. Sam handed him the rope of the toboggan. "Here, you can borrow it now to give the boys a ride." Sam tugged on Felicity's hand. "Come on. Let's get something to drink."

Felicity balked. "Leave your sister alone for a moment. Nothing could possibly happen to her standing over there talking to some boys. Geez, Sam, you aren't her father."

"No, I'm her brother. She's too young to be hanging out with boys."

"She's fifteen. By next year she'll be getting into cars with them and dating them. Are you planning on going along for the ride?" Felicity sat down on one of the tree stumps dotting the area.

Coop almost felt sorry for the boy. He couldn't imagine what it would be like to have two younger sisters. He looked over at Felicity, and whatever she had been smiling about a moment ago was gone. The girl was pouting. Felicity was pouting a lot lately, but then again every time he saw her and Sam together, Sam's sisters were right there, and his father was in the other room, usually flirting with Dorothy.

He sympathized with Felicity. Dating in a crowd wasn't conducive to romance. He looked at Jenni's boys and had to smile. All three had chocolate mustaches.

Last night had been Jenni's and his time together, and it had been perfect, but short. He hated driving her home at midnight, as if she was Cinderella. Her snow boots hadn't been made out of glass, but it hadn't mattered. Jennifer Wright had stolen his heart as surely as Cinderella had stolen the prince's.

He was falling in love with not only a beautiful, intelligent woman, but a mother of three small boys.

"What?" Jenni was looking at him strangely. "What's wrong?"

Coop shook his head. "Nothing's wrong." In fact, everything was beginning to look right in the world.

"Can we go on the toboggan now?" Chase asked as he tossed his empty cup into a waste barrel.

"Yeah," cried Corey.

"Yeah," echoed Tucker as he pitched his empty cup.

"Felicity, would you mind watching Tucker while Coop and I take Chase and Corey down a few times?" Jenni looked at her middle child. "Until Tucker learns to listen, I'm afraid he's going to be missing out on all kinds of things."

Coop was proud that Jenni was taking a firmer stand with Tucker, even though he could see that it was killing her inside. His own heart had nearly stopped beating when he saw Tucker go sailing through the air. Tucker could have been badly hurt.

"Mom?" moaned Tucker in dismay.

"Not one word"—Jenni folded her arms—"or else."

"Yeah," groused Tucker. He pointed to the parking area where the SUV was, saying, "My butt will be there." His finger indicated the cove. "And my head will be there."

Chase and Corey's eyes grew round in their little faces. It was quite obvious that Jenni didn't usually threaten the boys.

"Right, and don't you forget it. Stay away from that part of the sledding hill."

Felicity slapped her snow-crusted mitten across her mouth and started to laugh.

Dorothy heard the cars pull up out front and the boys' shouts before they had even hit the porch. The family was home from their sledding adventure. She glanced into the dining room at the man who had kept her company all afternoon: Eli. The man was easy on the eyes and good for her spirit. Eli Fischer made her feel like a woman.

A young, desirable woman.

A woman whom she was not. There were mirrors in the house; she knew what she looked like—a grandmother of three rambunctious boys. Thanks to Estelle's magic, though there still was gray in her hair, it was camouflaged with highlights, and the new carefree hairstyle suited her. Estelle had talked her into buying a firming moisturizer for her face, but while her skin actually felt smoother, the wrinkles around her eyes were still there. To top it all off, in one month she would be fifty, and the hot flashes were getting worse. None of that seemed to matter to Eli.

The man was not only blind, he was nuts. As it turned out, he also was six years younger than she. She had asked.

Eli, who was perched on top of a ladder, must have felt her gaze, because he looked right back at her and winked, just as the front door flew open with a bang. The man was incorrigible. And oh-so very tempting.

All afternoon he had playfully flirted with her while helping make the big pot of chili bubbling away on the back burner. He also had managed to take down over half the wallpaper in the dining room. Eli claimed he was going to redo that room as payment for all the meals he and his daughters were mooching.

"Wow, Eli, you got a lot of it down." Jenni surveyed the work as she stripped off her gloves and hat. "Are you sure I can't pay you for all this work?"

"Dorothy's paying me in the most delicious cooking I have ever had, both for me and my kids." Eli winked at her mother-in-law. "I need the physical work to keep all the added weight off."

Dorothy huffed. Eli didn't have an extra pound on him. In fact, she was taking it as a personal challenge to put a couple pounds on him. "He told me he'll have it done for our Christmas Eve meal." She didn't see how, but she had humored him and brought home three wallpaper sample books from a store over in Franklin yesterday morning before the snow started. Jenni and she had come to an agreement that she would go through the books first, and Jenni would pick something from her choices.

"Well, make sure you eat early, because you won't

want to miss the Festival of Lights." Coop entered the room and glanced around at what Eli had been doing. "Will you be running new electricity, Eli?"

"Pete's doing that, and I'll be helping him put in the new windows in this room and the bathroom upstairs next weekend."

"Who's going to be doing the wallpapering?" Coop asked.

"What's the Festival of Lights?" Jenni looked at Dorothy as if she might have the answers.

"Got me." She'd never heard of it. "What's it got to do with Christmas Eve? Is it something to do with the church service?" She had seen in the church bulletin that the Christmas Eve service didn't start until nine at night. How would that affect their dinner?

"Wow, that's right, Felicity. You've never seen it."

Felicity had tugged off her boots and was now peeling off the snow pants she had on over her jeans. "What is it?" Felicity dropped everything on the canvas cloths Eli and she had spread out earlier in the afternoon.

"It's the boats," Faith said as she stood in the doorway with her sister, Hope.

Eli got down off the ladder as the boys dashed into the room from the kitchen. "What boats?" asked Chase.

"Can we go on them?" Tucker asked as he went to survey the room.

Dorothy watched as Coop moved closer to Jenni. Her daughter-in-law gave him a soft, dreamy smile. Something had happened last night on their date, and she really didn't want to think about it, but Jenni had had a certain glow about her when she came downstairs for breakfast this morning. Her daughter-in-law was moving on with her life. She should be happy. Jenni had been devastated by Kenny's death and had grieved for her son. Jenni was such a sweet, loving woman who deserved nothing but happiness in her life.

So why was Dorothy scared to death that Jenni was moving on without her? What was she going to do if Jenni found love with another man? Where would she fit in to Jenni's life? Where would she fit into her grandsons' lives? This wasn't even her house. Where would she go?

"Dorothy, did you hear?" Eli was standing right in front of her looking at her with concern in his pale blue-gray eyes.

"Hear what?" She rapidly blinked, hoping to hide the tears that had pooled.

"About the Festival of Lights?" Eli moved closer, protectively blocking everyone's view of her. "What's wrong?" he whispered. "Are you okay?"

God, she felt like such a fool. An old, selfish fool. The tears refused to be blinked away. For the first time, she admitted, "It's nothing, just a hot flash." She turned and hurried from the room, straight across the kitchen and right through the sliding patio doors in the family room to the outside.

Dorothy stared up at the darkening sky and admitted to herself that she was scared. She was losing Jenni, and with her the boys. Where would she and Felicity go when it was time to leave?

It took her a moment to realize she was in her slippers standing in a snowbank. When she did, she started to cry in earnest.

Chapter Thirteen

Jenni snuggled closer to Coop on the couch. It was just after ten, and the television was on low. The boys were in bed asleep. Dorothy was up in her room either reading or watching her television, and Felicity was camped in her room probably talking to Sam on her phone instead of doing her homework. It had been a busy day, and the boys had been exhausted from all the fresh air and sledding. "This is nice."

"What's nice—the peace and quiet or the company?" Coop nuzzled her neck.

She smiled and tilted her head to give him better access. "A little of both." With all the creaks and groans in the house, they would definitely hear someone walking around upstairs and heading for the steps. Besides, they weren't really doing anything. She could feel Coop's smile against her skin.

"Are you sure you can't come back to my place for a couple of hours, or maybe a week?" Coop brushed aside her long hair and explored the sensitive area at the nape of her neck.

"That's the best offer I've heard all day." She'd hated leaving the warmth and softness of Coop's bed last night to head back out into the cold.

"What about my invitation earlier? You remember, we were about to go down Suicide Hill alone. I told you I would get you down that hill." He playfully nipped a tender spot.

She remembered his very casual invitation for her and the boys to spend a weekend up at his family's cabin in the mountains. She had had her arms wrapped around his waist and her thighs clamped around his hips. She had been holding on for dear life and debating if she should close her eyes or not. Coop had promised her the ride of her life.

They had crashed on the second turn, and she had ended up facedown in a snowbank, eating the white stuff. For the rest of the afternoon, she had refused to go back down the hill without the boys on the toboggan. Somehow Coop managed never to have the toboggan going too fast when the boys were on board.

"You were serious?" She had been playing that invitation over in her mind all afternoon, but since Coop had never brought it up again, she thought it was just one of those things. They had been talking about the toboggan runs that were up in the mountains with the ski resorts and he'd just casually thrown out that invitation.

Coop sat back and looked at her—really looked at her. "Why wouldn't I be? The boys would love it."

"I'm sure they would." She tried to think, but her mind was pulling blanks. Coop really wanted to go away for the weekend with her and the boys, just like a real family. It was too soon. Too fast. Oh, hell, they had just spent the entire afternoon like a real family and the boys had loved it. Of course, Sam, Felicity, and Hope and Faith had been there too. But at the cabin they would be alone. Just the five of them.

Okay, maybe not *that* alone.

"I think you would like it there too." Coop straightened up and released her hair. "It takes some getting used to; it's on the primitive side. There is no cell phone service, and the electricity is supplied by a generator."

The boys would love going to the mountains. None of them had ever been on an adventure before. They had all been too small when their father had died. Vacations back then had consisted of a couple days on the coast, and once when she was five months pregnant with Corey, they had taken Chase and Tucker into Boston for a couple days. Neither of the boys remembered the trip. "What about a bathroom?"

Coop grinned. "Indoor plumbing. My mom wouldn't have it any other way." Coop reached out and covered her hands. "Showers have to be quick, and you have to wait about fifteen minutes for the water tank to heat back up, but it's beautiful up there. Not another soul in sight, and if we're lucky, we might spot a moose."

"Really?" Now, that the boys would love.

"What has you hesitating, Jenni? The sleeping arrangements?" Coop softly raised her hand and placed a kiss in the center of the palm. "There's one bedroom there, Jen. It's yours. As much as I would love to be sharing it with you, I understand. The boys and I will be bunking down upstairs. The entire second floor of the cabin is wall-to-wall beds, and an occasional dresser thrown between them for clothes. If I was looking for a romantic weekend getaway, I wouldn't be inviting the boys."

Okay, that answered that question. But there were still a million more. She gazed into his dark brown eyes and tried to find those answers. She couldn't.

"What is it, Jen?" Coop squeezed her hand. "What has you so concerned? The fact that we haven't known each other for that long of a time? What's it been, six weeks?"

"Halloween. I met you on Halloween." She remembered that horrible afternoon when she had been covered in pink shaving cream and dirt. "You fixed the porch post." He was right, it had been only six weeks, but it seemed longer. What would she do without him in her and the boys' lives? He had rescued Tucker from the roof and found Corey when he had wandered off. Coop had even helped Chase with his homework tonight while she gave Tucker and Corey their baths.

For the first time in over two years, she felt like a woman. A desirable woman. Cooper Armstrong had given her that gift.

"The roof was about to cave in on your heads." Coop brushed a lock of her hair behind her ear. "I couldn't allow that to happen."

"You were very sweet."

"Were?"

"Are. You *are* very sweet." She leaned forward and placed a quick kiss on his mouth. "Did I ever thank you properly for fixing that post?" She loved the way Coop's eyes darkened when he stared at her mouth, something he did all the time.

"No, but Dorothy gave me cookies."

"So you're satisfied with sugar cookies?" Her fingers

teased their way up his arm. Coop had rolled up the sleeves of his green flannel shirt, and she toyed with the dark feathering of curls on his forearms. Her breath hitched as she remembered the way the hair on his chest had felt beneath her fingers last night.

"I was satisfied last night"—Coop leaned forward and brushed her lower lip with his mouth—"twice."

She smiled against his mouth. "Hmmmm." She remembered every vivid detail of their first night together, including the part where she'd had to leave his warm bed to go back home to her boys. Her boys needed her. They were her top priority in life, but darn, it had been so hard to step back outside into a snowstorm. "You do know that can't happen very often."

"I don't know about that." Coop's mouth skimmed her jaw. "With you in my bed, I think it has a very good chance of happening quite often."

She chuckled. "I wasn't referring to that, even though that's a very nice compliment." Coop did amazing things to her self-confidence in that department. She'd never considered herself a sexy or desirable woman before. She had a mirror; she knew she wasn't ugly or repulsive. But sexy? Never. Jennifer Wright was a typical girl next door, or in reality the mother of three hooligans who lived next door.

"What were you referring to?" Coop gave a playful nip to her earlobe and then moved away.

"The boys." She curled her feet up under her and reached for her now-cold cup of coffee. She drank it anyway. She was used to drinking it cold. "I don't like leaving them like that, Coop. They don't understand dating and being left at home with Dorothy or Felicity.

This morning Tucker wanted to know why he couldn't have come to dinner at your house with me. He thought you didn't like him."

"Of course I like him." Coop frowned. "What did you tell him?"

"That of course you liked him." She grinned. "I tried explaining how adults like to have some alone time, to talk about things only adults like to talk about, and to watch adult movies, but I don't think he got it." She twirled the empty coffee cup around in her hands. "I know you understand that I come with three boys, Coop. Do you *really* understand what that means?"

"I will be the first to admit that I never dated a woman with children before, Jen. But, then, I never met you before." Coop brushed her mouth with a slow kiss. "I understand they are a huge part of your life."

"Huge?" She tried not to roll her eyes. "They *are* my life."

"What about Dorothy? Isn't she part of your life?"

"Of course she is." What a stupid question.

"And Felicity?"

"Don't be stupid." What was Coop trying to say?

"What about your company, Mistletoe Bay? They are all *part* of who you are, Jen. You're not just the boys."

Okay, he'd made his point. "Aren't you afraid to date a woman with three kids?" Any sane man would be running in the opposite direction as fast as he could. And that would be before he met Tucker.

"I knew you had three kids before I asked you out. I would have asked you out if you had ten kids, Jen." Coop's palm cupped her cheek. "Don't you understand that what I'm feeling for you is that strong?"

"The boys don't scare you?"

"Spitless, but they are part of you." He leaned forward and kissed her. "They aren't a complication, unless you make them one, Jen."

"Okay." She grinned. "If you wouldn't mind being spitless for the weekend, we'll go."

"Really?"

"Yes, really. But we can't go until after Christmas. There's just too much to do before then. There's the house to decorate, baking to be done, the business, Chase has to practice his role of an elf for the school play, shopping, the—"

Coop's kiss not only effectively stopped her from listing the thousand things that had to get done, it shut down her brain, leaving only the sensations of touch and desire.

Dorothy bustled around the kitchen singing along with the radio playing in the other room. Eli had turned his radio to a channel that was playing nothing but Christmas songs while he repaired the plaster walls, getting them ready for the wallpaper she and Jenni had picked out. It was the perfect evening to start her holiday baking and admire a strong set of shoulders.

Things were really shaping up in the Wright household. The dining room was being done, and Pete had finished all the tile work in her bathroom. The room was going to be gorgeous and she couldn't wait to use it. Showering with Buster the turtle staring at her bare bottom was unnerving, to say the least.

Eli had brought the girls over to help with the baking

while he worked on the walls. Hope and Faith were lovely girls, but they wouldn't be much help in the kitchen. Neither knew anything about cooking, except what they had learned in school in home economics class, or whatever they were calling it nowadays. Although both girls knew there were three teaspoons in a tablespoon, neither knew how to sift flour.

Well, they'd come to the right place. It wasn't their fault that their mother had deserted them, horrible woman that she must have been. What kind of mother sent her kids off to school one morning, packed her bags, and left behind a hastily scribbled note and arrangements with a neighbor to watch the kids until their father got home from work? Eli had been blind-sided by the desertion and the knowledge his wife had been having an affair for the past two years, but he'd held it together. It had been poor Faith, the younger girl, who had been traumatized by the whole thing. It had been Faith's first day of school.

Dorothy yanked her baking sheets out of the top cabinet with a little more force than necessary. If she ever met up with Eli's ex-wife, she'd throttle the woman.

"Can I help you get them?" Hope, who was taller than Dorothy, tried to take the trays from her. Hope had her father's height but probably her mother's coloring, like Sam. Sam and Hope both had rich brown hair and deep brown eyes, while Faith, who also inherited their father's height, had his coloring of blond hair and blue eyes.

"Thanks, but I've got them." She pushed those dark thoughts away and got down to business—cookie business. "Okay, you two, you each get to choose what kind of cookies you want to bake tonight." She pointed to the counter. "See that list? Each of you pick one."

This morning she had dropped the boys off at day care, and then spent the next three hours shopping. Her first stop had been Krup's General Store, where she had made a very impulsive buy. She had purchased eight plastic reindeers, a sleigh, and Santa himself. Thankfully a stock boy had come out and secured a couple of the boxes to the top of her SUV because they all couldn't fit inside.

Her grandsons had loved them on sight and wanted them up immediately. They all lit up and were supposed to go on the roof of the house. That idea had been vetoed by every male at dinner. The reindeers and Santa were going up on the porch roof this very minute. Coop and Sam were on the roof, with Felicity and Jenni doing the supervising from the front yard. The boys were all outside completing a snow fort by spotlight and keeping an eye on the grownups.

Not that Jenni and Coop would be doing anything questionable in front of the boys. It was Dorothy's own daughter and Sam who were turning her neatly highlighted hair grayer. They were growing entirely too close. They were too young to be in such a serious relationship. Both had their entire lives before them. It was time to have another serious talk with her daughter, or else she would be spending every free moment for the next several years in Estelle's Beauty Salon getting rid of the gray.

"Wow!" gushed Faith. "You can make all these kinds of cookies?"

"I can bake any kind of cookie that has a recipe, and some that don't." She wasn't tooting her own horn, but when it came to her passion, cooking, she knew her stuff.

Eli walked into the kitchen and smiled at the way his two daughters were hugging either side of Dorothy while they went over the list. "How about those orange ones with white chips in them?"

"Orange ones?" Dorothy smiled over at the man standing in the doorway wielding a tool covered in wet plaster. She refused to acknowledge the sudden heat that clutched her gut. Lord, he was magnificent, and he was in her kitchen asking for cookies. How could she refuse? "Orange as in color, or taste? What are they called?" She racked her brain for an orange cookie recipe.

"I don't know." Eli frowned, causing her heart to flutter. "One of the other mechanics' wife brought some in last year. They were the best cookies I ever tasted."

She raised a brow at that.

"I mean besides yours, Dorothy, my sweet." Eli flashed a boyish grin. "Do you want me to call her and ask what they're called?"

Both of his daughters giggled.

"No, just tell me what they tasted like." She glanced at the one open shelf in the kitchen. About thirty of her cookbooks were jammed onto it. The rest of her cookbook collection was upstairs in a bookcase in her bedroom. She pored over cookbooks like Felicity poured over fashion magazines.

"Those ice cream bars." Eli looked like he was concentrating. "You know the ones, they're orange on the outside and have white creamy stuff on the inside."

"Orangecicles?"

"Those are the ones." Eli flashed her a heated look that melted her knees.

"If you have our dining room done in time for our Christmas Eve meal, I'll serve Orangecicle cookies for dessert." She'd never heard of them, but there wasn't a recipe she couldn't find.

"I take it we're invited for Christmas Eve dinner?" Eli looked hopeful.

"Smooth, Dad," groused Hope with a roll of her eyes. "Why don't you just kiss her and get it over with?"

Dorothy flushed a brilliant scarlet as she stared at the girl. Was what she felt for Eli that apparent?

"Hope, apologize to Ms. Wright. You just embarrassed her." Eli frowned at his eldest daughter.

"I'm sorry, Ms. Wright." Hope looked to be the embarrassed one now.

"It's okay, and call me Dorothy, please." She refused to turn around and face Eli. "Your father isn't interested in me that way, Hope. He's only after my cooking." She gave the girl a big smile and winked. "Besides, I'm much too old for your father."

Hope looked unsure about that and Eli muttered something under his breath as he left the room and went back to the plaster.

"Now, which batch of cookies do we do first?" She didn't want to think about Eli or kissing. "Faith, you get to pick the first batch." She reached into the pantry and started to pull out the flour and the sugar while the girls made up their minds.

Felicity walked into the house and couldn't believe it. She smelled cookies baking. Her mother had started baking the Christmas cookies without her. Impossible.

It was their tradition. She had baked the holiday treats with her mother ever since she could remember. Hell, she probably had been rolling dough in her high chair.

She hurried to the kitchen and stared in shock. There was her mother, singing Christmas carols, off-key as usual, with Hope and Faith right beside her. Peanut butter cookies were cooling on racks and they were loading up the trays with chocolate-chocolate chip—her favorite. Her mother knew they were her favorite.

"Felicity," cried Faith, "look what your mom is teaching us to do." Faith looked so pleased and thrilled with herself. There was a swipe of flour across the young girl's cheek, and half a pound of it on her clothes. Faith looked like she had been rolling around in the stuff.

Felicity didn't blame Faith or Hope for baking the cookies and ruining the one holiday tradition she had thought wouldn't change. Her nephews were still too little to be baking cookies. She blamed her mother.

Her own mother was replacing her.

"Felicity, do you want to help?" Hope carefully and precisely placed the next mound of cookie dough onto the baking sheet in front of her. "Your mom said we have time for one more batch."

She felt her throat work, but no words were coming out.

"Felicity?" Dorothy glanced at her daughter with concern. "What's wrong?" She dropped the spatula she had been using to scrape the bowl and walked toward her. "Are you all right?"

Tears filled her eyes. No, she wasn't all right. Suddenly she felt sick to her stomach. If her mother wanted to bake cookies with Sam's sisters, well, fine. Let her. "I'm coming down with something." It was the truth. "I think I'll go to bed now. Tell Sam I said goodnight." She ran from the room and up the steps as fast as she could.

She could hear her mother calling her name, but she didn't slow down until she was in the bathroom and slamming the door. If they thought she was sick, her mother would give her the privacy.

The whole family was going insane. She purposely had come in from outside to see if her mother wanted to bake a batch of cookies for the guys. Coop and Sam were freezing their butts off putting up the reindeer and sled her mother had bought this morning. She personally thought they were stupid-looking, but the boys thought they were cool, so who was she to spoil Christmas for her nephews?

Someone had to enjoy this festive holiday season, because it sure wasn't going to be her.

Tears poured down her cheeks as she sat on the side of the tub. The one thing she had been looking forward to was baking cookies and listening to her mother try to sing. It was the one happy memory she had of the holiday season. And now it was gone.

She reached for a tissue and glared at Buster, who was in the tub munching on a piece of lettuce. Buster ducked his wrinkled old head back into his shell as soon as he saw her watching him.

Great, freaking great. Not even the stupid turtle wanted her there.

"Dorothy, please sit down. Relax for a moment. The kitchen can wait. It's been a long day. I'll help clean up in a minute, just let me sit for moment." Jenni was tired, sore, and worried. "I think we need to talk."

The house was in shambles. Between the dining room furniture, boxes of decorations, and tins of cookies, she could barely walk from room to room. Her legs ached from being up on them all day making soap. She had a headache from the smell of polyurethane and Tucker's endless list of stuff he wanted from Santa. But more important, her body longed for Coop. She wanted nothing more than to spend a week in his bed. A few quick kisses under the mistletoe were only frustrating her more.

"About?" Dorothy grabbed the last cup of decaf in the coffeemaker and sat. The kitchen and the rest of the house smelled like polyurethane. Eli had finished with the dining room floors tonight. All they had to do was wait until they were dried, and then they could wallpaper and move the furniture back in. Christmas Eve dinner was definitely going to be in the formal dining room.

"Felicity. I'm worried about her." Jenni frowned when she thought about her niece. "She's not acting like herself. Haven't you noticed?"

"She said she was coming down with something. I checked on her earlier, and she wasn't running a temperature. Maybe she and Sam are having a fight."

"I think Sam's concerned too, but he's not saying anything." Felicity had been awfully quiet today in the shop. Usually she and the two new girls she had hired part time were nonstop chatter and laughter. Three nights ago Felicity had said she was coming down with something. Whatever it was, her sister-in-law should have had it by now.

She had bid Coop a quick goodnight so she could go to Felicity, but the girl had already been in bed—not at all like her late-night self. Maybe they should make a doctor's appointment.

"Sam's just worried that football season is now over, and he's not the star of the basketball team like he had been on the football team." Dorothy drank her coffee.

"You don't like Sam, do you?" She knew her mother-in-law wasn't thrilled with how close Sam and Felicity seemed to have become, but she had thought Dorothy had finally accepted the fact that her baby was growing up.

"Of course I like Sam." Dorothy seemed shocked that Jenni would think such a thing. "Why would you think that?"

"Maybe because every time I turn around you're telling Felicity she shouldn't be that involved with him. Sam seems like a nice kid, Dorothy. No tattoos, no piercings, and he does pretty good gradewise in school. Felicity's seventeen, beautiful, and totally normal. She's going to have a boyfriend. Why not Sam?"

"I know she's going to date. I told her she can start dating at last year." Dorothy looked defensive.

She reached out and covered one of her mother-in-law's trembling hands. Jenni loved the woman like her own mother. "I'm not criticizing you, Dorothy. Nor am I telling you how to raise your own daughter."

"Thank you for that." Dorothy squeezed her hand.

"So what has you so scared?" She could see the fear in her mother-in-law's eyes. "That Felicity will become pregnant? Decide not to go to college after all? Get her first broken heart?" Something was making Dorothy act this way, because she knew for a fact the woman loved her daughter more than life.

Tears filled the older woman's eyes. "I'm an old, foolish woman, Jenni."

She snorted. "Yeah, and the moon is made of cheese. Give me another one."

Dorothy cracked a quick smile, and then it was gone. "Okay, I'm a stupid old woman."

She raised a brow. "Out with it."

"Okay, I'm scared." Dorothy pulled her hand out from under hers and crossed her arms.

"Of what?" She had known Dorothy for ten years, and while she had seen her bent over with grief, she had never seen her scared.

"That my daughter is growing up much too fast and soon she'll be out on her own." Dorothy wiped at her tears with a snowman-printed napkin. "She won't need me any longer. She won't be my baby. I'll be alone."

"What about me and the boys? We need you." Jenni smiled. She now had a better understanding of what was bothering her mother-in-law. Hormones and a case of the self-pities. She could handle this.

"You?" Dorothy snorted. "You don't need me, Jenni. You never have."

Okay, maybe she couldn't handle this. "Of course I need you. When haven't I?" She didn't know what she would do without Dorothy. She waved her hand to indicate the entire house. "What would I have done without you?"

"You would have managed just fine, Jenni. I'm more of a hindrance than a help." Dorothy looked around the room and shook her head. "Look at this place."

"It's well lived-in." She didn't mind the clutter too much. The dining room would be put back in order in a couple days, and then they could finish decorating. "When have you been a hindrance? If it wasn't for your cooking, Eli wouldn't be smitten and redoing the dining room for you." She grinned at the flush of embarrassment creeping up Dorothy's face.

"Let's not forget Pete."

"What about Pete?" Dorothy frowned.

"Everyone in town is talking about it."

"About what?"

"How Pete has been working here for almost two weeks now. He isn't known to be sober, if not conscious, for that amount of time." Cathy Bailey had questioned her about Pete Van de Camp just that morning when she had dropped the boys off at day care. Cathy wanted some work done at Kiddie Kare and she was curious as to how Pete was working out.

"What's that got to do with me?"

"You feed him." She laughed at the look on her mother-in-law's face. "You think I don't know you warm him up leftovers every day for lunch, or how you ply the guy with goodies on his way out the door in the evening? Last night it was a loaf of cranberry bread that had mysteriously disappeared from the kitchen."

"He has only stayed for dinner once." Dorothy looked unconvinced.

"That's because Eli kept glaring at him all through the meal. I'm sure Pete didn't want to cause any problems between the two of you."

"There is no 'two of us.'" Dorothy rolled her eyes. "I think the reason Pete is still on the job is the boys. You should see how his eyes light up when they get home from school."

"He lost his three children along with his wife in a house fire almost twenty years ago." She had never told

Dorothy why Pete tended to fall off the wagon. Dorothy had had enough heartache in her life; she didn't want to remind her of how Kenneth had died.

"I know, he told me." Dorothy eyes grew misty. "He asked me one day if it was true that the boys had lost their father in a fire. I told him yes, and I even showed him the picture of Kenny I keep on my nightstand." Dorothy rapidly blinked away the tears. "He said that Chase and Corey looked just like Kenny."

"They do." She saw Ken in his two sons all the time. Corey had his father's smile, and Chase's ears stuck out a little more than they should have. "Tucker has my coloring, but Lord knows where he gets daredevil the gene from."

Dorothy chuckled. "Pete noticed that too."

"He would have to be blind not to." Jenni hoped that whatever Tucker was going through, he would outgrow it. She kept telling herself it was only a phase, but she was afraid Tucker's phase was going to land him in military school.

"So, Jenni, how serious are you and Coop?" Dorothy nervously toyed with the handle of her empty cup.

Touchy question. How was she supposed to answer Ken's mother on that one. "We're just dating, that's all." It wasn't a lie, yet it wasn't the whole truth. There was no way she could tell Ken's mom that she and Coop were lovers.

"Coop's a very nice man, Jenni." Dorothy looked Jenni in the eye and smiled. "I like him."

"So do I." She did more than just like him; she had a horrible feeling she was falling in love with him. What was she going to do then? "You're not upset that I'm dating?"

"No, I knew you would one day." Dorothy sighed. "Life goes on, Jenni. You and I both know that. You're young, beautiful, and intelligent. What man wouldn't want to sweep you off your feet?"

"I'm also the mother of your three grandsons. They aren't baggage, Dorothy, they're crates, fifty-ton crates that own my heart."

"As mine." Dorothy's smile looked sincere. "Coop doesn't seem to be running in the opposite direction."

"Not yet. Let Tucker recondition the upholstery of his truck with dog shampoo, and we'll see how fast the man can run." Tucker had cleaned her seats once. It had taken her an entire weekend with an upholstery cleaner to get all the bubbles out of the fabric.

Dorothy muffled her laughter with her hand.

She loved seeing her mother-in-law laugh. It made her green eyes dance, and she appeared to be younger. Eli Fischer was making Dorothy laugh a whole bunch lately. "Do you realize what a wonderful woman you are?"

Dorothy blinked. "Me?"

"Yes, you." She reached and grabbed Dorothy's hand. "I have a feeling that maybe I haven't been telling you often enough how much I appreciate everything you do for me and the boys."

"Nonsense. It's you that holds us all together, Jenni. I throw together the meals and toss clothes into the washer."

"You do more than that, and you know it." Jenni could feel her smile wobble under the weight of unshed tears. "When Kenny died, you were the one who gave me the strength to go on."

"How? I was a complete mess. I crumbled, Jenni, and

you were the one to pick me back up. I needed you so desperately then."

"I know, and that was what pulled me through, Dorothy. Don't you realize that being needed by you at that time saved me? Between you and the boys, I was forced to get out of bed every morning. Forced to live until I could manage my own grief." She remembered those bleak, dark days. "Then a year ago I told you of my dream of starting the Mistletoe Bay Company, and do remember what you told me?"

"Not really. Probably something like, 'that's nice.'"

She shook her head. "You said, 'go for it.' Then you told me you would help any way you could. Why would you do that, Dorothy?"

"Because you are a daughter to my heart, Jenni. Ken was taken away from both of us, but you still had the ability to dream. I wanted you to have that dream."

"So you sold your home, uprooted Felicity, and moved two hours away with me to a rundown house on the coast of Maine. Why would you do that?"

"You needed me," said Dorothy in wonder.

"I did. I do." She left her chair and hugged Dorothy. "And you wonder why I think you are the strongest woman I have ever known." She squeezed her tight. "Don't ever change."

"If I'm so strong, why is it that I feel so weak most of the time?"

"It's your heart."

"My heart?" Dorothy stopped and looked at her.

"Yep, it's all squishy and soft and filled with love" —for the first time she called Dorothy what she had become to her over the years—"Mom."

Chapter Fourteen

Jenni glanced at the three bickering boys in the back-seat, and then at the man driving her SUV. Coop Armstrong was grinning like a fool and seemed to be enjoying himself. His smile was infectious. Who would have thought shopping for a Christmas tree would be so much fun? She glanced behind them, and spotted two other pairs of headlights. Not only were Sam and Felicity following them to Kreider's Christmas Tree Farm, but so was Eli, his two daughters, and, amazingly, Dorothy, who was riding shotgun.

"Are we almost there yet?" asked Tucker.

"How much farther?" asked Chase.

"Less than five minutes." Coop chuckled. "Can't you guys wait?"

"Tucker, stop kicking the seat," she said. Her middle child was antsy, and he was taking out his lack of patience on the back of her seat.

"Mr. Brown," said Corey, not to be silenced by his brothers, "Mom says we're getting two trees this year."

Coop chuckled, gazed over at her, and winked. "So I heard."

"Santa only delivers presents under the one, boys. There won't be stacks of presents for each of you in different rooms." That many toys she couldn't handle.

She had wanted to use Dorothy's heirloom decorations on their tree, while her mother-in-law wanted to use Jenni's. She had wanted the tree in the living room, near the fireplace and the stockings that would be hung. The boys wanted it out in the glass-enclosed family room so they could see it snowing when they opened their presents from Santa. Why they thought it would be snowing come Christmas morning was beyond her logic. Maybe they had been watching too many Christmas specials on TV. She had settled the argument by saying they were getting two trees.

That started a host of other problems and arguments. The boys mistakenly thought two trees had meant two deliveries from Santa. Dorothy still wanted to use Jenni's mismatched, hodgepodge, kiddie assortment of ornaments on the living room tree, while she thought Dorothy's heirloom decorations should be used in the more formal of the two rooms. Calling the living room formal was a joke; the only room in the house that fitted that description was the dining room. Eli had done an outstanding job, and the stubborn man refused to take so much as a dollar for all his hard work. Eli claimed that he probably still owed them another room or two for all the food Dorothy had been feeding his family over the past month.

Dorothy had spent the past two days hand washing china, polishing the furniture, and hanging new drapes.

Last night Eli had even helped her re-cover the seats of the dining room chairs with a fabric that coordinated with the new wallpaper. The room now looked like it belonged in a house-and-garden magazine.

The boys were under threat of death not to enter the room.

"Here we are," said Coop as he pulled off the highway and onto a side road.

She could see bare lightbulbs strung everywhere. There had to be hundreds of Christmas trees cut and waiting to be bought. They also weren't the only family out tree shopping tonight. The place was doing a brisk business.

"Wow, look at them all!" shouted Corey.

"Can we get a big one, Mom?" Chase had his nose pressed to the side window as Coop pulled into the parking lot.

"We can get one as tall as our ceilings allow us—and that will fit in the back of Sam's truck." The living room ceilings were ten feet tall, while the family room's were only eight. They were going to be some big trees.

"I want a tall one," said Chase as he unsnapped his seat belt.

"I want a really fat one," Tucker said. "That way Santa can fit more presents under it."

"I want a green one," Corey said as he grinned at Coop, who had turned around in his seat now that the car was parked.

"And I want you guys to stay with your mom and me. No wandering off on your own."

"No wandering off at all," she clarified. "You don't say 'on your own,' Coop. Last time I did, Tucker took Corey with him and went wandering off."

"Sorry, Mom," Tucker mumbled as he lowered his head.

She would have bought his pitiful apology if she hadn't seen the gleam of mischief that had been in his eyes before he could duck his head. But she had to admit, lately the boys, especially Tucker, had been on their best behavior. Of course, that didn't count the trick Tucker and the Higgin's twins had planned to pull. She had been forewarned and had easily spotted Fred in Tucker's backpack.

Santa was coming soon, and the boys all knew that the big guy didn't leave presents for naughty boys.

"Let's go find our trees and try not to act like barbarians who have never seen a tree before." She undid her seat belt and opened the door. Coop's chuckles filled her heart.

The boys piled out the back doors, and she grabbed the back of Corey's coat before he could dart out into the parking lot. "Careful, Sam's pulling in." She watched as Sam parked his truck. Eli had already parked two spaces down. She smiled as Dorothy joined her. "So how was the ride?"

"Comfortable, why?" Dorothy gave her a look that dared her to say anything.

"Just wondering, that's all." She tried to hide her smile as Eli joined them. Eli was on a mission, and it wasn't to buy a tree. It was to get her stubborn mother-in-law to see that a six-year difference in their ages didn't make him too young for her. Jenni thought they made a cute couple. Dorothy had other ideas.

Hope grabbed Corey's hand. "Come on, Corey, let's go see the trees." Faith had already run ahead to catch up with Chase and Tucker, who were in the first row of trees not so patiently waiting for the adults.

Coop reached for her hand and started to tug her toward the waiting boys. "Now remember, Jen, just because you have a ten-foot ceiling doesn't mean you have to get a ten-foot tree."

"I know that." She turned around and frowned at Sam's pickup truck. Neither he nor Felicity had gotten out of the truck yet, and by the looks of their silhouettes, they appeared to be discussing something. Her sister-in-law kept shaking her head. "Dorothy has an antique porcelain angel that has to go on top, so nothing over nine feet."

Eli and Dorothy had already joined the kids and were checking out the trees.

Jenni frowned and dug in her heels. "Let's wait for Sam and Felicity." Her sister-in-law hadn't even wanted to come on this outing; it had been Sam who had convinced her to come. Now it looked like he was trying to get her out of the truck.

Coop glanced over at Sam's truck. "Jen, leave them alone. They're fine. They're teenagers, they live on drama."

"I don't know, Coop. Felicity hasn't been herself lately." Dorothy was brushing off her daughter's behavior as nothing, but Jenni wasn't too sure about that.

"Well, you have to cut her some slack, Jen. She's dealing with a lot on her plate right now." Coop pulled her toward the trees and out of the parking lot.

"Like what?"

"Like everything." Coop lowered his voice so they wouldn't be overheard. "You can start with a new school, new friends, new boyfriend, new house, grades, learning how to drive, college applications, living with her nephews and sister-in-law, and to top all that off, Fred likes her room better than his cage."

"Well, putting it like that, I can see where she might be moody." Maybe Felicity was still adjusting to everything. It was a lot to ask of a seventeen-year-old.

Coop lowered his head further and nodded in the direction of Eli and Dorothy, who were standing really close to each other arguing over a tree. "Now, add on the fact that her boyfriend's father is hitting on her mother."

Jenni felt her heart sink. Why hadn't she thought of it that way? Instead she had been concentrating on how Dorothy has changed since Eli appeared on the scene. Her mother-in-law had been smiling more and truly enjoying herself. At first Jenni had thought it was because the boys were in day care and Dorothy had the day to do whatever she wanted. Dorothy might not admit it, but she liked Eli and all that male attention. She had even gone to Estelle's the other day and had a manicure. The only other time she remembered Dorothy getting her nails done had been the morning of her son's wedding.

"This isn't going to have a happy ending, is it?" Jenni leaned closer to Coop. She wanted to rest her head against his chest and cry for both her mother-in-law and Felicity. All she wanted was for them both to be happy, and right about now that looked impossible.

"No one can predict the future, Jen." Coop cupped her chin and gazed into her eyes. "I never would have predicted falling in love with a woman with three children."

Jenni stared back into his dark eyes and knew he was telling the truth. Her heart fluttered, and all her breath seemed to leave her lungs at once. Coop loved her! How could it be? How could it not be?

She sucked in a deep breath. Cold, fresh air once again filled her lungs as joy exploded in her heart. The smile she gave Coop came from the heart.

"Mom!" shouted Tucker. "Come see this one. It's real fat. Santa can fit my new bike under it."

"I want a new bike," cried Corey. "I asked first."

"You have a bike," yelled Tucker. "Ask for something else."

Her heart screamed in protest as her dream of a life with Coop faded. She turned and glanced at the bickering boys. Hope was hauling Tucker out from between the towering evergreens while Chase seemed to be inspecting every tree on the lot. Corey stuck his tongue out at Tucker as she slowly buried her face in her chilly hands and shook her head.

She gave Coop the only advice she could. "Run."

Her dream not only faded. It had crashed and burned. The next sound she would hear over her breaking heart was Coop starting up the car and driving away. The man might think he was in love, but he wasn't suicidal. She listened for the sound of the starting engine and peeling tires as he rushed from the parking lot.

What she heard was a far cry from squealing tires. She peeked out through her fingers and dared to hope. What she saw sent her heart soaring. Cooper Armstrong stood there with his head thrown back, laughing like a fool.

"Coop?" She slowly lowered her hands. The crazy man wasn't running.

Coop picked her up and swung her around in a circle.

Her arms gripped his wide shoulders and she could read every emotion on his handsomely chiseled face. Coop had no intentions, of running.

"My turn, my turn," cried Corey as he hurried over to them. "I want a turn."

Coop slowly lowered her to the ground, gave her a wink, and reached for her son.

The smile that had been plastered across her face slowly faded as she spotted Felicity and Sam standing at the entrance. Felicity had her arms crossed and was staring right at her. Her sister-in-law did not look happy.

Dorothy dashed into the house to start the coffee for the adults and hot chocolate for the kids. The men were outside getting the trees out of the truck, and everyone was freezing. Oh, but what a wonderful time they'd all had.

Eli had shocked Dorothy by pulling her into the shadows, while trying to find the perfect tree, and giving her a quick kiss. She had been too stunned to respond. By the time her senses came flying back in a rush, Eli had joined his daughters and declared that the tree they were holding upright was perfect.

It hadn't been perfect and just to teach the kiss-stealing sneak a lesson, she had taught his daughters how to pick out the proper tree. Eli had stood there grinning like a big ox while she explained how you had to make sure that the trunk was straight and that the tree was evenly filled out. She had even bent needles and shook the tree to test for dryness. The girls had been impressed and went searching for the perfect tree for their house.

Eli had tried to drag her back into the shadows, and she might have gone too, if Tucker hadn't jumped out from between a group of trees, growling like a maniac and nearly giving her heart failure.

All the way home in the car, she watched Eli's strong, capable hands on the wheel and wondered what they would feel like against her skin. What he would feel like in her bed. Wicked thoughts. Delightfully wicked thoughts. Eli Fischer might be six years younger than she, but the man was old enough to know what he wanted. He obviously wanted her.

She was tired of arguing with him. Tired of running from her feelings.

She tossed her coat on the back of a kitchen chair and got to work filling the coffeepot. If Eli ever tried to kiss her again, she'd make sure it was a real, proper kiss—one that would curl his toes and make him have these same crazy butterflies that were dancing in her stomach. She didn't like being the only one walking around with them.

She grabbed the milk out of the refrigerator as the men carried in the trees and once again the house was in total chaos. She couldn't say she liked the chaos, but she was getting used to it. With the coffee flowing and the milk warming she went in search of the cookies she had baked this morning. Dreamsicles was the name of the cookie Eli had been raving about. They were orange-flavored cookies with white chips. She had never made cookies with Tang before, but she would be the first one to admit they tasted just like the ice cream bar Eli had been talking about.

"Grandmom, can we have a cookie?" asked Corey as he sprinted into the room.

"In a little while." She loved spoiling her grandsons as much as she always did, but she was now making conscious decisions to cut back on too many goodies. Last night she had made them banana milkshakes using bananas and yogurt. Today, with the trees going up and little hands and feet frozen from being outside so long, they needed a celebration. A warm celebration. "Why don't you go see if Coop or Eli need any help setting up the trees?"

She was pawning off her grandson on the men, but she wanted to be alone to savor Eli's kiss. She frowned as she opened the tin and started to arrange the cookies on a plate. It hadn't been much of a kiss and there really wasn't much to savor, but it had been their first.

Dorothy shook her head at the absurdity of it all. She was acting like a teenager.

Warm, strong arms snuck their way around her waist and swiped a cookie. "Awh, Dorothy, you made them for me?" Eli's husky voice was low against her ear.

She closed her eyes, felt his warmth against her back and breathed in the scent of his aftershave. Eli used Old Spice, and the scent of it had been driving her nuts for weeks. If anyone walked into the kitchen, they might think Eli was playing around and teasing her for a cookie. She knew better. "You can have just one."

"One what?" Eli whispered and moved a step closer.

"Eli?" She watched as her fingers trembled against the ceramic platter shaped like a penguin.

"No one is here but me and you, Dorothy." Eli's voice was still low as he turned her around in his arms. "See?"

She glanced over his shoulder, but she couldn't see

anyone. They were alone—an amazing feat in this house. "We won't be for long."

"True." Eli brushed another fleeting kiss across her mouth. "I think it's time for me to repay you for all those dinners you've been feeding me."

The kiss had been too quick, but the butterflies weren't slow dancing any longer. They were doing the mambo. "You did repay me, and quite wonderfully. I love the dining room, Eli."

"That's good, but I was thinking about dinner, say, Saturday night?" Eli's fingertips traced her lower lip. "Please say yes, Dotty."

How could she not when Eli looked at her as if she was the most beautiful woman in the world. "Yes."

Eli lowered his head and kissed her. Really kissed her.

This time she stretched up onto her toes, wrapped her arms around his neck, and kissed him back.

Neither one of them saw Felicity standing in the kitchen doorway.

Friday night in the Wright house, and Bing Crosby was on the CD player in the family room and the Grinch DVD played on the television in the living room. The trees needed to be decorated, and a light snow was falling outside.

"I want to put that one up," Tucker said to his older brother.

"Pick another one." Chase hung on to the plastic moose. "This one is mine."

"Boys, please be careful. Some of those are break-able." Jenni stood on one side of the tree as Coop, who was up on a stepladder, tried to string the multicolored lights on the family room tree.

"Dorothy, are these all the lights you have?" asked Eli, frowning at the two strings of white lights in his hands.

Dorothy stepped around a box and smiled when she saw what Eli was holding. "So that's where those were. I knew I saved two strings from last year. I was looking for them."

Eli glanced around the room and raised a brow. "And you couldn't find them? Amazing."

She chuckled. A small elephant could be hiding in the family room and she doubted she would be able to find him. How did two women end up with so many holiday decorations? Between Jenni and herself, they had enough to deck out the White House and its fifty-foot tree in the front yard.

"Somewhere in this mess, Eli, are five boxes of brand-new lights. I picked them up the other week."

"Can you give me a hint on what color the boxes are?" Eli shook his head. "What do you need these for if you bought new lights?" Eli examined the string of lights before handing them to her.

"The boxes are green, but the bag they are in is white, I think." How was she supposed to remember what color Krup's General Store's bags were? She had bought them almost two weeks ago, and she was having trouble remembering what she ate for lunch today. Life in the Wright house was happening at a breakneck speed. She was holding on for dear life and loving every minute of it. She had never felt so alive.

Eli groaned. "White?"

"I think." She glanced over at Hope and Faith, who

were sitting in the middle of the chaos oohing and ahhing over Dorothy's collection of mercury glass ornaments. The girls were handling each like it was made of the finest crystal.

Eli's daughters were sweet, most of the time. Like normal kids they bickered about things, and Hope tended to wear too much makeup if Eli wasn't paying close attention. The one thing she did know about his daughters, they craved a woman's touch and she could barely keep them out of her kitchen.

"Dorothy, could you help us at our house with our tree?" asked Faith. "Dad isn't very good at decorating."

"Hey!" Eli looked insulted, but she could see the glint of amusement in his gaze.

"Dad, face it, you're hopeless when it comes to making a bow or wrapping the garland around the banisters." Hope joined her sister in the teasing. "Last year, Dorothy, he went out and bought nothing but gift bags so he wouldn't have to wrap one present."

She had to admit she was curious as to what Eli's home looked like. The way the girls always complained about all the stuff around the house their father made them do, it had to be neat and orderly—obviously not decorated, but tidy. Maybe she would go and help the girls add some feminine touches to the holiday decor, if Eli didn't mind. She might even teach the man how to make a proper bow.

She placed the strings of lights to the side and started to search for the lights that had to go on the living room tree first. Jenni had won that argument with logic. Dorothy's decorations would be going on the nine-foot tree taking up the entire corner of the living room. The boys were allowed to watch television in the living room, but they weren't allowed to roughhouse in the room. Rolling around and acting like idiots was to be done outside and in the family room, since the weather didn't cooperate at this time of the year.

Jenni had said that chances were, some pillow or toy would land in one of the Christmas trees this holiday season. It would be better if it smacked into the one with mostly plastic ornaments and shatterproof balls. Dorothy couldn't argue against such logic.

"Grandmom," asked Tucker, "can you fix this for me?" Her grandson handed her a tangled mess of red plastic beads.

She glanced down at the string of beads and wondered how they could have gotten so tangled. "What happened to them?"

"Corey did it." Tucker gave her that innocent look that she had grown to know.

She looked over at Corey, who was lying on the floor and keeping busy by lining up all the ornaments that could stand. He had quite a collection of Disney characters before him. Her gaze took in the room until she spotted Bojangles, trying to worm his way under the couch. It was an impossible fit, even if the mutt didn't have red plastic beads tangled around his back legs. "Tucker, go save Bojangles, and then I'll untangle the beads."

"Jen, are you sure all these bulbs were lit before I put them on the tree?" Coop asked. "I see at least one blue and one red out."

"Mom, can I hang this one now?" Chase asked, holding up a Santa.

"I'm hungry," Corey said as he sat Scooby-Doo, wearing a Santa hat, on top of a three-inch reindeer. "When do we eat?"

"As soon as Sam gets here. He had basketball practice after school." Eli popped his head up from behind a stack of boxes. "Found it!" Clutched in his hand was the white plastic bag containing five green boxes of Christmas lights.

Dorothy smiled at the look on Eli's face. The man sure looked proud of himself for finding one simple bag.

A knock sounded on the front door, and Tucker sprinted to go answer it. She glanced down at Bojangles, who was still trying to work his way under the couch, and sighed. Poor baby. If she believed in reincarnation, she would have to wonder what he had done in a previous life to come back as the family pet to her grandsons. She made a mental note as she dropped to her knees to rescue the bejeweled mutt to put something extra special into his Christmas stocking. A big thick bone tied in a ribbon would do the trick.

"Hi. You guys look busy." Sam grinned as he looked around at the chaos and stepped over a box. "Where's Felicity?"

Dorothy glanced up and frowned. She had forgotten to call Felicity down to help decorate. She had been on the way to the stairs to yell up when Eli had sneaked a quick kiss. Felicity had slipped her mind.

Jenni looked at Sam in confusion. "I thought she was with you at practice."

Dorothy jerked her head around and stared at Jenni. "What do you mean, you thought she was with Sam?"

"Yeah, why would Felicity be at my basketball practice?"

Jenni frowned. "Yesterday she asked if she could have this afternoon off work. Said something about helping decorate the gym with school-spirit banners for your upcoming games."

Sam looked at Dorothy. "Did she come home from school on the bus?"

Dorothy shook her head as her heart sank. "I don't know. I wasn't here. I was food shopping, and then I picked up the boys from day care." Why would her daughter lie to Jenni? "She must be upstairs in her room."

"You don't know?" Sam sounded angry. "What kind of mother are you that you don't know where your own daughter is?"

"Enough!" snapped Eli as he reached down to help Dorothy back up onto her feet. "Apologize to Ms. Wright this instant. She didn't deserve that crack. Felicity is seventeen, hardly the age where her mother has to be waiting for her every day to get off the school bus."

She reached out and laid her hand on Eli's arm. She could feel the tension radiating in him. "No, Eli, Sam's right. I should have at least checked on her when I got home with the boys." She blinked back the tears threatening to overflow.

"Sam, could you please do me a favor and go upstairs to see if Felicity would like to join the family and decorate the trees?"

Sam still looked upset. "Fine." He turned and stormed out of the room.

She pushed a box of silver garland to the side, made room to sit, and then lowered herself to the couch. What kind of mother was she? What kind of family were they that they hadn't even noticed that Felicity hadn't joined them? She had been about to decorate the tree without her own daughter. Impossible—Felicity always helped her decorate the tree. It was a tradition.

"Dorothy"—Eli squatted down in front of her—"it's okay."

She glanced over at Jenni, who was pale and biting her lower lip. Jenni knew it wasn't okay. Her daughter-in-law had tried to tell her something was up with Felicity, but she had chalked it up to teenage angst. The problem hadn't been with Felicity, it had been with her mother.

The boys, sensing something was wrong, hurried to their mother's side. Corey reached for Coop's hand.

In the distance she could hear the pounding of Sam's feet as he headed back downstairs. She could hear only one set of feet. Felicity wasn't going to come down.

Sam hurried into the room, clutching a piece of kiwi-colored paper. "She's gone."

Dorothy stopped breathing.

"What do you mean, gone?" Eli stood up.

"She left a note wishing us all a merry Christmas." Sam stepped forward and held out the paper to Dorothy.

She couldn't raise her hand to take it. If she didn't read it, it wouldn't be true.

Jenni stepped forward and took the note. Jenni gave it a quick glance. "She doesn't say where she went."

Corey started to cry. "Where's Felicity? I want Felicity."

Coop scooped the boy into his arms. "Don't worry, Corey, we'll get her back."

Eli placed a hand on Dorothy's shoulder offering comfort and support. "Sam, where do you think she would have gone? You know all her friends. Which ones would she go to?"

"I don't know." Sam was pale and shaken. "She left a pile of presents on her bed. They're all wrapped and there's one for each of us."

Dorothy looked at Sam and saw the tears in his eyes. Sam really did care for her daughter, and all this time she'd kept trying to break them apart. She had kept trying to put some space between them. She put her face into her hands and started to cry. How was she going to get Felicity back if she didn't know where she went? How was she ever going to make this better?

Eli pulled her to her feet and wrapped his arms around her while she sobbed. "Shhh . . . Dorothy, we'll find her. It will be okay."

"How, Dad? How are you going to make this okay? Don't you get it, Felicity doesn't feel like she is wanted here. She told me she felt invisible, that no one cared or paid any attention to her. How are you going to fix that, by dating her mother? Yeah, that's going to help Felicity one hell of a lot."

She cried harder upon hearing Sam's words.

"Not now, Sam. We'll figure out the how and the why after we have her home, safe and sound."

Eli cupped Dorothy's chin and forced her gaze to meet his. "Do you have any idea where she would go?"

She could see the worry on Eli's face. He did care about her daughter. "Sam. She would have gone to Sam." She glanced over at the young man, who looked crushed. "I'm sorry."

Sam nodded. "I'm going to check with all the kids she knows in school. Someone has to know something, or seen her. I'll have my cell phone, call me if she shows up here first." Sam turned and walked out of the room.

Chase and Tucker now were crying too. Jenni was brushing away tears and trying to comfort the boys. Hope and Faith started to cry.

Eli and Coop looked at each other. Neither looked comfortable in a room full of crying people.

"Okay, here's the plan," Eli said, stepping up to take charge of the situation. "Coop and I will head into town and check out the shops and anywhere else we can think. With the two of us, we can cover double the ground."

Coop nodded his approval.

"Jenni," Eli continued, "could you please call the sheriff and just advise him to keep a lookout for Felicity. He'll probably want a description of what she might be wearing. I don't think there's anything he can really do just yet, but he'll notify his deputies. It will mean extra eyes out there looking for her."

Jenni nodded and seemed to pull herself together. "I can do that. But keep in contact with us, and we'll call you if she shows up here."

Coop gave Jenni a hug and a quick kiss. "We'll find her."

Eli looked at his daughters. "I want you two to help Dorothy and Jenni take care of the boys until I get back, okay?"

Faith wiped her eyes. "Okay, Dad."

"We'll play a game or something with them." Hope held her younger sister's hand.

Faith cried harder as her lower lip trembled. "I'm sorry, Daddy. I didn't mean to make Felicity mad."

"You didn't, sweetie." Eli gave them both a hug. "It's not your fault. Call me if you need me. I'll be with Coop, okay?"

Both girls nodded their heads.

Dorothy wanted to die. Sweet, innocent Faith once again thought she had done something wrong to make someone run away—just like her own mother had done to her on her first day of school.

Eli gave Dorothy a long, concerned look but didn't pull her back into his arms before hurrying from the room to join Coop.

She slowly crumbled back onto the couch to do the hardest thing she had ever done in her life—wait.

Chapter Fifteen

Jenni glanced at the clock on the microwave; nine forty-eight p.m. and still no word on Felicity. Where in the world could her sister-in-law be? More important, whom was she with and was she okay? Sam had called five times within the past three hours. So far none of the kids from school had seen her, but he was still out looking.

Every horrible news report she had ever heard on missing teens came flooding back. She felt sick to her stomach.

She glanced over at Dorothy sitting at the kitchen table cradling a cup of lukewarm tea. The tears had finally stopped, but her mother-in-law's hands still trembled. Eli was trying to talk to her, but she had a feeling Dorothy wasn't listening.

Eli looked frustrated as all hell. She didn't blame the man.

The boys had all fallen asleep watching a movie with Hope and Faith earlier. She had carried Corey to his bed, but Tucker and Chase had to be awakened and prodded up the stairs and into their beds. She had managed to get their jeans and socks off, so they were sleeping in shirts and undies and hopefully having peaceful dreams. She doubted anyone else in the house would be.

Eli's girls were now out in the family room trying to straighten up the mess of Christmas decorations that had all been pulled from their boxes earlier. No one had felt like decorating the trees after Eli and Coop had left, so the boxes had been abandoned.

"What can I do to help?" asked Coop as he came up behind her to give Eli and Dorothy a bit more privacy.

A fresh pot of coffee was brewing, and she had lunch meat and cheeses sitting in front of her. Both Coop and Eli must be starving; they had checked everywhere in town and out of town for Felicity. No luck. They had been so determined to find the girl that they hadn't even stopped to pick something up for dinner.

"What kind of sandwich do you want?" She didn't even know if Coop liked mayonnaise or mustard. "You have to eat something."

"I'll fix it. Why don't you go ask Eli what he wants?" Coop took the loaf of bread from her hands and set it on the counter. Coop's hands were gentle and warm as they cupped her cheek. "Don't worry, Jen, she's going to be okay."

"How do you know?" She should have been more understanding with Felicity. She should have made more time. Ha, now there would have been a good trick— making time. There weren't enough hours in the day to do everything that needed to be done now. How was she going to make more time for Ken's little sister?

"Felicity's smart. She knew exactly where she was going and had it all planned out, Jen. Don't you see?

She told you Thursday she wanted this afternoon off."
Coop pulled her into his arms.

She rested her head against his chest and listened to
the strong, sure beat of his heart. Her hero had once
again tried to come to her rescue. Granted, he hadn't
found Felicity, but he had been there out searching
everywhere and never once balked or passed judgment.
She slipped her arms around his waist and held him
tighter. "How can you stand this family?"

Coop's chest vibrated with his chuckle. "Oh, Jenni,
my love, don't you understand yet?" He tilted up her
chin so he was gazing into her eyes. "They're part of
you. How could I not love them?"

She finally allowed herself to believe him. Coop
loved her. All of her; crazy family and all. He wasn't
going to go running and screaming into the night, dragging her broken heart behind him. Love for this man
filled her heart.

The ringing of the telephone brought them both back
crashing to the ground.

Dorothy flew out of her chair and ran to pick up the
phone. Before it could ring twice, Dorothy had answered it. "Felicity?"

Jenni held out hope, but it was slim. Every time the
phone rang tonight, it had been either Eli or Sam checking in to see if Felicity had come home. Since Eli was
sitting at the kitchen table, it couldn't be him, but Sam
was still out there searching.

She watched as Dorothy's face started to light up,
only to be crushed.

"She doesn't want to talk to me, Mitch?"

Jenni frowned but noticed Eli and Coop were both

glancing between Dorothy and her, so she filled them in. "Mitch is Dorothy's brother. He lives in Boston." How in the world had Felicity ended up in Boston?

Both men mouthed the word "Boston." She nodded and listened to Dorothy's end of the conversation. Mitch and Dorothy might be brother and sister, but they weren't really close. Mitch and his wife had six children, and though they were all in their twenties and thirties now, they all still relied on Mom and Dad to fix their problems. Mitch had his hands full. Dorothy and Mitch only saw each other for weddings and funerals.

"Bus?" Dorothy frowned harder. "Are you sure she's okay?"

Felicity must have taken the bus into Boston, then somehow made her way to her uncle's house.

"I see." Dorothy had tears in her eyes but was holding up. "Mitch, thank you for being there for her, for me." There was a brief pause. "Okay, I'll talk to you then. Could you please tell her I love her? That we all love her." Another pause, and then, "Goodbye, and thanks." Dorothy slowly hung up the phone.

"She's in Boston with Uncle Mitch?" Jenni asked.

Dorothy nodded but didn't take her gaze off the white wall phone. "He's making her something to eat and Karen's making up the sofa bed in the den for her. She's safe."

Eli joined her by the phone. "Coop, can you call Sam and tell him she's safe and in Boston? Tell him I'll talk to him at home later."

Coop pulled out his cell phone.

For the first time, Jenni noticed Hope and Faith both standing in the doorway to the family room. They must have overheard their conversation, because although neither was smiling, they seemed relieved. Jenni gave them each a big smile.

"Come on, Dorothy, now will you eat something?" Eli reached for her hand.

Dorothy moved her hand back, away from his outstretched fingers. "Thank you for looking for my daughter, Eli."

Eli frowned at the polite, distant tone in Dorothy's voice. "I didn't do it for a thank-you."

"I know." Dorothy was staring off into the distance. "I think it's time for you to take your sleepy daughters home, Eli." Dorothy wouldn't meet Eli's gaze. "Felicity's safe; that's all I care about."

Eli's frowned deepened. "I realize that our dinner date for tomorrow night might have to be postponed, so tell me what I can do to help."

Dorothy's shoulders slumped. "I'm sorry, Eli, but dinner will have to be canceled, not postponed."

"I'm not going to accept that." Eli had the appearance of a very determined man. "Don't you deserve some happiness in your life?"

Dorothy gave Eli a look that nearly broke Jenni's heart. Her mother-in-law really did have feelings for Eli, strong feelings. "I'm sorry, Eli." Dorothy turned and started to walk out of the room.

"So that's it?" Eli looked stunned. He looked like a man whose world was crumbling at his feet.

Dorothy's whisper was low, but everyone in the room heard it. "That's it."

Jenni watched as Dorothy left the room. For the first time she could ever remember, her mother-in-law not only looked her age, she looked older. She could hear Coop still talking with Sam on the phone, but it was Eli who held her attention. The man looked heartbroken.

She placed a hand upon his forearm. "Give her some time, Eli."

"Time for what?" Eli asked, still staring at the empty doorway Dorothy had just walked through.

"Time for her to come to her senses." What else could she say? Dorothy was a very stubborn woman when she put her mind to it.

"Okay, I'll give her time, for now." Eli tried to smile but failed miserably. "Come on, girls. Go get your stuff. It's time to go home."

Jenni watched as Uncle Mitch surveyed her shop and she gathered up some goodies for him to take back to Boston with him tomorrow morning. Doing the driving twice in one day was just too much to ask, so he was bunking down in Chase's room for the night. Chase would be joining his brothers in their room. Felicity was home, safe and sound. "So what do you think?"

"I think you're a genius." Mitch smiled as he smelled a bar of oatmeal cranberry soap.

"Thank you." She grinned. "But I was referring to Felicity."

"Oh." Mitch shrugged. "What the devil do I know?"

"You do have six children of your own." Anyone with half a dozen kids should know something about the workings of a teenage mind. Felicity and Dorothy were talking in the kitchen. To ensure their privacy, she took Mitch on a tour of her shop and gave the boys colored water in spray bottles. They were currently turning their once white and wonderful snowman into a psychedelic nightmare.

"Making them is the easy part; raising them is a whole different ball game."

"Tell me about it. You've met Tucker." Her son had greeted Mitch with an iguana on his shoulder and a plastic pirate sword in hand. Tucker had been demanding loot, gold, and wenches. She knew her son had no idea what "wenches" were. Sam must have taught him that one. Mitch had thought Tucker was adorable.

"You're doing a great job with the boys, Jenni." Mitch smelled another bar of soap. "It must be hard without their father."

"We're doing okay. I'm dating a very nice man, Coop Armstrong. You'll be meeting him tonight at dinner." It seemed so natural to tell Mitch about Coop. Life did indeed go on.

Mitch smiled. "Good."

"So no advice on Felicity?"

"Nope. I learned long ago that what works on one child won't work on another. Kids will do what they want to do, and it's our job as the parents to teach them right from wrong." Mitch lowered the bar of soap back onto the tray. "The rest of the time we pray that they remember those lessons."

"You do know that Dorothy is blaming herself for all of this?" She had never seen her mother-in-law so beaten before. Grief-stricken, yes; beaten, no. Dorothy had barely said a word all morning long while waiting for Mitch and Felicity to arrive.

"I know." Mitch frowned as he looked around the

shop. "I couldn't help but overhear the beginning of their conversation. I can't imagine what my sister did that was so terrible that made Felicity run away. Dorothy loves that child."

"We all do, but lately things around here have become more hectic than normal. Maybe having Dorothy and Felicity move in with me and the boys was a mistake."

Mitch snorted. "I've never met two women who liked to blame themselves for every little thing in the world that has gone wrong more than you and Dorothy." Mitch raised a brow. "If you did something wrong to Felicity, make it right. If you didn't, stop blaming yourself. Tell my thickheaded sister that too." Mitch zipped his coat, signalling the end of the tour.

"I will." She buttoned her coat and turned out the lights as she opened the door. The sun was going down, and the wind had picked back up. Time for the boys to come in. "Thank you for driving Felicity all the way home." It was at least five hours of straight driving.

"Been meaning to get up here to check up on my sister, Felicity, you, and the boys for a while now. Never seems to be enough time."

"You can say that again."

"There never seems to be enough time." Mitch gave her a teasing wink, stepped outside, and headed for the edge of the bay.

Jenni scraped the dishes and loaded the dishwasher while Dorothy put away the leftovers. It had been the same nightly ritual for months, until Coop, Eli, and his daughters had shown up on the scene. Then things had been different. It had been happier, with a lot of teasing going on, and the smiles had been genuine.

Tonight Dorothy's smiles hadn't been real. Oh, the corner of her mouth tilted up, but that was about the extent of it. Dorothy had been putting on a show for her daughter, but she hadn't been fooling anyone.

Uncle Mitch had headed home right after breakfast, and Coop had eaten dinner at his parents'. Coop wanted to give the family some alone time with Felicity. It had been awfully sweet of him, but she missed him something terrible.

Felicity carried over the last of the dirty dishes from the table. "I have to go do some homework."

"Okay, hon. Do you need anything?" Dorothy asked.

"Do you need the computer?" Jenni asked. She had planned on doing some paperwork for the business tonight, but if Felicity needed it, she'd gladly let the girl use it first. Dorothy had been holding off buying Felicity her own computer until she was ready to leave for college. The way technology changed, whatever was purchased this year would be almost obsolete in two years.

"No, it's just some studying." Felicity had been awfully quiet since her return. The girl dried her hands on a towel and then left the room.

"She's still not happy." Dorothy frowned at the empty doorway. "I don't know what else to do." There was a whole lot left unsaid in that statement.

"Give it time." She hesitated to approach the subject, but someone had to. "Dorothy, have you considered moving back to Augusta? It's not too far, and I and the boys will come visit all the time." She gave her mother-in-law an encouraging smile. Felicity was always talking about her friends from back there.

"You don't want us here?"

"Never!" She put a plate into the dishwasher with a little more force than necessary. "How could you say that? We love you here. *I* love you here." She softened her tone when she saw the look on Dorothy's face. "I just thought I'd be the one to say it first. Don't tell me that idea hadn't occurred to you."

Dorothy looked away. "If I thought it would solve this problem, I'd go tomorrow. Felicity says she likes it here now."

It took all her willpower not to say the obvious to that one. "Okay, second thought; what about you buying your own house, just for the two of you again, in town?"

"Maybe." Dorothy snapped the lid on the storage container. Tonight had been lasagna, Felicity's favorite, and the girl had barely touched her plate.

"I can check in with the zoning authorities to see if I can sell you a small piece of this property. You could build your own home and have us for neighbors." She was sincere and selfish. She didn't want Dorothy and Felicity moving back to Augusta or even into town.

"You would do that for us?" Dorothy looked like she was ready to cry.

"Name the day. The boys and I would miss your cooking, and Fred would miss Felicity, but we'll survive." She walked over to Dorothy and gave her a big hug. "Think about it. It's not a decision to make lightly."

"I'll think about it."

"Good. Now can you do me a favor and keep an eye

on the boys? I think it's time for me and Felicity to have a little talk."

"Maybe you should wait."

"For what? A lot of Felicity's problems were caused by me and the boys. I need to talk to her, to get it all out in the open. Then maybe a solution or two might become clearer."

"Okay." Dorothy wrung out the dishcloth and started to wipe down the table. "Good luck."

Three minutes later Jenni was standing outside Felicity's bedroom door knocking.

"Come in," Felicity called.

She stepped into the girl's room and closed the door. Felicity was flopped across the bed listening to some horrible-sounding music. The history book beside her wasn't even open. So much for studying. "Hi. Can we talk?"

Felicity shrugged, so Jenni took that as a yes. She sat down in the overstuffed chair next to the bed and resisted the urge to straighten something up.

"You're partly right, you know." Jenni had no idea how to talk to this angry young woman. This was not the sweet little girl Ken had introduced to her nine years ago. "While no one purposely ignored you or forgot about you, you were the silent one that fell through the cracks."

"So if I acted like Tucker, I would get more attention?" Felicity rolled her eyes.

"Is that what you want, attention?"

Felicity shook her head.

"Living together as one large family means you are going to have to speak up for yourself."

"And if no one listens?"

"Speak louder." Jenni grinned at the girl. "I have one hundred percent faith that you can make us listen—not that we'll approve of what you're saying, only that we will listen." She leaned forward in the chair. "This is a major adjustment for us all, hon. I'm not used to living with your mother and you, just like you're not used to living with me and boys."

"Don't forget Fred."

She smiled. "How could I ever forget Fred? He missed you."

"I was only gone one night." Felicity glanced around the room as if the green reptile would be poking his head out from behind something any minute now. "He's in his cage, isn't he?"

"Last I saw him, he was sunning himself under his heat lamp. I do believe he was naked so he doesn't get tan lines."

Felicity cracked a smile.

She liked seeing the smile back in Felicity's eyes. "So we have an understanding? You talk to me if something the boys or I do is upsetting you?"

"Yes, I'll talk, scream, and kick my feet if need be, to get someone's attention."

"Good." Now for the hard part of this conversation. "What about your mother. Doesn't she deserve some happiness in her life?"

"What are you talking about?" Felicity sat up on the bed, and that stubborn, mulish tilt of her chin was back.

"Haven't you noticed how happy your mother has been since Eli showed up on the scene?"

Felicity sat up straighter and looked away.

"Don't worry, Felicity, she sent him away. Your

mother chose you over Eli. It wasn't even close. You won hands-down."

"It wasn't a contest." Felicity's lower lip pouted. "Eli is Sam's father. My boyfriend's father. Don't you understand how yucky that is, Jenni? It's freaky and disgusting, and a thousand other things."

"It's none of those things. It is strange and a highly unusual situation, but running away wasn't the way to solve it. If you want to be treated as an adult, then you have to act like one. Mature, responsible adults don't run away from their problems, they talk them out."

"What's to talk out? I saw them kissing in the kitchen the other night."

"Your mother is an adult, Felicity. If she didn't want Eli kissing her, she would have said no." She tried to hide her smile. Felicity wouldn't see the humor in this for years to come.

"It looked like she was the one doing most of the kissing." Felicity sounded disgusted.

She bit the inside of her cheek to keep from grinning. "Eli's an adult; he could have said no." She wanted to cheer Dorothy on. "So what has you so upset, that she was kissing a man? Or that it was Eli she was kissing?"

Felicity hesitated.

"What do you think is going to happen to your mother when you go off to college in two years, or get married, or even move out on your own? Is your mother supposed to stay single and lonely while waiting patiently for you to stop in and visit her? Doesn't she deserve a life?"

"Mom will always have you and the boys. She won't be lonely."

"What if I meet someone special, fall in love, and get married? What happens when the boys grow up? Why must your mother's life revolve around everyone else? Don't you think she should have a life of her own? It won't mean that she will stop loving you, or me, or the boys."

Felicity cracked a smile. "Is that someone special Coop?"

She couldn't answer that question without giving away the fantasy running through her mind. Coop was indeed that someone special, but she hadn't gotten around to telling him yet. She didn't want this conversation to be about her. It was all about her sister-in-law. "What about Sam?"

"What about him?"

"Have you talked to him today?" She had heard Felicity's cell phone going off all day long. Not once had she seen the girl answer it.

"Not yet." Felicity started to bite one of her fingernails. "I'm not sure what to say to him."

"You hurt him. When you ran from this family, you ran from him too."

"I didn't mean to hurt him."

"Then you'd better talk to him. Call him, or at least answer his calls." She stood and stretched the tension out of her neck. Their talk had gone better than she had dared to hope. "Hon, I have known you for nine years and love you like a sister. Never once in all that time did I ever think you were spoiled or selfish, until now. Think about it."

She left Felicity sitting on her bed.

* * *

Coop glanced around his apartment and tried not to laugh. It looked like Santa's workshop, and he was one of the elves. He had only himself to blame for that one. It had been he who insisted on putting together not one but two bicycles. He had argued with Jenni not to pay the extra forty-five dollars on each bike to have the store assemble them. How hard could putting a bike together possibly be?

The room filled with parts gave him his answer—impossible. The instructions were written in five languages, and one appeared to be English but he'd be damned if they made any sense to him.

"Are you sure I can't help you with that?" Jenni stopped wrapping a present and smiled over at him.

"I've got it covered." She didn't have to know he was definitely dropping Corey's bike over at his dad's on the way to work tomorrow morning for his father to put together. His father would love the challenge. Tucker's bike was scattered everywhere and if he was lucky, it might be together by Christmas Eve. "Remember our agreement—I'll do the bikes, you do the bows."

"The way you were frowning at the instructions, I thought maybe you had a problem." Jenni took a long gold ribbon and wrapped it around the box. She knotted the ends and then proceeded to make a perfect bow.

"How did you do that?" He stood up and walked into his kitchen. Rolls of wrap, tape, tags, and ribbons were everywhere. "I still remember my mom making me stick my finger on top of the knot to keep it tight."

"Ribbons improved the last decade." Jenni grinned. "I appreciate you letting me store all the kids' presents here, Coop. You have no idea what Tucker is capable of when there are presents in the house."

He chuckled. "No problem. I don't mind sharing my bedroom with them." All the wrapped presents were stored on the floor between one side of the bed and the wall. He no longer could get out on that side of the bed. "Of course, I'd rather be sharing it with a certain someone."

"Oh yeah, who?" Jenni wrapped a silver ribbon around his neck and pulled him down for a quick kiss. "Naughty boys don't get anything in their stockings for Christmas. How naughty have you been?" Jenni playfully nipped at his lower lip.

"That's it. I'll show you how naughty I can be." He swept her up into his arms, carried her into the bedroom, and dropped her onto the center of the bed. He followed her down and let his arms take his weight. Jenni was a tiny thing. "How long can you stay out?" He felt like he was a teenager again and his girlfriend had a curfew.

"Eleven or so." Jenni tugged on the ribbon, bringing him closer. "Felicity's watching the boys tonight for me."

He nuzzled the side of her neck. "Remind me to buy her something special for Christmas, like a BMW." His hands started unbuttoning Jenni's blue, silky blouse. "Did I tell you today how beautiful you are?" His lips caressed warm, smooth skin as they followed his fingers. He could feel Jenni trying to tug at the buttons on his shirt.

"Twice, and one of those times was in the action-figure aisle of the toy store." Jenni pushed her hands in between their bodies. Giving up on his buttons, she reached for his belt. "You nearly gave the stock boy a lesson he shouldn't be getting until at least the twelfth grade."

Jenni's fingers weren't playing fair. "Who's being naughty now?"

"Me," purred Jenni. "I already got what I wanted for Christmas—you hard and wanting me."

"That was your Thanksgiving present." His eyes crossed as her fingers started to stroke his zipper. With a flick of his fingers, he undid the front clasp of her bra. His gaze feasted on two perfectly formed breasts. He swirled his tongue over one extended nipple, then gave the other one the same treatment. He smiled at the way Jenni's hips arched up. "Now be a good girl and tell me what you really want for Christmas."

"You, I want you." Jenni's fingers wrapped around him, and he was the one to arch his hips this time.

"You already have me." Christmas was four days away, and he hadn't gotten her a gift yet. He had been to the mall twice, but nothing seemed special enough. He had haunted three jewelry stores with big-haired and bigger cheesy–smiling clerks, looking for that special gift. At all three jewelry stores he had ended up at the same spot, in front of the engagement rings.

How could he ask a woman he'd just met on Halloween to marry him? It was too soon. Jenni hadn't once said she loved him, even though he was positive that she did. He could see it in her eyes.

Jenni's fingers tightened. "I don't have you where I want you, Coop."

He smiled against the gentle swell of her breast. "And where would that be?" His fingers got busy on their own, unsnapping her jeans and tugging them down. He groaned when Jenni released him to help.

Coop rolled onto his back and started to yank off his own clothes. Since Jenni was already half undressed, she was naked before him. Her hands were strong and sure as they pulled his shirt over his arms and tossed it on top of the presents. He grinned. This was his Jenni, so wild, sweet, and wanting him.

Jenni captured his hands and straddled his thighs. Her grin was sexy and hot as she stared down at him. "I'm going to put you where I want you, Coop."

His breath slammed out of his lungs as he tried reaching into the nightstand drawer. "There is a Santa Claus, and he delivered early."

Jenni slowly shook her hair as she lowered her mouth toward his. "Santa won't be here for another four days." Silky dark hair teased the sides of his face. "It's just me and you." Jenni's breath played across his waiting mouth.

Coop could have easily reversed their positions, but why spoil all her fun? He was rock-hard and ready for anything Jenni might want to do. "Good, because I don't think I can wait four more days." He'd be lucky to last four more minutes. His fingers clutched a foil packet.

Jenni's nipped at his chin and then trailed her moist lips down his throat. "How long can you last?"

Plump breasts skimmed his chest and stomach as Jenni moved lower. His thighs started to tremble when he realized she wasn't stopping. "I ummmm . . ."

Jenni smiled against his stomach. "That's what I thought." She moved lower.

With a flick of her tongue, his hips arched off the mattress and he nearly embarrassed himself. He closed his eyes and swallowed when he felt the heat of her mouth engulf him. The woman was trying to kill him.

With a loud growl, he grabbed Jenni's shoulders, pulling her up and over onto her back. "Enough!"

Jenni wrapped her arms around his neck and smiled. "Not yet, it isn't."

He could feel the satiny smoothness of her thighs as they clutched his hips. "Now where exactly do you want me, Jen?" He positioned himself between her thighs but kept his arousal away from her. "Here?"

"No." Jenni arched her hips, trying to bring him closer.

He barely teased her opening with the head of his penis. "What about here?"

Jenni wrapped her legs around his hips and locked her ankles. "Deeper," came out in a hoarse plea as her head moved side to side.

"Like this?" He felt his arms tremble as he slowly started to enter her. He was using every ounce of self-control not to sink into her heat.

"More." Jenni's breath was fast and shallow. "Please."

He could no more refuse her than breathe. With a groan of pure pleasure he slowly pulled out of her and then plunged.

Jenni cried her release as he thrust deeper, and then deeper still.

The sweet convulsions that tightened around him sent him over the edge. He arched his back and climaxed.

Chapter Sixteen

Jenni snuggled closer to Coop under the comforter. Lying with Coop was fantastic. Okay, the sex had been fantastic; the afterglow was warm and wondrous. She trailed her fingers over his chest and smiled. "I didn't get all the wrapping done."

"There's still time left before the big day." Coop's fingers were toying with the ends of her hair.

"Time for you to get the bikes together?" She glanced at the bedside clock. She had an hour yet before she turned into a pumpkin.

"Right after I get my mechanical degree." Coop chuckled softly. "How they can make something so simple so complicated is beyond me."

"You'll figure it out."

"You have that much faith in me?" Coop seemed curious.

She lifted her head and looked at him. "Yes, one hundred percent." Plain, simple, and the truth.

Coop's expression fell and his body stiffened. "Don't

keep looking at me as if I'm some type of hero, Jenni. I'm not perfect."

"I never said you were." She sat up, bringing the sheet with her. Something was bothering Coop; she had seen a flash of pain pass across his face. "What's up?"

Coop wouldn't meet her gaze. "There's something we need to talk about."

"Like?" She had a horrible sick feeling in the pit of her stomach.

"Let's get dressed and then we'll talk."

"No, let's talk now." Coop looked like he was ready to run. Naked men usually didn't run, and besides, Coop was on the side of the bed with all the presents. He would either have to look like a fool crawling to the bottom of the bed, get past her, or stay put.

Coop sighed but stayed where he was. "I got a feeling Sam never told you. I was a chicken by hoping that he would so I didn't have to."

"Told me what?" What did Sam have to do with anything? Felicity and Sam were seeing each other again, and both seemed happy. Dorothy put on a great front, but she was miserable as all get out. Eli had been out of the picture for over a week now.

"Remember I went in to the high school the one evening and talked to the football team after practice?" Coop pulled himself up into a sitting position and used the headboard as a backrest. His portion of the sheet was covering his lap, but his chest was bare.

"Vaguely." How did Coop expect her to remember her own name when he was sitting naked less than two feet from her and looking so scrumptious?

"I go into high schools a lot to talk to the athletes."

"That's nice." She frowned when she spotted a red scratch on Coop's chest. She must have just done that while they were . . .

"Would you stop looking at my chest when I'm talking?" Coop grabbed a pillow and held it in front of him like he was protecting his virtue.

She grinned. "It's a nice chest."

"Thank you, but pay attention. You might not think it's so nice when I'm done."

Now that put an end to her wicked thoughts. "Continue." What she wanted to say was to hurry the hell up and get to the point. Why wouldn't she like him? Hell, she was in love with him.

"Didn't you ever wonder why I dropped out of college, gave up football, and moved to California?"

"Sure, I just figured you'd tell me about when you were ready." Coop couldn't have done something really bad. His parents still loved him. Sam's football coach had been thrilled to see him at their game. "Why did the hero worship die from Sam's eyes? What did you tell them?" Come to think of it, when the entire football team had been at her place, the day Corey had gone missing, they all had been friendly and polite toward Coop. But they hadn't been hanging on Coop's every word, like they had been at that Friday-night game.

"The truth."

"What truth?"

"I used drugs." Coop watched her closely.

She blinked. "Excuse me?" She couldn't have heard right. Coop wasn't a druggie. He was her UPS man. He was Misty Harbor's football hero with the most receiving yards, or something like that.

"I used steroids, Jen."

"Isn't that illegal?"

"Yes." Coop sat there and watched her.

A thousand thoughts flashed through her mind. She was sitting naked in bed with an illegal-drug user. Impossible! She looked at Coop and the resolve upon his face. Was he expecting her to leave just like that? Coop had another thing coming. She was made of stronger stuff than that. She wanted the story, the whole story, and then she would make up her mind if she would leave or not.

"Want to start at the beginning?"

"You're not leaving?" Coop relaxed just a bit.

"I'm Tucker's mom. You're going to have to do better than that if you're trying to frighten me away."

Coop grinned and relaxed further. "You know most of it already. Local high school football star gets offered a full scholarship at a semi-decent college."

"Semi-decent?"

"It wasn't Ohio or Penn State, but said football star figured he would shine enough that one of the major football colleges would pick him up in his last two years." Coop shook his head. "Said football star was a fool."

"To be seen." She clutched the sheet to her breasts with one hand and waved the other. "Continue."

"Going from high school to college ball was a whole different ball game"—Coop gave her a lopsided smile—"pun not intended."

She rolled her eyes and waited.

"Coach Rawlins took me under his wing, you could say. He was going to show me how to shine. How to improve my game. How to get to the NFL." Coop gave a self-deprecating laugh. "How to use steroids to reach those goals, and make himself look good in the process."

Her stomach turned. "Your coach encouraged you to take steroids?"

"Encouraged, no. To Coach Rawlins's thinking, it was mandatory. Who do you think got us the stuff?"

"Us?" Now she knew she was going to be sick.

"Four of us. The four shining stars." Coop closed his eyes but not before she saw the pain again.

"How long were you taking the stuff?"

"A little bit over a year. We were at the end of our regular season. Last game and we were undefeated. The team we were going up against was also undefeated and, if push came to shove, probably better than us. Push was going to come to shove. Brian Dole was our quarterback and a shining star. He was from some hick town in Tennessee and desperately needed to prove himself. Three days before the big game he got ahold of the coach's supply and figured if one syringe was good, three would be better."

She closed her eyes and wanted to close her ears.

"They found him dead in the weight room later that night. Everything broke loose. I stuck around long enough to testify and then took off for California."

"Why not come home to Misty Harbor?"

"Sullivan, my parents live in Sullivan." Coop shook his head. "I couldn't face the town, or my parents. I had known it was wrong, yet I took the drug anyway."

"But you were just a kid. You were—what?—eighteen?"

"Nineteen. Old enough to be away at college and making my own decisions."

"But it was your coach who gave it to you."

"I could have said no." Coop's lips were twitching.

"He could have kicked you off the team. You would have lost your scholarship." She glared at him. "Why are you laughing at me?"

"I'm not laughing, Jenni." Coop reached out and cupped the back of her head. "I did something that was illegal, and you're defending me." Coop forced her mouth closer to his. "I love you, Jennifer Wright" was whispered across her lips right before he kissed her.

Jenni felt herself sink into the kiss. The sheet slid down her chest as Coop hauled her up onto his lap—his very hard lap. She broke the kiss and slapped her hand onto his chest. "Don't you ever do anything so stupid again. Do you have any idea what that stuff can do to your body?"

Coop grinned and held up his fingers in the Boy Scout–promise position. "Promise."

She nodded, then blinked as a new thought came to her. "Is that why you're so good at . . ." She swept her hand toward the rumpled sheets and wiggled her butt on the hard evidence of his arousal.

Coop grinned, then threw back his head and laughed himself silly.

Felicity glanced at the clock and tried not to allow her excitement to show. She had a very special Christmas present for her mother, one that couldn't wait till Christmas morning, nor would it fit under the tree.

"What do you think, Felicity? Should we have dessert now, or wait until we get back from the Festival of Lights?" Dorothy smiled at her daughter as she straightened up the kitchen.

She put the last glass in the dishwasher. "Since it's only four now, let the boys have some cookies if they're hungry. After the festival we can make up sandwiches with all the ham that was left and you can serve your cake then." She was getting tired of her mother asking her opinion on every little matter.

The age-old saying was true: Be careful what you wish for; you just might get it. Well, she had been the one who wanted to have a bigger part in this family. She had been foolish enough to run off to Boston to prove it. Her mother was only granting her wish by seeing that everything met with her approval.

French toast and blueberry pancakes were now served every morning for breakfast. Her laundry was done to perfection and there was always an abundance of bath towels in their bathroom. Her mother had taken her clothes shopping twice for Christmas, and even Fred hadn't made an appearance in her room since Uncle Mitch had brought her home.

If she hadn't checked it herself, she would have sworn her mother had welded Fred's cage closed.

It was enough to make Felicity scream. She couldn't take one more day of being cuddled and coddled by her mother. At least Jenni treated her about the same. Her mother needed a hobby—one that didn't include her.

Sam walked into the room and gave her a wink. It was time. Only Sam knew of her surprise. She ducked her head as the doorbell rang.

"I'll get it," shouted Tucker from the back room.

"I will," yelled Corey.

Both boys raced for the door. Tucker had the speed, but Corey was finally starting to exert himself. Her littlest nephew grabbed onto the back of Tucker's sweatshirt and hung on for dear life.

She watched as her mother left the kitchen to go see who was at the door. Sam grabbed her hand and pulled her after her mother.

Tucker yanked open the front door. "Yeah?"

"Tucker James, that is not how we . . ." Dorothy's voice trailed off when she saw who was standing there.

"Eli!" shouted Tucker.

Corey picked himself up off the floor, where he had slipped, and grinned at Hope and Faith standing on the front porch. "Hi, we're going to go see the boats."

Felicity rolled her eyes when she realized her mother wasn't going to invite Eli and the girls in. She stepped farther into the room. "Come on in Eli, girls."

Eli was holding a tall crystal vase filled with red roses and baby's breath. He held it out toward Dorothy. "These are for you."

"Me?"

"Yes, Mom, he said they're are for you." Felicity could tell Eli was nervous and not quite sure what was going on. The roses were gorgeous, but she liked the bouquet of pure white tulips that had been gracing the buffet in the dining room when she got home from school the other day. Her mother never said where they had come from, but Felicity had known. She looked over at Jenni, Coop, and Chase, who had come to see what the commotion was all about. "Mom, I invited Eli and the girls over."

"You did?"

"Yes." Inviting Sam's father over had been one of the hardest things she had ever done. By all rights, the man should have been furious at her, but he wasn't.

"Eli, I want to give you your Christmas present now." Felicity smiled at the man who wouldn't, or couldn't, take his gaze off her mother. "You don't even have to unwrap it."

Eli's gaze cut to her. "I thought you said your mother knew about us stopping over."

She shrugged. "I fibbed."

Sam reached for her hand and pulled her to his side. "She lied, but it was for a good reason."

"What reason?" Eli asked.

"To give you your present." The man was turning stubborn on her.

Eli glanced around. "What present?"

"This one." she grinned and squeezed Sam's hand harder. "Eli Fischer, I give you permission to date my mother."

Eli's gaze flew back to Dorothy. "You do?"

"Two conditions." She held up two fingers of her free hand. "One, you hurt her in any way, shape, or form, and we are sending Tucker to come live with you." She ignored Coop's chuckle from the back of the room. "Two, no mushy stuff around me."

"Deal." Eli smiled.

She glanced over to Jenni, who was grinning and nodding her head in approval. She knew the situation was going to be awkward, but she also knew it was the right thing to do. Her mother truly did deserve some happiness in her life, and if Eli was the one to do that, who was she to stop it?

"Give me those. I'll put them in the kitchen for you, Mom." Dorothy still hadn't reached for the vase.

"Hope, come see our tree," said Tucker as he pulled on the girl's hand.

Corey reached for Faith's hand. "Coop set up a train under the tree. It's cool. Come see."

The kids all hurried from the room. Jenni and Coop followed.

Sam started to steer her from the room toward the kitchen. "We'd better put them in water, Felicity."

"They are in water." She held the vase up for Sam to see."

"It needs more." Sam groaned, trying to hurry her from the room.

"Sam, what are you doing?" She wanted to make sure her mother was okay with her surprise.

"You said no mushy stuff in front of you." Sam practically pushed her into the kitchen. "In case you didn't notice, there was mistletoe hanging right above their heads." Sam's voice was filled with laughter.

"Oh, yuck."

Coop tugged a laughing Jenni all the way to her shop. It was freezing outside, but neither of them seemed to care. He had slipped Hope a ten-dollar bill to keep an eye on the boys for a few minutes. He had something very important to ask Jenni.

"We could have gotten our coats," teased Jenni as she unlocked the door.

"They were in the foyer." Coop hurried her through the door as soon as it opened. "Eli and Dorothy are in the foyer."

Jenni laughed. "I wonder if they are doing any of that

mushy stuff." Jenni reached for the lights, but Coop's hand stopped her.

"Leave them off." There was enough light given off by the low-wattage bulbs Jenni kept on all the time. He pulled Jenni into his arms and briskly rubbed her back and arms. "Warming up?"

Jenni wrapped her arms around his neck and teased his chin with quick kisses. "A little."

He allowed his hands to rub lower while tilting up her hips against his growing need. "What about now?" He tried to capture her teasing mouth. He hadn't pulled Jenni away from her family for this, but he couldn't let her freeze.

"Getting there." Jenni's hungry mouth slid over his.

He could never get enough of this woman. He wanted Jenni day and night, and not just in his bed. Letting her out of his bed on these cold winter nights was one of the hardest things he had ever done. He didn't mind sharing her with the boys, Dorothy, or even Felicity, but he wanted something more. He wanted a life with her.

He tenderly cupped her cheeks and held her wandering mouth still for a moment. "I love you, Jen."

Jenni's smile was beautiful as she whispered the words he had been hoping to hear. "I love you, Coop."

The soft, dreamy expression on Jenni's face told him she was telling the truth. Jen loved him. His Jenni loved him. There really was a Santa Claus, because he was given the most precious gift of all—Jenni's love.

He slowly lowered his head and kissed her.

Jenni opened her mouth and seductively raised more than his body temperature. The more she gave, the more he wanted. He pressed her up against the wall and took it all.

"Coop." Jenni's mouth was everywhere, begging and teasing him beyond thought.

He cupped her bottom and raised her off her feet. The warmth of her legs encircled his thighs. There were too many clothes between them. He needed her now.

His hands tunneled their way under her sweater. He caressed the warm, silky skin of her back as his tongue tangled with hers.

"Mom!" shouted Tucker from the other side of the door. "Are you there?"

Coop jumped back so fast that Jenni nearly tumbled to the ground. His quick reflexes caught her before his brain could comprehend what was happening.

Jenni's blush was beet red as she tugged down her sweater. "Yes, Tucker, I'm here." Jenni gave Coop a slow sweet smile that stole his breath. "You're naughty," she whispered while playing with the clip holding up her hair. "Santa won't leave you anything tonight."

"He already did." He grinned as he opened the door to Jenni's son. "Hey, Tuck, what's up?"

"Eli says it's time to leave, or we're going to miss the boats." Tucker's eyes gleamed with excitement. "Come on."

Coop and Jenni left the shop, locking the door behind them. "Okay, buddy, we're hurrying." Tucker was practically running back to the house.

Before they reached the house, Hope came hurrying out the sliding doors of the family room. She came to a sudden stop when she saw Tucker tugging on his mother's hand. With a hopeless sigh she apologized. "I only turned my back for one second."

Coop laughed. "Don't worry about it. It's fine."

"Hurry up, Mom!" shouted Chase from the doorway. "Everyone's ready to leave."

Jenni glanced over her shoulder at Coop. "You ready to go?"

"As soon as we get our coats."

They hurried into the house, grabbing coats, keys, mittens, and hats.

"Felicity and Sam already left. They said they'd meet us down there." Dorothy stood next to Eli with a radiant smile upon her face and happiness dancing in her eyes. She was either blushing or having a hot flash.

"Coop," Eli said, "we might have to park on Spruce or White Pine streets. Anyone who can walk to the docks usually does, but in this weather, most drive. Last year we got there late and ended up on Hamilton Street."

Jenni undid the clip in her hair and tugged on a hat. Fashionable she wasn't, but she wanted to stay warm. "Boys, last potty call, and grab your scarves before heading out." As sure as she knew Santa was coming tonight with way too many presents, one of the boys would need a bathroom as soon as they got to the docks.

She dug in her purse and then flipped Coop her keys. They couldn't all fit in Coop's pickup, and, besides, it was filled with the presents Santa would be bringing tonight. Coop had purposely parked away from the boys and their prying eyes. "Why don't you warm up the car while I handle the boys."

Coop gazed at the mistletoe above his head, wiggled his brow, and grinned.

She shook her head. "Don't even think about it." Dorothy, Eli, and the girls were already in their car waiting for them. If Coop kissed her again, they would miss the festival.

"Spoilsport." Coop headed out the door with Chase.

Tucker was already in the powder room.

Corey banged on the door. "Hurry up, Tucker."

She patiently slipped on her gloves. Knowing those two, this could take awhile. She was pleasantly surprised when not a moment later Tucker sprinted past her and out the door. "Come on, Mom" had been shouted over his shoulder.

"I'll be right there." A moment later, she and Corey headed out the door to see their first Festival of Lights in Misty Harbor.

Forty minutes later, she spotted the first boat off in the distance. A soft, light snow had begun to fall, giving everything a peaceful and quiet feel. She moved closer to Coop. It felt like Christmas Eve.

"I see a boat," shouted Tucker as he jumped up and down on the dock.

"Shhh . . . you're not supposed to yell, hon. Everyone can see the boat." Her hand reached out and pressed his shoulder downward so he would stop jumping and people would stop staring.

"What are we supposed to do?" Tucker frowned and glanced around.

"Just watch the boats come in, hon. That's all." She gave her son a big smile. "Enjoy how pretty they look on the water all lit up like that." The first boat was all decked out in white and green lights that reflected off the sea.

Tucker gave her a look that expressed what he

thought about that. Her middle son didn't do "pretty."

"Where's Grandmom?" Tucker asked.

"With Eli." She had seen Eli's daughters walk off with a bunch of teenagers when they had first arrived at the docks. Eli and Dorothy had headed in the direction of the restaurant, the Catch of the Day. She still hadn't caught sight of Felicity and Sam, but she wasn't looking that hard.

"Can I go with them?"

"No, you are to stay with us." Coop had wanted to find a quiet place along the shoreline that might block some of the wind. The boys had taken one look at the wooden-planked dock with all the other kids and families on it and insisted that was where they wanted to be.

"There's another one," whispered Chase, who was closer to the edge than she liked.

"It's all yellow," Corey said. Her youngest son was holding Coop's hand and keeping his distance from the edge.

"It's gold," Chase said. "They don't make yellow Christmas lights, only gold."

Leave it to Chase to point that one out.

"How many lights do you think are on that boat, Chase?" Coop gaze was off in the distance. "Has to be thousands, I would think."

Chase frowned. "Maybe."

"Here comes another one," Tucker said in loud voice. It wasn't a shout this time, but it wasn't a whisper either. "This one is all white."

She watched as the boats slowly and almost silently made their way into the harbor. It was one of the most perfect sights she had ever seen. "It's beautiful."

"That it is." Coop wrapped his arm around her waist and tugged her closer. "Are you warm enough?"

"Toasty." She stuck out her tongue and caught a big fat flake. She closed her eyes and tasted the drop of water that had been the flake. She opened them again and grinned. "I love the taste of falling snow."

Coop's eyes were dark and full of promises as he followed her every move. "You're playing with fire, Jen."

"That's why I'm toasty." She loved the way Coop made her feel, all hot and needy.

In her quest for the snowflake and to tease Coop, her hand had released Tucker's shoulder. The boy now was standing next to Chase, much too close to the edge of the dock. There was a good six-foot-drop before a person would end up in the frigid water below. Before her feet could follow the warning her brain was screaming, Tucker saw another boat come into view.

Tucker twisted around to tell her and lost his footing. With flailing arms he teetered on the edge of the dock, about to go over into the darkness below.

She opened her mouth to scream, but before a sound could emerge, Coop had a hold on the back of Tucker's jacket and was pulling him to safety. Jenni had never seen anyone move that fast in her life.

"Hey, Coop," someone about ten feet down the dock shouted, "nice catch."

"Thanks," Coop shouted back.

"Still has the hands," shouted another.

Coop shook his head and looked pale as he frowned down at Tucker. "You stay away from the edge."

Chase, who had witnessed his brother's near fall, took two giant steps back away from the brink.

Tucker's eyes were still wide and round from his near mishap. "Okay."

She grabbed the back of Tucker's jacket and suppressed the urge to hug him. He didn't deserve to be hugged. Tucker had just taken another year off her life, a life she wanted to spend with Coop. Using her low, no-nonsense mother voice, she whispered in Tucker's ear. "If you so much as move a muscle, I will personally see to it that Santa does not come down our chimney tonight."

Corey moved closer to Coop.

"Hey, Corey, can you see okay from down there?" Coop asked as he squatted to the boy's height.

Corey shook his head.

Coop swung Corey up and placed him on his shoulders. "There are perks to being the youngest."

"What's perks?" Corey asked, in awe of his new height.

"It means you get to ride on Mr. Brown's shoulders, where your brothers can't." She grinned up at her youngest.

Corey seemed quite pleased with himself.

Coop glanced out over the water and watched as another boat came into sight. This one was lit up in red and white lights that seemed more powerful than the other boats. He hadn't realized until tonight how much he had missed this over the years. Somewhere up on one of the hilltops his parents were in their car, drinking their coffee and enjoying the view. It was a yearly tradition with them.

He wanted to start a yearly tradition with Jenni and the boys.

He wanted candlelight and champagne tonight. Jenni deserved them and a whole lot more. There was a question on his tongue burning to be asked, and a jeweler's box

scorching a hole in his pocket. He noticed the death grip
Jenni had on the back of Tucker's jacket and prayed that
wouldn't be part of their yearly tradition. His heart had
stopped when he spotted Tucker about to go into the water.

He tugged Jenni closer and whispered in her ear,
"What do you think of the lights?"

"It's the most beautiful thing I've ever seen." Jenni
leaned her head against his shoulder and continued to
stare out onto the harbor. "Thank you for saving
Tucker." Snowflakes were melting on Jenni's cheeks.

"I'll always save Tucker."

Jenni turned her head and looked at him. A snowflake
clung to one of her lashes. "Will you?"

"If you let me." He could see forever in Jenni's gaze
and knew her answer before he even asked his question.
"Will you marry me, Jen?"

Jenni's smile was radiant.

That night over a dozen boats made it into the harbor
and Santa was extra generous at the Wright house on
Mistletoe Bay.